Rebecca was in trouble

Mac was as sure of this as he'd ever been sure of anything. She was in terrible trouble somewhere up ahead.

Sled dog racing! he fumed. *Whoever thought up such a ridiculous sport?* "All right," he bellowed to his team. "Get up." His voice had an edge to it that he'd never used with his dogs before. They struggled valiantly against the ferocious wind and swirling snow.

Where the hell was the summit? They must be getting close. Mac looked ahead into the stormy darkness. Was that a sled in front of him? He reached out, and his hand connected with the solid wood of the driving bow. "Hey," he shouted. "Rebecca?"

The top line of the sled bag ripped open in the fierce wind, and a man sat up. "Rebecca's somewhere down below. She and her whole team got blown over. I don't know how far they fell."

Mac stared at the bottomless void. She could be anywhere along this slope or she could have tumbled clear to the bottom. How in God's name would he ever find her in this whiteout?

He turned and plunged through the snow to the front of his team. He unhooked his lead dog from the gang line.

"Merlin, come!" he shouted over the howl of the wind. Then he turned his back on the dog and began a careful, step-by-step descent of the slope, panning his headlamp back and forth as he went.

He had to find Rebecca!

Dear Reader,

The Yukon Quest Sled Dog Race is without a doubt one of the toughest in the world—an epic journey covering one thousand miles of rugged wilderness terrain in temperatures that often reach minus sixty degrees Fahrenheit. It is the ultimate proving ground for mushers and their teams, and the cumulative effort of race volunteers, veterinarians, sponsors, handlers, families and friends. All of the characters in this story are fictional. I have taken a few liberties with both the race route and the rules, but have tried for the most part to give you, the reader, a sense of what it's like to travel down a long trail behind a team of incredible canine athletes. And a hint of the camaraderie that can develop between the mushers themselves.

The history of the north country is written in the paw prints of the intrepid sled dogs who hauled freight, food, medicine and mail over thousands of miles of winter trails in some of the worst conditions imaginable, for the benefit of mankind. We owe them our esteem.

Nadia Nichols

Across a Thousand Miles
Nadia Nichols

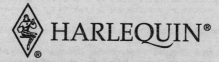

TORONTO • NEW YORK • LONDON
AMSTERDAM • PARIS • SYDNEY • HAMBURG
STOCKHOLM • ATHENS • TOKYO • MILAN • MADRID
PRAGUE • WARSAW • BUDAPEST • AUCKLAND

ISBN 0-373-71043-7

ACROSS A THOUSAND MILES

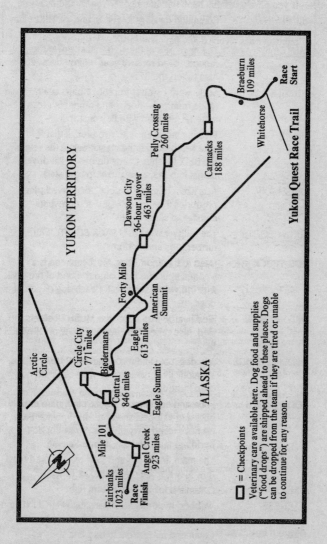

YUKON TERRITORY

Arctic
Circle

Braeburn
109 miles

Race
Start

Whitehorse

Pelly Crossing
260 miles

Carmacks
188 miles

Dawson City
36-hour layover
463 miles

Forty Mile

Circle City
771 miles

American
Summit

Biedermans

Central
846 miles

Eagle
613 miles

Eagle Summit

Mile 101

Angel Creek
923 miles

Fairbanks
1023 miles

Race
Finish

ALASKA

☐ = Checkpoints

Veterinary care available here. Dog food and supplies
("food drops") are shipped ahead to these places. Dogs
can be dropped from the team if they are tired or unable
to continue for any reason.

Yukon Quest Race Trail

GLOSSARY OF MUSHING TERMINOLOGY

ALL RIGHT! Command for dogs to get up and go. HIKE! may also be used.

BASKET The main part of the sled that sits over the runners. Used to carry gear, injured dogs, etc. Also called the BED.

BOOTIES Socks worn by dogs to protect paws against ice. Made from polar fleece and other high-tech material. Secured with Belcor strips.

BRAKE Pivoting metal bar with two prongs that is attached between the stanchions at the rear of the BED. Musher stands on bar, which drives points into the snow and stops the sled.

BRUSHBOW Acts like a bumper or deflector. Curved piece protrudes from front of sled and prevents damage to sled.

BUNNY BOOTS The military version of PACK BOOTS. White rubber tops and bottoms.

DOG TRUCK Used to transport dogs. Most common is a wooden structure built onto the bed of the truck with individual sections for each dog or pair of dogs.

DRIVING BOW Sled handle with which the MUSHER steers the sled. Also called the HANDLE BOW or DRIVER'S BOW.

DROPPED DOGS Any dog that cannot continue may be dropped at an official checkpoint or at an assigned dog-drop location.

FOOD DROPS Food and equipment, bagged in burlap or poly bags and shipped ahead to checkpoints. Bags cannot exceed sixty pounds. Straw (for dog bedding) must also be shipped ahead.

GANGLINE The main line. Dogs and sled are attached to this. May also be referred to as TOWLINE.

GEE! Command for leaders to turn right.

HARNESS Webbed material, fits dogs snugly. TUGLINE and NECKLINE are attached to this.

HAW! Command for leaders to turn left.

LEAD DOG	Leader of the team. Intelligence and drive are important qualities. Teams can have one or two LEAD DOGS.
MUSHER	A person who drives a sled dog team.
NECKLINE	Short line—no more than twelve inches—attached to HARNESS and GANGLINE. Keeps dogs in place.
ON BY!	Command to go by a potential distraction such as another team.
PACK BOOTS	Felt-lined insulated boots. Usually rubber soled with leather or Cordura uppers.
PEDALING	Standing with one foot on the sled runner while pushing against the snow with the other.
POINT DOGS	These dogs run behind the LEAD DOGS. Sometimes called SWING DOGS.
RUNNERS	The two skilike "feet" that slide along the snow. Usually made of wood and covered in plastic.
SAFETY LINE	Extra line from sled to GANGLINE
SNOW HOOK	Double-pronged metal hook. Can be pushed into the snow and used as an anchor to halt the dogs for short periods of time without tethering them.
SNUB LINE	Attached to the end of the GANGLINE. Can be tied to an object (tree) to hold the dogs when the snow is too soft to use SNOW HOOK.
STANCHIONS	The upright pieces that form the framework of the sled. They hold the runners to the rest of the sled.
SWING DOGS	Either the same as POINT DOGS or may refer to the two dogs running between the POINT DOGS and the WHEEL DOGS.
TEAM DOGS	Refers to all dogs other than LEAD DOGS, POINT DOGS, SWING DOGS and WHEEL DOGS.
TUGLINE	Connects the dog's harness to GANGLINE.
WHEEL DOGS	The two dogs running directly in front of the sled.
WHOA!	Command to stop the team.

To my beloved sled dogs, past and present,
my heroes and my best friends, who have taken me on
some of the greatest adventures of my life
and who have always brought me safely home.

CHAPTER ONE

Now promise made as a debt unpaid, and the
trail has its own stern code...

> Robert Service,
> from *The Cremation of Sam McGee*

THE MAN WHO DROVE his truck up Rebecca Reed's rutted dirt drive was a stranger, and her dogs let her know it long before she stepped out of the arctic entry to her small cabin and onto the front porch. She shrugged into her parka which had been hanging in the small pre-entry room as she watched his approach. The afternoon was chilly in spite of the sunlight, and the limbs of the aspen and willow were silvery and bare. Ravens were calling along the river and the wind played a lonesome song through the spruce behind the cabin. It was late autumn and the taste of snow was in the air.

He was tall. She could see that quite clearly as he climbed out of his truck. Even if his truck—with the dog box bolted to its rusting bed—hadn't given him away, his clothing would have. "Uh-oh. Another crazy dog driver," she commented to Tuffy, the small black-and-tan Alaskan husky who had followed her onto the porch. In her prime, Tuffy had been Bruce's favorite lead dog, but she was old now, her muzzle graying, her movements stiff, and her eyes a bit cloudy. "I'll lay odds he's after a load of dog food and he'll want it real cheap,"

Rebecca said. "But how on earth did he get past my truck?" Tuffy looked at her quizzically and flagged her tail.

The stranger was dressed like a typical musher, and as he walked up the path toward the cabin, he paused for a moment to brush the worst of the mud off his drab-colored parka. His clothes were dog-eared, dog-chewed and dog-dirty. His insulated boots were patched with rubberized tool dip, his tawny shock of hair needed trimming, he was at least two days unshaven, and heaven only knew when he'd last had a decent bath. A bush dweller and a musher. A dangerous combination. He walked to the foot of the porch steps and paused there, looking up at her. "Hello," he said with a nod and the faintest of grins. "Your truck was blocking the road and I moved it. Hope you don't mind, but the hood was left up as if something was wrong so I took a quick look."

"I went out to get the mail yesterday and it stalled on me," Rebecca explained. "The battery went dead, but it shouldn't have. It's fairly new."

"Well, your battery was fine, but the ground-wire connection was loose. I tightened that up, and she started like a champ, so I moved her down the drive a ways into that little pullover near the blowdown. I'll drive her in for you if you like."

Rebecca was taken aback. "No, thank you. I'll walk out and drive back. Thank you very much for fixing it. My wallet's inside. Hold on a moment, I'll get it."

He grinned and shook his head. "No, you won't. I was glad to help and that was a real easy fix. The reason I'm here is that Fred Turner told me you sold dog food. He said you had the best prices in the Territory, so I thought I'd swing by your kennel on my way into Dawson."

"I do sell dog food," Rebecca said warily. "But it's *good* dog food. I don't sell the cheap stuff."

"Good dog food's what I'm looking for," he said. He rubbed the back of his neck and glanced around her yard. "You've got quite a few dogs yourself," he said.

"Forty," she said.

"Forty!" He glanced up at her, and she noticed that his eyes were exceptionally clear and bright, a shade of gray that hinted at blue or green, she couldn't tell which. "My name's Bill MacKenzie. Most folks call me Mac."

"Rebecca Reed," she said, with a curt nod. "How much food were you looking to buy?"

"Well, I only keep fourteen dogs myself, and I have plenty of chum salmon to carry them through the winter. I was thinking along the lines of forty bags, if you had that much to spare. That should see me through till spring."

"I could sell you that much food," Rebecca said, "but that truck of yours is only a half-ton, and it isn't even four-wheel drive. I doubt it could haul that heavy a load."

"Well, I know it doesn't look like much," Mac admitted. "But it's a tough truck, sure enough. She'll carry a ton of food, easy, four-wheel drive or no."

"How far do you have to take it?"

"Thirty miles or so. Not far. Hell, if it would just hurry up and snow, I could ferry the food back with my dog team. It'd be good training for them."

Rebecca smiled faintly. "It'll snow soon enough. You said you were on your way to Dawson, so I guess you'll be wanting to pick the food up on your way back to wherever it is you live?"

Mac nodded. "That'd be great. I'm bringing a dog to the veterinarian for a checkup. She's a good dog but she's been off her feed for nearly a week. My appointment isn't until four, so I thought I'd spend the night in town and get an early start tomorrow. I could be here by eight-thirty, if that's all right with you.''

Rebecca shrugged. "Fine by me. I suppose if Fred Turner told you I sold dog food, he probably also told you that I don't extend credit. My husband started this business five years ago and he gave credit to every Tom, Dick, and Harry that came up the trail. Couldn't say no to anyone. When he died he left me in an awful mess. I'll sell you however much dog food you need, but you'll pay cash at pickup, same as everybody else. Twenty-five dollars a bag.'' Rebecca narrowed her eyes as she spoke, aware that her words were hard and businesslike, and aware, too, that MacKenzie probably didn't have two dimes to rub together. Probably didn't even carry a checkbook or a credit card.

"I understand," Mac said, nodding. "That's good business.'' He patted the flat, frayed pocket of his parka and grinned again. "Not to worry about my finances,'' he assured her. "I've got me a good little jag of cash, what with all the furs I've sold. I could pay you right now if you like.''

"You can pay at pickup,'' Rebecca said. "You're a trapper?''

"I run a trapline up along Flat Creek.''

"Really.'' Rebecca frowned. "How long have you been living out there?''

Mac paused, his eyes suddenly intent on searching the ground at his feet. The color in his windburned cheeks deepened. "Well, not that long,'' he admitted. "Since early August. Actually my brother's the trapper and they were his furs, but he's gone to Fairbanks to finish his degree at the University of Alaska. He asked me if I'd like to spend a winter in the Yukon, taking care of his dogs and running his trapline. The timing was perfect, so here I am.'' Mac grinned again, raising his eyes to hers. ''They're real good dogs. He ran the Yukon Quest with them last year and finished third. He told me to sell the furs and buy dog food for them.''

''Ah,'' Rebecca said. ''You're Brian MacKenzie's brother.''

''Yes. You know him?''

''He and my husband were friends.''

Mac nodded. ''Well, he wants me to run his dogs this winter, so I expect I will. There's not much to it, really. He gave me a some lessons before he left, and I've been working with the dogs for a few months now. We should be able to do really well at some of these races. I'd kind of like to win the Percy DeWolf. It's only 210 miles and those dogs of my brother's will eat that up like it was nothing.''

''Had you ever driven a dog team before you came out here?'' Rebecca asked.

''Nope. But I'm a quick study and my brother's a good teacher. What about you? Are you planning to run any races this season?''

Rebecca shrugged again. ''Depends on the training, I guess, and my work schedule.'' She straightened up and zipped her parka. ''You'd better get headed for Dawson. It'll be pitch-dark soon, and I've still got chores to do.''

''Need any help? I could give you a ride out to your truck,'' he offered.

''No, thanks. I can manage and I like the walk.'' She started to turn away and then paused. ''Be careful of that soft spot in the drive just before you get to the main road. Keep to the left of the deep ruts and you should be okay.''

Rebecca watched him turn and walk back toward his truck. Her eyes narrowed speculatively. "Early thirties," she said to Tuffy, who had remained at her side. "See the way he walks? Definitely military. I should have guessed he was Brian's big brother when he told me his name." She laughed softly, the first time she'd laughed in forever. "Win the Percy DeWolf? He's awfully arrogant, wouldn't you say, Tuffy, for a cheechako who probably doesn't know a dog harness from a doghouse!" Tuffy, as always, cheerfully agreed.

MacKenzie's truck started hard, with much grinding and groaning. It took several tries for him to turn around in Rebecca's yard, backing up into the irregular gaps between the spruce trees and the dog barn, and the dog yard fence and the cabin porch. At length, with a burst of black exhaust, he was gone, and the sound of the old truck's engine faded into silence.

Rebecca gazed beyond her late husband's dog yard, at the wall of rugged mountains that made up the Dawson Range. *Bruce Reed,* she thought, *I miss you like crazy and I hate you for leaving me here with a pack of forty sled dogs to look after and a business that's still in the red....*

Her eyes stung with tears, and a sudden chill made her wrap her arms around herself as she stood on the cabin porch. Tuffy leaned her small but solid weight against Rebecca's leg. Rebecca sniffed and let one hand drop to stroke the dog's head. "I don't hate him, Tuffy," she said softly. "I'm just mad at him, that's all. I want him back and he won't come, but that's not really his fault, is it?"

She might have stood there feeling sorry for herself indefinitely, but there were chores to do. There were dogs to feed, a wood box to fill, water to haul and, finally, her own supper to cook. Tomorrow she had sled dogs to train, more chores to do, more wood and water to haul, and the guest cabin needed a good cleaning in preparation for the steady stream of clients that would inhabit it once the snow came, some flying in from as faraway as Japan to spend a week in the Yukon behind a team of dogs. Bruce's outfitting business, now in its fifth year, had gotten off to a slow start, but if Rebecca's figures were correct, this year it would actually turn a profit. Nearly all of the available dates were filled with clients seeking a northern adventure. More than half of them were repeats. Between the food sales, the guided trips, and the small sums she earned writing a weekly column for a Whitehorse newspaper, Rebecca, without her husband, was managing to scrape by.

As she mixed the dog food in the big galvanized washtubs, three of them set side to shoulder inside the cabin door, she caught herself thinking about Bill MacKenzie. "He'll never make it," she said to Tuffy as she mixed the ground meat into the kibble and added copious quantities of warm water from the huge kettles steaming atop the woodstove. "He'll never last out the winter in Brian's shack up on the Flat. He may think he's Jeremiah Johnson, but he doesn't have a clue. This country will eat him up." She shook her head and laughed for the second time that day. "Ex-military. He probably has a hard time tying his bootlaces without a drill sergeant instructing him." She scooped the warm, soupy mix of meat, kibble, fat, vitamins and water into five-gallon buckets, hoisted two of them with hands that were calloused and arms that were necessarily strong. She pushed the door open with a practiced kick of her booted toe, did likewise to the door from the arctic entry and emerged from the cabin to the wolflike chorus of forty huskies howling for their dinner.

Halfway through her chores she paused for a moment, pushed a stray lock of hair from her forehead with the back of her wrist and shook her head. "Boy, I feel kind of sorry for his dogs."

"WE'LL NEED TO TAKE X rays to see what's going on," the veterinarian said, removing his stethoscope and laying it on the side table. "From what you're telling me and from what I'm hearing inside her, it sounds like some sort of intestinal obstruction. Does she eat rocks?"

"Rocks?" Mac stared down at the small sled dog that he steadied in his arms. "Why would she do that?"

The veterinarian laughed. "You'd be amazed at the things we find in a sled dog's intestines. Rocks are the most common. They start out playing with them and then for some unfathomable reason they swallow them."

"Rocks," Mac said. He shook his head. "I guess there's a lot I need to learn about these dogs. Okay, so what happens now?"

"We'll knock her out, take some pictures and if there's an obstruction, we'll go ahead and surgically remove it. She'll have to stay overnight for observation, and I'd like to get some IV hydration into her."

"And if you don't find anything?"

"I'll do some blood work and we'll take it from there. The other option is to keep dosing her with mineral oil the way you've been doing and hope the obstruction works its way through. But she's pretty dehydrated right now and she's lost a lot of condition. There's also the possibility of a rupture of the intestine, which would cause massive infection. It's up to you. If you want to wait a little longer…"

Mac shook his head. "Go ahead and do whatever needs to be done. I don't want to take any chances with her. Can I call here tonight and find out how she's doing?"

"We should know how we're going to proceed as soon as we see what the problem is. If you leave a number where you can be reached, I'll give you a call."

"I'm staying at the Eldorado," Mac said. He stroked the dog's head one final time before leaving her to the vet. "You're a good girl, Callie," he said. "You'll feel better soon." Sick as she was, Callie wagged her tail at his words and tried to follow him out of the examination room, which made him feel worse than ever. If someone had told him three months ago that he would be so attached to a pack of sled dogs, he would have laughed in disbelief, but abandoning Callie at the veterinarian's launched him into a state of high anxiety.

He paced the lobby at the Eldorado for nearly an hour before the phone call came. The X rays showed a large obstruction, probably a rock. They were commencing surgery and would phone again to let him know how things went. Another ninety anxious minutes later, he got word that the operation had been successful and that Callie was fine. "That rock was as big as a hen's egg," the vet said. "I saved it for you."

Mac's relief was followed by intense hunger. He ate a huge and satisfying meal, then had a couple of cold beers while watching some of the locals shoot pool in the barroom. His thoughts kept returning to Rebecca Reed. Try as he might, he couldn't get her out of his mind. Fred Turner was a taciturn old cuss, but he'd divulged a good deal about her when he'd stopped at Mac's cabin for a visit two weeks back. "Terrible sad story," Fred had said, shaking his head and blinking the sting of a large swallow of Jack Daniel's from his eyes. "She came here with her husband, oh, must be five, six years ago. Quiet little thing. Shy. Hard worker, though. Worked right alongside her man, never shirked. Good with the dogs, too. She helped Bruce train, ran some races herself and did real well.

"Bruce, he ran the long races. The Iditarod and the Yukon Quest. Those are thousand-mile races. Tough races. Rebecca ran some of the shorter ones. Two, three hundred milers like the Fireplug, the Copper Basin, the Percy DeWolf. They started up a business giving tours by dog team and selling dog food. Best prices in the Territory on dog food. And then Bruce went and got himself killed. Hit a moose with his truck coming back from a supply trip to Whitehorse. We all thought she'd pack up and leave, but by God she's stuck it out, all by herself. Folks say she hasn't smiled once since Bruce died, and she's got no family to turn to, just a mother back East who thinks she's crazy livin' way out here in the wilderness."

Mac leaned his elbows on the bar and cradled the beer bottle between his palms. Fred hadn't mentioned that Rebecca Reed was an arrestingly beautiful woman. Long, dark hair plaited in a thick braid, high forehead, wide-set blue eyes, straight nose, expressive mouth that wanted to smile but wouldn't, and a determined chin with a little dimple in it. The thought of her living in that cabin all by herself, grieving for her husband, disturbed him more than he cared to admit. Divorced for several months, his own experiences with women had led him to conclude that most of them were fickle. Loyalty simply did not abide in them. Yet how could he explain this woman living in voluntary seclusion, this young widow who hadn't smiled since her husband died? And might things have turned out differently for him in that military courtroom if he'd had the love and support of a wife like Rebecca? Would he have fought harder for his exoneration?

Mac sighed. Taking care of forty dogs must be a hell of a lot of work for a woman! Caring for his brother's dogs turned him inside out, and getting away from them for just one day was more of a vacation than a three-week holiday used to be. How on earth did she manage all by herself?

"Hey, mister." A man leaned on the bar beside him, olive-drab wool cap with the ear flaps turned up, wind-burned complexion, black eyes, red-and-black-plaid flannel shirt, green wool pants with bright orange suspenders. "Barkeep tells me you play a mean game of pool and you're looking for some action."

Mac finished his beer and straightened. "Well, I don't know how mean it is, but it's pretty good, I guess."

"Good enough to place a bet on?"

"Maybe." Mac followed the woodsman to the pool table, thinking smugly, *Ha! Easy money!*

Six hours later he opened his eyes and stared up at an unfamiliar ceiling. For a moment he couldn't remember where he was or why he felt so awful. Pool... He'd played pool with a guy named Joe Redshirt, and Joe played a pretty mean game of pool himself. Whiskey. Joe had bought him several shots over the course of the evening. One of the last coherent memories Mac had was of an easy rail shot he'd pooched, and Joe's deadpan voice drawling, "Don't worry, son, I couldn't make those shots when I was young, either."

Mac closed his eyes, moaned, then opened them again, realization flooding through him. "Dammit!" He swung his legs over the edge of the bed and stood, not overly surprised to find himself fully clothed. He held on to the nightstand for a moment until his legs steadied beneath him, then staggered to the chair. His fingers dug into the frayed pockets of his parka with frantic movements, and he knew a moment of wild relief when he drew forth the carefully folded envelope that held the dog-food money. He spilled the bills out onto the coverlet and counted them. Sweat beaded his brow. He counted again, as if more might appear the second time around then sank onto the edge of the bed. By nature he was neither a gambler nor a heavy drinker, but betting on a game of pool had seemed like such an easy way to win money to help pay both the vet and the hotel charges, and Joe Redshirt had kept handing him those shots of whiskey…

…and somehow Mac had gambled away half his dog-food money.

One hot shower and thirty minutes later, he was standing in the vet's office counting those same bills again. Then he pushed all but sixty dollars toward the receptionist. She counted it primly before writing him out a receipt. "I'll get Callie for you now," she said, and disappeared into the back room. Mac stared at the remaining bills in his hand with a feeling of doom. "Oh, God," he said to the empty room. "I'm flat broke."

When he finally got Callie comfortably ensconced in the passenger seat of his old truck, he was stunned to realize that it was nearly 10 a.m. He had an early-morning appointment to pick up nearly a ton of dog food from a beautiful widow named Rebecca Reed, who lived about an hour outside of Dawson…and who didn't sell dog food on credit.

"Oh, God," he said again, putting the truck in gear

and heading down the Klondike Highway. "I'm a dead man."

"YOU'RE LATE! Rebecca said, hands on her hips. I could have trained three teams of dogs in the amount of time I've spent waiting around for you."

A stiff wind bent the tops of the spruce, and the overcast sky gave off an ominous thundering. "I'm sorry," Mac said. He stood at the foot of the porch steps looking about as apologetic as she'd ever seen a man look. Those broad military shoulders were hunched, and his hands were shoved deep into his parka pockets. His tawny hair was tousled, though clean and freshly trimmed, and he had obviously shaved, revealing more clearly the strong, masculine planes of cheekbone and chin, but his eyes mirrored his abject guilt.

"Well, I'm not going to help you load the dog food. That's your job. Back your truck up to that door on the end of the dog barn. Your food is on pallets stacked to the right of the door. Forty bags, though I seriously doubt your truck will take the load."

He nodded again, looked over his shoulder at the old rusted truck, then dropped his gaze to the toes of his worn-out pack boots. He stood silently at the foot of the cabin steps until Rebecca felt a knot forming in the pit of her stomach.

"What is it?" she said.

He sighed and dug his hands deeper into his parka pockets. He lifted his shoulders and let them fall. A snowflake fluttered down from the leaden sky and brushed over his shoulder unseen. "Well, the thing is, I'm a little short of cash," he said in a low voice, speaking to the ground at his feet. "The vet bill turned out to be higher than I expected. You see, Callie ate this big rock..." He raised his eyes and pulled one hand out of his pocket, fingers unfolding to reveal the smooth egg-shaped stone cradled within.

Rebecca stared at the rock and crossed her arms in front of her. The wind was cold, but a curious feeling warmed her blood. "I see. Yes, that certainly is a big rock. So. You spent all your money on what had to be the most expensive surgery ever performed in the Yukon, and I suppose now you want me to extend credit to you?"

Mac shook his head. "I have enough left to buy a couple of bags. I can come up with more money. I'll sell some stuff up at the cabin. A couple of bags will hold me over till I can hock my watch. I have a good one. A Rolex." He bared his wrist to display the watch, but Rebecca was unimpressed. Another snowflake whirled through the air, a tiny dance of white, a promise of winter. He watched it land and disappear, then raised his eyes to hers. "I'm not asking to buy on credit. I'll get the money. Callie's okay, and right at this moment that's all that matters."

Rebecca's arms tightened against herself. Bruce would have done the same. He would have sold his soul to the devil to save one of his dogs. And truth be known, so would she. "Take the food," she said shortly, "and pay me when you can. Your brother, Brian, did very well with his trapline. I expect you'll be able to make good on this loan in a month or so. I can't abide the thought of those good dogs of Brian's going hungry, and they can't live on chum salmon...and egg-size rocks."

Mac stared at her until she felt the cold knot in the pit of her stomach return with a vengeance. "What is it now?" she demanded.

"Trapping." His eyes pleaded with her to understand,

and the flush across his cheekbones deepened. Rebecca waited, grim-faced, for him to continue. "I tried trapping. I set the traps like Brian showed me. For a while there was nothing, and then I caught a fox," he said. "When I came to check the trap, the fox was… It had…" He half turned away from her and rubbed the back of his neck with his hand. His shoulders rose and fell around a silent sigh. "I let the fox go. It just didn't seem right."

Rebecca looked at him for a moment and then turned her back abruptly, raised her hands to her mouth and coughed behind them to hide her smile.

"I don't know what I'm going to do to earn the money, but something's bound to come up."

She turned around, her face composed, and nodded curtly. "I'm sure you're good for it. Load the dog food. You have a long trip ahead of you, and it's starting to snow."

She watched him back the old truck up to the barn door and let her hand drop to rest on the head of the dog who was forever by her side. "He can't trap wild animals, Tuffy," she said softly, a bemused smile curving the corners of her mouth. "Who can figure the heart of a man?"

IT TOOK MACKENZIE a good thirty minutes to load the bags. Rebecca spent the time mixing her own batch of dog food for the evening feeding. The cabin was warm, and she lit an oil lamp against the early twilight. The hardest part of living in the north was the lack of daylight in winter months. It wasn't so bad now, but come December the nights would be endless, and sunlight all but a precious memory. She gave the stew pot a stir and poked the pan of sourdough bread rising on the warming shelf, shifting it to a cooler spot. A light tap on the door drew her back onto the cabin porch. MacKenzie stood humbly before her. "Thank you," he said. "I'll be off now."

"Good," she said.

He nodded. "I'll pay you within the month."

"I'm sure you will."

She couldn't keep the edge of sarcasm from her voice. He nodded again and turned away, walked down the three steps and crossed the yard to where his truck was parked. He paused before climbing into the cab. "Need any mechanical work done on your truck?" he asked hopefully.

"Nope."

"Two weeks," he said. "I'll have the money in two weeks!"

She didn't reply, and he climbed into the cab and slammed the door. The truck started right up, but he had to work to get it into first gear. He pulled ahead with a lurch that stalled it. He started it again, waved his arm out the side window when the engine finally caught and slowly rumbled out of the yard, the old truck's springs sagging under the heavy load. As he drove cautiously down the long rutted track that led to the main road, it began to snow in earnest, the flakes whirling past on a strong westerly wind. By morning there would be a foot or more. Winter came all at once in the north country and stayed for a very long time.

She stepped inside to fill the buckets with dog food, hurrying now to beat the darkness and the storm. The dogs howled with delight as she reemerged bearing their supper, which she ladled into the feed pans attached to the sides of their houses. "We'll run tomorrow, Thor," she promised the black lead dog, another of her hus-

band's favorites. "Maybe even with the sled." She'd
been training the dog teams with a four-wheeler since
the weather had cooled in August, letting twelve dogs
pull the ATV down miles of dirt roads, and while rig
training was important, she couldn't wait to get back
onto the sled. Nothing compared to a fast run behind a
good team of well-trained dogs. Rebecca had come to
love the dogs and the lifestyle they represented. She had
come to love this little place on the edge of the wilderness, the timeless cycle of the seasons, the ebb and flow
of life, and the hard, harsh laws of the wild. If not for
the aching loneliness that had hollowed her heart since
losing Bruce, she would be quite content here.

"Okay, Quinn, I'm coming with the chow. Hold your
horses!" She dished out the food quickly, moving
amongst the whirl and dance of the excited animals with
practiced ease, speaking each dog's name as she fed it.
Finally she dropped the scoop back into one of the
empty buckets with a weary sigh. "Done and done."
The snow was already turning the ground white, and
strong gusts of wind lifted it up in streamers. "Wild
night ahead."

She wondered how MacKenzie was making out on his
long drive home, and no sooner did this unbidden
thought enter her mind than the dogs erupted into a
frenzy of barking, all eyes focused on the dirt track that
led to the main road. She followed their gaze and after
a few moments picked out the dark shape of a man moving through the thick veil of wind-driven snow. "It can't
be!" she said.

But it was. MacKenzie trudged into her yard and
veered in her direction. His hair was plastered with
snow. "I'm sorry to bother you," he said over the roar

of the wind. "My truck broke a U-joint about half a mile from here, just shy of the main road."

Clutching both empty buckets in one mittened hand, she stared at him. "I guess it was too heavy a load," she couldn't resist saying.

"I guess," he said.

"You got into that soft spot, didn't you?" she said. He nodded. "Well, what do you want me to do about it?"

"I was wondering if I could borrow your phone."

"You're assuming I have one. Who do you plan to call?"

"God," he said.

"I don't have *that* kind of a phone. Mine is a limited-signal radio phone, and the best you can do with it is to call over to Sam and Ellin Dodge's place. They have a ham radio and can call into Dawson for a wrecker, but nobody will come out tonight with a storm brewing. And even if someone does, a wrecker won't get you home with a load of dog food for a pack of hungry dogs."

"No, ma'am, probably not."

"And if you don't get home tonight, who's going to feed your dogs?"

"Fred Turner. He's staying at my place till I get back."

"Fred Turner?" Rebecca glared at Mac. "Fred Turner's about as dependable as one might expect an alcoholic amnesiac to be. If you left any liquor in your cabin, he's drunk it all by now. Lord only knows what shape your dogs'll be in when you get back."

"I can fix that U-joint in jig time. All I need is the right part. I noticed you had an old, broken-down Ford parked behind the dog yard..."

"That old, broken-down Ford is my snowplow, mister, and you aren't laying a hand on it! Sam Dodge has some junkers over at his place. He may have the part you need. Like I said, you can use my phone to call him, though you won't be able to do much in the pitch-dark.''

"I have a headlamp in my truck," Mac said. "Hell, I could work blind if I had to. I'm a fair enough mechanic. How far away do these folks live?"

"Sam and Ellin? Not far. Five miles down the trail, east of here.''

"Which trail?''

"That one." Rebecca raised her free hand and pointed. "If you hurry you could get there and back in my four-wheeler before the snow gets too deep, but we'd better call ahead first.''

"I appreciate this," Mac said, following her into the warmth of the cabin. He stopped inside the door and looked around while she hooked the radio phone to the twelve-volt battery. She noticed him staring at Bruce's clothing on the wall pegs near the door and the pair of man-size Bunny boots behind the wood cookstove. "You have a real nice place here," he offered. She said nothing, dialing Sam and Ellin's number by heart and hoping that they had their phone turned on.

They did. Ellin answered on the second ring. Her voice was always warm and welcome to Rebecca's ears. "'Becca! Sweetheart, how are you? I hope you're all ready for winter, my dear, because its here!''

Rebecca quickly filled Ellin in, and within moments Sam was speaking directly to Mac about parts and pieces and tools and time. Finally, Mac handed her the phone and grinned. "All set!" he said. "They have the part I need. All I have to do is pull it, bring it back here, and fix my truck. Callie should be all right in the meantime.''

"I could drive you over," she offered, albeit grudgingly. She had chores to finish, a column to write and a deadline to meet.

"No need, if I can borrow your four-wheeler."

Relieved, she led him back out into the brumal blast, zipping her parka against the cold. It was rapidly growing dark. The four-wheeler was parked inside the barn, and she swung the door wide and held it open against the force of the wind while he started up the vehicle and drove it out. Once again she pointed at the mouth of the trail that led directly from her yard into the thick spruce forest. "Just follow that trail. You can't possibly get lost. It takes you right into Sam and Ellin's yard. Don't worry about Callie. I'll bring her into the cabin and keep an eye on her."

"Thanks," he said, visibly relieved. He shifted into first gear, and was swallowed up instantly by the darkness and the storm.

CHAPTER TWO

THE WIND MADE a noise in the eaves that sounded like a dying man's moan, and Rebecca fed more sticks into the stove to thwart the deepening cold that worked its way through tiny cracks between the cabin logs and radiated up from the floorboards. It was nearing midnight, and still no sign of Bill MacKenzie. The storm had intensified, and more than eighteen inches already covered the frozen ground in some areas. Rebecca poured herself another cup of tea, her fifth of the night. Maybe it was time to get out of the dog-food business. The markup was so small, just fifty cents a bag. For the privilege of selling Bill MacKenzie forty bags, she had earned the tidy sum of twenty dollars, not even enough for one bag of food for her *own* huskies. And that was assuming he ever paid her.

It simply wasn't worth the aggravation.

And where was he, anyway? He had her four-wheeler, a Honda that Bruce had spent a small fortune on four years ago. If he hurt that machine… "Okay," she said to Tuffy. "He left here around four o'clock. It's five miles to Sam and Ellin's. He has to go out back and remove the parts he needs from the junkers Sam collects and that's going to take some time. One, two, three hours? Even if Ellin feeds him—and she surely will—he should have been back at least three hours ago. The snow is too deep now for the four-wheeler, which means he's stuck out there somewhere and freezing to death.''

Rebecca paced the small confines of the kitchen with mug of tea in hand. Tuffy raised her head and watched intently. "I can't call Ellin," Rebecca told the dog. "I thought he'd be back by nine so I didn't phone before and now it's too late, Sam goes to bed early and if I bother them now..." She took a sip of tea. "I have to! If he's lost out there we'll have to find him. It's ten degrees standing temperature, but way below zero with the wind chill.''

She set her mug down with a thump on the kitchen table and plugged the radio phone into the battery. "Ellin? Ellin, it's Rebecca! Where on earth is Bill Mac-Kenzie!''

Ellin's voice was drowsy with sleep. "Why, he's right here! He's spending the night. It was late and the weather was far too nasty for him to head back after he and Sam had gotten the parts, so we made him bed down in the boys' bedroom.'' Ellin's voice lowered to a naughty whisper. "My dear girl, wherever did you find him! He's a treasure!''

"Ellin, for your information I did not find him! He bought a load of dog food from me, and his truck just happened to break down on my road! Do you mean to say that all this time he's been *sleeping?*''

"Like a baby. We tried to call, but as usual your phone was unplugged. Don't be mad, my dear. I must tell you that we've enjoyed his company immensely. I even helped Sam fix that old Bombardier of ours, he's that good a mechanic! I must say, you've got yourself quite a man there, Rebecca.''

"Ellin, he's not my man! I'm sorry to have woken you but I thought... I just didn't know..." She glanced at Callie, who was curled on a blanket behind the stove, sound asleep. "I mean, it's a bad storm and he—"

"You were worried. I understand completely." Ellin's grandmotherly voice soothed and reassured. "But worry no more, my dear. We're taking good care of him and we'll get him back to you safely first thing in the morning. Now go to bed and get some sleep."

Rebecca couldn't be angry with Ellin, and as she climbed the steep stairs to the cabin's sleeping loft, she surprised herself by laughing for the second time that day.

BY MORNING the storm had blown itself out, and at 8 a.m. Sam and Ellin arrived, riding double on the wide-track Bombardier snowmobile and towing a sled. Bill MacKenzie was driving Rebecca's Honda behind them. Rebecca had finished watering and feeding the dogs, and she invited the elderly couple into the cabin for a cup of coffee. Mac came inside briefly to check on Callie and then went out to rummage in the sled behind the Bombardier. She could see several mysterious tools protruding from the canvas wrappings he pulled out.

"Mac's a darn good mechanic," Sam said, as he settled himself into a chair at the kitchen table. Sam was in his seventies, lean and trim and bursting with the health and vitality of a man who had lived most of his life in the outdoors. Ellin's hair was as white as her husband's, and she was also in shape. They had lived in the Yukon all of their lives, had raised four boys in their cabin, home-schooling them with such success that all four had gone on to successful careers.

"He's Brian's older brother, and I remember Brian telling us he was in the military. I don't recall which branch," Rebecca said, pouring the coffee. "He's taking care of Brian's team for the winter.''

"Well, he certainly knows his stuff. He knows airplanes, too,'' Sam said. "You should've seen his eyes light up when he saw my old Stearman! Said he'd help me get her back in the air this spring if I wanted. I guess I wouldn't mind having some help.''

"I've never known you to refuse help,'' Ellin said to her husband. "Now,'' she turned to Rebecca. "Let me give you a bit of advice—''

"Ellin, before you start, let me just say this,'' Rebecca interrupted firmly. "I'm not the least bit interested in Bill MacKenzie. I hardly know him.''

Ellin sat up straighter. "It's been a long time since—''

"I wouldn't go there if I were you, Ellin,'' Sam advised his wife. "Rebecca knows her own mind.''

"Thank you, Sam,'' Rebecca said.

"She can't spend the rest of her life grieving.''

"When it's time to move on, she'll know it,'' Sam replied.

"I doubt it. Rebecca's one of the stubbornnest people I know,'' Ellin said.

"Now, just a minute!'' Rebecca nudged the sugar bowl in Sam's direction. "I wouldn't call myself—''

"Well, you are, my dear, and you might as well admit it. Trying to make a go of it alone here, running Bruce's business—''

"*My* business now, Ellin, and I'm doing just fine with it. Better than Bruce did, if the truth be known.''

"It's too much! You need help. Especially with the dogs and the tour business. What if you were out on a training run with a team of dogs and something went wrong? What if you never made it back home? Who would know you were missing? Who would know to come looking for you?'' Ellin leaned over the table, her blue eyes earnest. "My dear girl, the lowest possible denominator in this part of the world is two. You simply can't go it alone!"

Rebecca sighed and lifted her coffee cup. "Ellin, just what are you getting at? You want me to marry this man? This stranger?"

"He's not a stranger. He's Brian's brother!"

"This conversation is getting a little too weird for me," Sam said, pushing out of his chair. "I think I'll go see if I can give Mac a hand."

"Yes, you do that," Ellin said, waving him away as if he were an annoying fly and turning her attention to Rebecca. "Not marriage, my dear. At least, not until you know each other a little better."

"Thank you for that much, at least," Rebecca said.

"I think you should hire him."

"What?"

"Think about it. He owes you money. He told us the story about the dog food and also that he couldn't pay Sam for the truck parts. So to work off the parts, he's going to help Sam with some odd jobs. Maybe he could work off what he owes you for the dog food. You need a man's help around here. He could get in your firewood, help with the tours, pick up the food in Whitehorse, help take care of the dogs—"

"No!" Rebecca said.

"Oh, I know what you're thinking. Where will he live? He can't stay in your guest cabin because most of the time it'll be occupied with paying clients. Well, don't you worry, I've thought it all out. He can stay with us. We have that log cabin the boys built. It needs some fixing here and there, but he's perfectly capable of making it livable, and it has a good roof. He can move the junk that's stored there into the hangar, and in his spare time he can help Sam with mechanical things, like keeping the snow machines up and running, and working on that old wreck of an airplane.'' Ellin sat back in her chair with a self-satisfied smile. "Don't you see how perfectly that would work out for all of us?"

"No!" Rebecca repeated. "No, I don't. If you want to hire him, Ellin, you go right ahead. Be my guest!" She nodded to give her words emphasis. "But I want no part of it."

SAM FOUND Bill MacKenzie wedged beneath the rear axle of his old truck, his booted feet sticking out into the snow. "Well," Sam said, hunkering down on his heels and peering beneath the truck's frame. "How does she look?"

"She looks like a broken U-joint to me," came the muffled reply. "As a matter of fact, she looks just as broke today as she looked yesterday."

"You'll need to jack her up," Sam suggested mildly.

"Damn straight, and if I had a jack I would, but this old truck of Brian's doesn't seem to be blessed with one, and to tell you the truth, I think I'd rather be horsewhipped than ask Rebecca Reed if I could borrow hers."

"Well, now, son, I don't see why that should bother you. Rebecca's a good woman."

There was a thump, a grunt of pain, and then, with much wriggling, Mac squeezed out from beneath the truck and sat up. A thin trickle of blood ran from a gouge over his left eyebrow. "I'm sure she is," he said, rubbing the wound and smearing it with grease. "But that woman dislikes me and I don't blame her. We've hardly known each other two days and already I owe her a lot of money. I've never owed anybody anything in my entire life. It's no wonder she thinks poorly of me."

"Oh, now, she don't think bad of you."

Mac laughed. "Well, if she doesn't, she sure puts on a good show." He climbed to his feet and brushed the snow off his pants. "I can't do anything without getting the hind end of this truck off the ground. I better just bite the bullet and go ask if I can borrow her jack. She probably has three or four of 'em, all heavy-duty monsters capable of lifting a Mack truck.

"She has at least two that I know of," Sam agreed. "I'll ask her, if you want."

Mac shook his head. "Thanks. I'll do it. Her opinion of me can't get much lower."

They both heard the approaching truck at the same time, and moments later Rebecca's old red Ford lumbered into view, plowing up a wave of snow before it. She cut the engine as she drove around Mac's truck, opened the cab door and dropped to the ground. "Gosh! I thought for sure you'd have it all fixed by now," she said.

"Couldn't jack her up," he said. "Couldn't find the jack…"

"Ah," she said, nodding calmly. "Well, I've got one. A good heavy-duty one." She turned and walked back to the truck and Mac watched her, admiring the way she moved, her self-possessed grace, wishing more than anything in the world that he could do just one thing right in this woman's presence. He saw her struggling with the heavy jack and moved to help her.

"This is great!" he said as he took it from her hands. "This'll do the job. Thanks."

"You're bleeding," she said.

"Bumped my head." He turned back toward his truck. In a matter of minutes the vehicle was jacked up enough for him to crawl beneath it with his tools and spare parts spread on an old blanket beside him.

"How about a light?" Sam said.

"Oh, he doesn't need one," Rebecca said. "He told me he could work blindfolded, he's that good."

"Well, there's a headlamp on the front seat," Mac said. "if you wouldn't mind passing it to me."

He heard her footsteps march up to the driver's side. She wrenched open the door. Long pause. "I don't see any lamp."

"Look under the stuff on the passenger's side," Mac called out, picturing the horror in her beautiful eyes as she beheld the heaps of trash in the cab of his brother's truck. "It's buried in there somewhere."

She climbed into the cab, and as she did so, the truck began to move.

"Hey!" Mac shouted. Seconds later the vehicle shifted just enough for the jack to kick out from beneath the bumper. The back of the truck banged down hard, making him cry out as the air was driven from his lungs. He tried to move but couldn't. The undercarriage of the truck pressed against him as one of the tires slid more deeply into a rut.

"Mac? Mac! Are you okay?" he heard her ask as her feet hit the ground.

"I'm fine," he managed. "But…I'm kind of…pinned… under here…"

"Help me, Sam!" Rebecca sounded scared. "We've got to get this thing back up! Chock the front wheels again, front and back! Hurry!" Mac heard the frenzy of coordinated movements as they got the jack under the rear bumper and worked the long handle. The rear of the truck rose slowly, and he felt the pressure against his chest ease, though breathing was still difficult. "I think that's enough!'' Rebecca said. "Mac? Can you move at all?''

"Yeah,'' he said, the word more gasped than spoken. "I'm fine. I just got wedged in a little too tightly.'' He slowly inched his way out and just as slowly pushed himself into a sitting position. He looked at her…and felt as if he were gazing into the face of a beautiful angel that was drifting slowly away from him and into a gathering darkness.

"Mac?'' Rebecca said, and then caught him as he slumped forward into her arms.

"WELL, BILL MACKENZIE, I think you'll live,'' Sadie Hedda said, corralling medical paraphernalia into her bag. "You'll be a little sore, but that's to be expected after being squashed by a truck. You're young and strong and in very good shape. Your blood pressure is stable, and I don't think there's any internal bleeding. Like I said, you have at least six cracked ribs and some pretty impressive bruising, so you'll be laid up for a while, and we'll have to keep the ribs taped. But I don't see any long-term complications unless you do something foolish, like puncture a lung.'' Sadie shrugged into her parka and tucked her flaming mane of shoulder-length hair beneath a thick fleece hat. Her broad freckled face broke into a smile, and she reached to give Rebecca's arm a squeeze, walking with her to the door. She lowered her voice to a barely audible murmur. "Jeez, Becky, you landed yourself a live one here! He's one handsome son of a gun!''

"He's not mine,'' Rebecca said stonily. "How long does he have to stay in bed?''

"If I were you,'' Hedda advised, "I'd keep him there as long as possible.''

"Sadie! I'm serious. My first clients of the season are coming to stay in this cabin very soon, and I need to do a lot of work on it before they arrive. I can't have it tied up as a hospital! Shouldn't we transport him into Dawson?"

"He'd be better off not moving. He'll need a week of bed rest, followed by another three weeks of recuperation."

Rebecca stared over Sadie's shoulder at the man who lay on the lower bunk on the cabin wall opposite the woodstove. He apparently felt her gaze and turned his head to meet her eyes. In the soft glow of lamplight his eyes were unreadable. She felt a twinge of guilt, but after all, she had a business to run.

"Look, Sadie, I'll have to take him into Dawson. He'll get a lot more attention at the clinic. I have too much work to do here."

"Well," Sadie said, "it's up to you, of course. I understand how things are. Can you possibly keep him here for two days? Yes? Good!" She pulled on her mitts and reached for her bag. "Becky, I wish you all the best, but I have to go. Roady Dan's woman is expecting any moment now, and I promised I'd stay near my radio phone." She looked over her shoulder. "I'll check on you tomorrow, Bill MacKenzie, and no getting out of that bed to fix your truck!" she said. Then, with Rebecca on her heels, she exited the guest cabin and walked to her pickup truck.

"Thanks for coming so quickly, Sadie," Rebecca said. "I appreciate it."

"No problem. Keep an eye on him, Becky. He's just the sort to try and crawl out of here under his own power. He really shouldn't be moving around at all for a while." With a cheerful wave, the nurse practitioner and EMT, who covered an area of some five hundred square miles, drove off.

Rebecca walked back to the main cabin where Sam and Ellin were waiting for Sadie's prognosis. She delivered it glumly, slumping into a chair and dropping her head into her hands. "I rue the day that man ever drove his truck into my yard."

"Now, Rebecca," Ellin said, "let's just be grateful that he wasn't more seriously hurt."

"I can't be grateful for that right now, because right now I've got to drive clear to Flat Creek, find his cabin, and feed his hungry dogs, who incidentally, probably haven't eaten for several days. Fred Turner was in charge of feeding them."

Sam cleared his throat. "I know where that cabin is. Been over that way a time or two to visit Fred. I expect I could show you the way."

"I didn't know you ever visited Fred Turner," Ellin said, her voice radiating surprised disapproval. "I can't imagine what the two of you have in common. Why, that man is nothing more than an alcoholic reprobate!"

"Well, now, Ellin—"

"Would you drive over with me, Sam?" Rebecca asked. "I'll feed my dogs before we go just in case we get back late. We can throw ten bags of food into the back of my truck and ferry it over."

"And what about tomorrow?" Ellin asked pointedly. "Who's going to feed those dogs tomorrow?"

Rebecca stared at her and then nodded slowly. "You're right." She slumped again, reconsidering. "Okay. Sam, here's what we'll do. We'll drive over with one bag of food. We'll feed the dogs, load them into my dog truck and bring them back here. Tomorrow I'll sort out the rest. At least the dogs will be safe and cared for.'' She pushed wearily to her feet. ''I'll get started with my chores.''

''And I'll run Ellin home on the snowmobile,'' Sam said, ''and be back directly.''

''You will not,'' Ellin retorted. ''What about that poor young man? Who's going to watch him? No, I'd better stay right here and keep an eye on Mac while you two do what you have to do.''

''Thanks, Ellin,'' Rebecca said gratefully. ''I guess we'll be back when we get here.''

As she lugged the heavy buckets around the dog yard, scooping out the evening feed a good two hours early to her surprised huskies, she reflected on how much more complicated life had become in the past two days. She finished her chores in record time while Sam filled the wood box and hauled a couple of buckets of water from the spring. They climbed into her dog truck and she gave the cold engine a good prime before turning it on. It caught instantly and roared to life. ''There's nothing like a Ford,'' she said to Sam, who returned with his usual, ''unless it's a Chevy.''

She was driving past the guest cabin when its door opened and that damn nuisance of a man emerged, pulling on his parka and weakly waving for her to stop. She did, nearly throwing Sam into the dashboard. She jumped out of the truck and charged toward him. ''Where do you think you're going! Get back inside!'' She raised her arm and pointed behind him. ''If you puncture a lung, don't expect any sympathy from me!''

MacKenzie finished pulling on his parka. ''If you're going up to my place, I figured I'd ride along. I can take care of my dogs better than anyone. All I ask is that you throw a few bags of food in the back of your truck.''

''I mean it,'' Rebecca warned. ''Get back into bed!''

"I feel fine. I can certainly ride in a truck for a couple of hours, and I can take care of my own dogs. You'll have your cabin back, too."

"I won't say it again," Rebecca warned.

"You won't have to," Ellin said, walking up behind MacKenzie. "Go on, Rebecca. You and Sam get going." She reached out and closed one hand firmly around MacKenzie's upper arm. "You may think you're big and tough, young man, but believe me, you don't have anything on little old Ellin Dodge."

Rebecca turned on her heel, stormed back to the truck and hoisted herself behind the wheel. Without looking back, she gunned the truck down the rutted, snow-covered track, causing Sam to clutch the dash with both hands.

"I'm so sick of arrogant, egotistical men!" Rebecca blurted.

"Well, I can surely understand that," Sam said, casting her a wry glance. "You see so darn many of 'em on a day-to-day basis!"

It took nearly two hours to drive to the MacKenzie cabin on the banks of Flat Creek, the last few miles of unplowed road a white-knuckled adventure. "There it is," Sam said, as the truck's headlights picked out a wall of gray weathered logs. No lights shone from the windows, no smoke curled from the chimney, but to Rebecca's relief the dogs appeared to be all right. She put on her headlamp and carried a bucket of kibble around the dog lot, giving each hungry animal a generous scoop. "This dog's name is Merlin," she said to Sam. "He's Brian's best leader and one of the smartest dogs I've ever known." She gave Merlin a friendly pat. "I'll water them when we get them home," she said. "They aren't dying of thirst, not with a foot and a half of snow on the ground.''

She went to the cabin door, noting that there were no tracks in the snow, and pulled the latch string. The door swung open. The cabin's interior was as cold as ice, and in the light cast from her headlamp she panned the small, low-eaved room. It was an unbelievable mess. Dirty dishes and cooking pans filled the dry sink. A frying pan with something still in it was atop the stove. Clothing was heaped and thrown everywhere and trash covered the floor. Three empty whiskey bottles stood upon the cluttered table. Fred Turner had obviously stayed long enough to drink all of MacKenzie's liquor before moving to greener pastures.

She slammed the door shut behind her and began the arduous process of loading fourteen dogs into her truck, gambling on which dogs could share a dog box without fighting. At length she and Sam had accomplished the task and the nervous growls and whines had faded into silence. It had begun to snow again. ''Well,'' she said to Sam, ''let's head for home.''

They left the MacKenzie cabin and crept slowly homeward in steadily worsening conditions. By the time her familiar turnoff came into view, three more hours had passed, and it was nearly midnight when they pulled into the kennel yard. Ellin had kept the lamps burning in the cabin, and the yellow glow shining through the frosted windowpanes warmed Rebecca's heart. ''Sam, take Ellin home in my plow truck,'' she said as they climbed wearily out of the cab. ''I'll start it and get it warming up for you. And thanks a million for helping out.''

''Anytime, Rebecca. You know that.''

Ellin was waiting at the door when she entered. "He's still alive," she said.

"What a relief," Rebecca said, scowling.

"It hasn't been easy for him. He's in quite a bit of pain, but he tries not to let on. His dog is in the cabin with him. She really wanted to be near him."

"Ellin, have you been holding his hand the whole time we've been gone?"

"No, but I looked in on him from time to time and kept the woodstove going. I brought him some supper, some of your stew. I hope you don't mind."

"Of course not," Rebecca said.

"He ate a little bit, but he doesn't look very good to me. I think you should check on him. Maybe we should call Sadie back."

"Certainly not. She has to drive nearly an hour to get here. If he's dying, I'll drive him into Dawson. If he isn't, he'll just have to suffer out the night. But first I'll need to let his dogs out of the boxes and water them. You two get on home. It's way past Sam's bedtime. And, Ellin?" She gave her friend a grateful hug. "Thanks. I owe you."

Rebecca spent the next hour tethering Mac's dogs on two picket lines she'd strung between the spruce trees in her yard. She gave them pans of water flavored with meat scraps and kibble, and they drank the offering eagerly. She left them outside in the gentle snowfall while she spooned down a plate of the moose-meat stew herself, and then she loaded the dogs back into the truck for the night. This was an arduous chore. Lifting a sixty-pound dog up over her head was no easy task, especially when she was so tired. When Mac's dogs were all bedded down, she checked on her own, and then on her way back to her cabin, she paused beside the guest cabin, debating whether to see how the patient was doing.

Finally she opened the cabin door quietly. Ellin had left a lamp burning on the table, which she'd moved closer to the bunk. Mac was asleep, and Callie was curled at his feet. His head was turned away from the table so that the lamplight shone on the back of his neck and his left shoulder. His breathing was shallow and rapid, but given the nature of his injuries, Rebecca thought that was probably to be expected.

Almost against her will, she moved closer to the bunk and gazed down at him as he slept. She felt a twinge of guilt at how she had treated him earlier. Aside from owing her a chunk of money, which he'd earnestly promised to repay, she had no real reason to dislike him so. Except…except that he was undeniably handsome, and she resented the fact that she was attracted to him. She was the widow of Bruce Reed, a man she had loved deeply and would for all time. She had no right to feel attracted to another man.

She turned away abruptly and fed three more good-size chunks of wood into the stove. With the dampers closed, the fire should hold through the night, especially since morning wasn't too far off.

She was walking toward the cabin door when Mac shifted, moved his head from side to side and moaned. His breathing became more rapid. Rebecca froze. He made a strangled noise in the back of his throat, and one arm knocked the covers down to his waist. Callie sat up, alarmed.

"No!" he gasped harshly. "I can't reach it! It's no good, I'm pinned! Mouse, get out! Get out! Can't breathe!" His arms thrashed and his breathing became even more labored. Rebecca found herself at his side, reaching down to stop his struggles, to wake him from the clutches of some awful nightmare, but the minute she closed her hand on his arm, he shot upright, smacking his head hard against the upper bunk. "Oh, God!" he gasped, grabbing her arm with a strength that both hurt and frightened her.

"Mac! It's me, Rebecca! It's all right, you were just dreaming. It was just a dream!" She put her hand over his, trying to reassure him.

"Mouse!" he said, his shoulders heaving as he gasped for breath.

"No, it's Rebecca! Wake up!"

He turned his head slowly and his eyes focused. "Oh, God!" he said again.

"It's all right, Mac! Everything's okay."

He released her slowly, raised a hand to his head and then slumped back onto the bunk, flat on his back, and moaned again. His skin was cold and clammy, and his face was pale.

"It was just a dream," Rebecca repeated. "A dream about a mouse."

"Not a mouse," he said, struggling for breath, remembering. "Mouse! Mouse is dead. His plane crashed."

"It was a bad dream," she reiterated. "Do you want another pain pill? Sadie left some for you." She rubbed her arm where he had gripped it.

He moved his head slowly back and forth. "I'm okay," he said.

"Try to relax. You have a bunch of broken ribs. Breathing's going to be tough for a while. I'm going to get you something to drink."

"I don't need—"

"I don't care what you think you need or don't need,"

Rebecca said. "I'm going to get you something, anyway, and you're going to drink it!"

She stood up, trying not to show how shaken she was, and quickly left the cabin. The cold darkness of the Yukon night braced her, and she welcomed the dry, clean sting of it. What if he died here in her guest cabin, especially after the miserable way she'd treated him? She rushed to her cabin and rummaged in the cupboards until she found a bottle of rum that Bruce had bought years ago. She tried to remember how to make a hot buttered rum, but for the life of her she couldn't. She melted a good chunk of butter in a small pan, added a cup of milk and finally a generous slug of the rum. She heated a mug with hot water and poured the mixture into it, wrapped a clean towel around it to keep it warm and carried it quickly to the guest cabin. His breathing had improved, she thought, and he was still awake. These were both good signs. He smiled faintly at her, but his face was still pale.

"Can you sit up?" she asked.

"I'm sorry to be so much trouble," he said.

She ignored his apology. Since sitting was obviously painful for him, she propped all the pillows behind him, until he was in a half-reclining position. "I made this for you. I figured it would help you sleep."

He accepted it and sniffed. "Rum?"

"Rum and milk. Is there such a drink?"

"If you made it, I guess there is." He took a sip and swallowed.

"Is it okay?"

"It's just fine."

"How are you feeling?"

He took another sip and considered her question carefully. "Like a half-ton pickup sat on my chest," he replied. "How are my dogs?"

"They're fine. You can see them tomorrow. They're out in my truck, fed and watered."

"Thank you. More than I can ever say."

Rebecca stood. "Can I get you anything else?"

He shook his head. "I appreciate everything you've done. And I'll be out of here soon, I promise you." She nodded and turned toward the door. "Hey," he said, and she looked back. "Was Fred Turner there when you got to my cabin?"

Rebecca shook her head. "There were no tracks in the snow, and your woodstove was two days cold. And you'd better lay in a few more bottles of whiskey for the winter. Looked to me like Fred found your stash." She smiled briefly and closed the cabin door gently behind her.

HIS DREAMS OPENED doors to his past that he kept tightly closed when he was awake. In his dreams he relived every awful moment of that awful time. When he awoke it took him minutes, hours, days, sometimes, to close all the doors, to rebuild and fortify the walls that kept him safe, kept him sane.

This morning he lay in soft-breathing stillness, staring up at the hand-hewn planks of the bunk above him. The stove still held a fire, but its warmth was ineffective. The light through the thickly frosted window was dim and gray. It was early, very quiet, and very cold. Callie shivered at his feet.

Mac moved tentatively, shifting his upper body on the hard, lumpy mattress, and caught his breath. No doubt about it. Having a truck fall on you was a seriously painful business. Of course, if he hadn't been so stupid about overloading his truck, none of this would have happened. Even worse that it had to happen right in front of *her*.

Rebecca regarded him as a cheechako and she was right. He was definitely the idiot of the North, completely out of his element. A few months ago he'd been in the Persian Gulf flying one of the most advanced technical fighters off one of the most advanced Nimitz carriers, and now he was lying on a bunk in Yukon Territory with a bunch of broken ribs at the mercy of a woman who didn't care for him one little bit, in a land so hostile that all he had to do was walk out into it and he could quite easily die.

He shifted his legs beneath the thick wool blankets. He couldn't just lie here. If he had to crawl back to his brother's cabin, he'd crawl. A man had his pride, after all. Sometimes it was the only thing in the world he had. The effort cost him, but he made it as far as the stove, where he fed two split chunks of dry spruce onto the bed of coals and closed the door. He knelt in front of it with the blanket around his waist, shivering, his breath making little frost plumes in the cold cabin air. If this was technically still autumn, what would winter be like? Would he still be alive then, or would wolves be gnawing on his bones?

The cabin door opened and he glanced up. It was Rebecca.

"What are you doing out of bed?" Stern, disapproving voice.

"Freezing to death," he replied.

She was carrying a coffeepot and two cups and looked bright and alert, as if she'd been awake for hours. She had walked bareheaded and without a parka from the main cabin, and her hair fell in a thick, glossy tumble clear to her waist.

"I brought coffee," she said, scrutinizing him. "How are you feeling?"

"I feel just fine," Mac said.

"Oh, yes, and you look just fine, too. Actually, your dog looks a lot better than you do. I'll bring her a bowl of food in a little bit." She set the coffeepot and mugs on the stove and then helped him to his feet with a strength that her small stature belied. "Get back into bed." She guided him to the bunk and steadied him while he sat. Sitting was still painful, but he didn't move while she poured him a cup of coffee, black, no sugar, and handed it to him.

"Thank you." He cradled the mug between his palms, relishing the warmth that radiated from it. The coffee smelled wonderful. Rich and fragrant. He tasted it, and something inside of him eased. "This is very good."

She poured herself a cup and gazed at him over the rim. Steam curled up and wreathed her face. She was without a doubt the most beautiful woman he'd ever laid eyes upon. Rebecca Reed had the kind of beauty that came from within. He lowered his eyes, afraid of what might be showing in them. "It's twenty below zero and clear," she said. "The rivers should freeze up soon."

His brother Brian had talked a lot about the rivers, one in particular. "My brother calls the Yukon a drifter's river," he said. "A river of dreams."

She smiled through the steam. "Bruce and I paddled a canoe down it from Whitehorse to Dawson. Everyone should do that at least once in a lifetime. It mellows the soul."

Bruce. Her dead husband. Mac took another swallow of coffee. It didn't taste quite as good this time. He glanced at her hand, noting the gold wedding band she still wore. "Must have been a good trip."

"It was a great trip. Our honeymoon." She fiddled with the stove's dampers and stuffed two more pieces of birch into the firebox. The stove began to roar like a blast furnace, the metal ticking rhythmically as it heated. "I should drive you into Dawson today for X rays."

"No need. I feel fine."

"You look flushed. My guess is you're running a fever."

"Can't be. I'm freezing to death. Where are my clothes, by the way?"

"Ellin took them. They needed a bath. Sam and Ellin have loads of hot water and a washer and dryer, thanks to a big propane water heater and a huge diesel generator. They have a shower, too, which Ellin forces me to use from time to time."

"That must be hard to take."

"Sheer torture. I can only stand it for about thirty minutes at a time." He noticed that she almost smiled. "I have a sauna here and it's great, my clients love it, but it's just not the same." She rose to her feet. "When I'm done feeding and watering, I'm going to run some dogs. I'll bring you breakfast before getting started and I should be back by two. Will you be all right by yourself?"

"I'll be fine. I'm sorry to be such trouble." Rebecca nodded and began to leave, taking her coffee mug with her. "Rebecca," he said. She paused and turned. "You have to believe me when I tell you I'm not usually like this."

Her eyebrows raised slightly. "Like what? Half-naked and freezing to death?"

Mac drew the wool blanket more tightly around his

waist, and felt his color deepen. "I'm not usually such a nuisance. I'm actually a fairly intelligent, capable, self-reliant man, and I have good common sense."

"You do?" she said.

"Yes, ma'am. I'm loaded with it."

This time the smile made it to her lips, and they curved in a most delicious way. "Well," she said, "you certainly couldn't prove it by me."

And then she was gone, taking her smile and its sunshine with her.

CHAPTER THREE

REBECCA WAS STILL SMILING three hours later, twenty miles down the trail. The dogs were trotting smoothly, moving through the fresh snow as if it wasn't there. She had put Cookie and Raven up in lead, two young females with loads of drive and intelligence, and they were doing a great job. The sky was a deep vault of blue, the sunlight bright, the air very still and very cold. Her eight-dog team was covering ten miles an hour, not bad at all on an unbroken trail and pulling about a hundred pounds of weight in the toboggan sled.

"Raven! Gee!" The main trail intersected with a cut-off that would loop around and take them home. Raven pulled to the right as ordered, taking Cookie and the rest of the dogs with her. "Good girl, Raven! Good girl."

Common sense? Hah! The man was hopeless. He would most certainly die out there in that trapper's shack on the Flat this winter. He would starve to death trying to feed his dogs. He would freeze to death trying to keep a fire in the woodstove. Common sense, indeed! What on earth possessed him to think he could come into this wild land and survive?

And now she was stuck with taking care of him and his dog team, all of which made her wonder just how much common sense she, herself, had. She laughed aloud, the noise startling her dogs and causing them to break their gait and glance back at her. "It's okay, gang.

Good dogs. All right." They faced front again and their tug lines tightened as they forged ahead. She could still picture Mac sitting on the bunk with that old wool army blanket pulled around him, his broad shoulders bared to the chill of the room. She hated to admit it, but Sadie Hedda had been right. William MacKenzie was one long, tall, handsome man—even if he didn't have one shred of common sense. He had something else, though, something she couldn't quite fathom....

Rebecca shifted her weight on the sled runners, bent her knees and bobbed up and down to warm up the backs of her calves. Her toes were cold even in her heavy boots. This was nothing new. Her toes and fingers were always cold from October until May. It came with the Territory.

"Okay, you huskies, pick it up!" Cookie and Raven broke into a lope at her words, and moments later they were heading home. The trip back would be quicker on the broken trail, and she'd have time to run one more team before she had to start evening chores. The other dogs in the yard heralded her arrival, and Rebecca was surprised to see her red plow truck parked in front of the main cabin. As she looped her snub line around the hitching post, securing the team, Sam stepped out onto the porch. At the same moment, Ellin emerged from the guest cabin. Ellin's face was radiant as she strode across the dog yard.

"Rebecca," she said as she approached. "We're taking Mac over to our place. Sam's rigged a sled behind the Bombardier for Mac to lie in so it'll be an easy trip for him. He can stay in the boys' room for now and move into the cabin when he's ready."

Rebecca unsnapped the dogs' tug lines and began stripping the polar fleece booties from their feet. "Ellin, you and Sam have enough to do without taking care of an invalid.'' She reached for the stack of galvanized feed pans and dropped one into the snow in front of each dog, then opened the prepacked cooler to give each some broth thick with chunks of liver.

"He won't be an invalid for long, Becca. Sam could use some help around the place, and the way I see it, God has provided it in the form of this nice young man.''

Rebecca straightened, one mittened hand pressing into the small of her back. She looked at Ellin and sighed. "You do have a way of looking at things.''

"He's going to be a big help to Sam. If he can do all the things Sam thinks he can, Bill MacKenzie will be worth his weight in gold. After all, he did fix the Bombardier, and that thing hasn't run since the turn of the last century.''

"He's a big man, Ellin,'' Rebecca cautioned. "Probably eats a lot.''

"I cook a lot. Can't get out of the habit after raising four boys. There'll be plenty to eat. And Sam has fixed up one whole end of the hangar for the dogs.''

"You're taking his dogs, too?''

"Of course! It'll be fun having a dog team around the place again. I miss them.''

"Take some of mine!''

"Becky, I've said it before and I'll say it again. This is too much for you. You can't go it alone.''

Rebecca bent to pick up the empty feed pans. "I have another team to run, Ellin.''

"Yes, I know,'' Ellin said curtly. "And another team after that, and then there are the chores to do. The wood to split, the water to lug, the dogs to feed.'' She sighed. "Well, my dear, I've had my say and as always, it's fallen on deaf ears. I really think all mushers have dog biscuits for brains!''

"I love you, Ellin Dodge, and I always will," Rebecca said, arms full of feed pans. "But I have to do things my way."

Thirty minutes later she was out on the trail again with another eight-dog team and Ellin's words echoing in her ears. Her neighbor was right. It was too much. There were days when Rebecca felt like giving up, days when everything piled up in front of her like an unscalable mountain, days when she was so lonely and exhausted that she would drop her head into her hands and weep like a baby. Those were the bad days, and while not all of her days were bad, they were all long and lonely and hard, and they were making her hard in ways she didn't like.

Bringing coffee and breakfast to Mac this morning was the first time she'd felt like a woman since Bruce's death. There was no denying that the simple act of handing Mac a cup of coffee had made her feel good inside. And the way he'd looked at her had made her feel... He had made her feel... Oh, for Pete's sake!

"Twister! Get up, you lazy beast!" she chastised a young wheel dog, whose job was to run directly in front of the sled. "I'll feed you to the wolves if you don't pull your weight!"

Ellin was right about Sam. He did need help. Sam and Ellin's boys had all become very successful, but none of them had wanted to remain in the Yukon. Sam had given up the mail route he used to fly two years ago. He probably shouldn't be flying at all, but she'd like to see anyone try to keep that old man out of the sky. And then he'd gone and bought that old wreck of a Stearman with the dream of restoring it to its former glory. Rebecca shook her head. It was true about men. They never grew up. They were just boys grown tall.

"Come on, Minnow, you can do it. Good girl!"

Well, anyhow, she was rid of Bill MacKenzie. He'd be gone when she got back and she could spruce up the guest cabin and get it ready for her first clients, who would be arriving in a few weeks—and none too soon. She desperately needed the money the dogsled tour would generate.

Three hundred yards from the cabin she stopped the team, snubbed the sled to a nearby spruce and loaded the toboggan bed with six armloads of the firewood that had been cut to length and stacked beside the trail. She used dog power to pull the load to the cabin and had barely finished watering, snacking and unharnessing the dogs when a familiar truck bounced into the yard. The cab door opened and Sadie Hedda jumped down, waved, then grabbed her parka and shrugged into it as she crossed toward the guest cabin, one hand clutching her medical bag.

"He's gone, Sadie," Rebecca called, tossing the wood from the sled onto the cabin porch.

Sadie turned to stare at Rebecca. "Gone? Gone where? My Lord, Becky, the man was seriously injured, and he was in no shape to be going anywhere! I know you didn't want him here, but surely you didn't drive him off!" She was walking rapidly toward Rebecca as she spoke.

"No, Sadie, I didn't. Ellin and Sam have adopted him. If you want to do a follow-up exam, you'll find him there."

Sadie was visibly relieved. "Rebecca," she said. "I know it's none of my business, but where did you find that guy?"

"I didn't find him! He came here to buy dog food." Rebecca continued to unload the firewood. "He's Brian MacKenzie's older brother and he's taking care of Brian's dogs for the winter while Brian finishes his degree at the university. He says he's going to race the team and expects to do very well. He thinks there's nothing to mushing, that it's easy as beans and anyone can do it. And, oh, by the way, he's also planning to win the Percy DeWolf."

Sadie grinned. "Where's he from?"

"Dunno. But he was in the military. Some kind of mechanic, I think."

"Mechanic," Sadie said, eyes narrowing appreciatively. "Mechanics can come in awfully handy around here."

"Yes. I'll be glad when he fixes his truck and gets it out of my driveway."

Sadie shoved her hands in her parka pockets and frowned at Rebecca. "I know he owes you money, but is that the only reason you dislike him so? I mean, you have to admit that he's the best-looking thing to step into the Territory in a dog's age. Does he smoke?"

"Nope. At least, I don't think he does."

"Good! I like the idea of a Marlboro man without the cigarettes. By the way, if you're throwing him back, throw him in my direction, would you?"

"He's a free man," Rebecca said as she threw the last log onto the porch. "But, Sadie, it wouldn't be a bad idea for you to stop by Sam and Ellin's. Your patient looked kind of off-color to me this morning. I think he might be running a fever."

"A fever! That's not good at all," Sadie said ominously. "I'd better get over there straight away." Without another word she marched back to her truck, jumped

in and roared off. Rebecca eased a cramp in the small
of her back as she watched Sadie disappear. She longed
to sit down in the rocker beside the woodstove with a
cup of hot tea, but there was no time. She had to mix
the dog food, fill the wood box, haul endless buckets of
water up from the springhouse, and then feed the dogs
before full dark. It was going to be cold tonight. She
needed to be sure that each dog had enough straw in its
house to make a warm bed.

No time for tea. No time for herself. And certainly no
time for anyone else, especially a helpless cheechako
like William MacKenzie.

IT TOOK FAR LESS TIME than Sadie had predicted for Mac
to recover from his injuries. Within a week he was up
and about, doing light chores over Ellin's protests, but
by the end of the second week he counted himself cured
and was taking care of his dogs when he wasn't helping
Sam work on the Stearman.

In his third week at Sam and Ellin's, he used Sam's
old Jimmy to haul his dog truck from Rebecca's driveway to Sam's hangar where, with Sam's help, he replaced the U-joint. The next day he drove his truck to
his brother's place on Flat Creek, picked up his few be-
longings, the two dogsleds, feed dishes, the harnesses,
gang lines and other assorted mushing paraphernalia,
and returned to the little cabin on Sam and Ellin's property. The day after that, he began training his dog team.

The trails around the Dodges' place were the same
trails that Rebecca trained on, so Mac had anticipated
that they'd run into each other frequently and had been
looking forward to it more than he cared to admit. But
during his first week, he saw no sign of Rebecca. He
finally mentioned her absence to Ellin.

"She's probably out on a trip with some clients," Ellin explained. "She usually heads down toward Guggieville or up toward Inuvik. You might swing by her cabin and see if Donny's old blue Chevy is there."

"Who's Donny?" Mac asked.

"Donny's a good kid. He takes care of Rebecca's kennel when she goes on her trips. He's Athapaskan."

Mac spent the rest of the afternoon splitting firewood for Sam and Ellin, but the next morning, bright and early, he was on his way to Dawson City, where he sold his Rolex for far less than it was worth. He drove directly back to Rebecca's with the money. She wasn't there, but Donny was.

"She could be gone two, three more days," the young man said in answer to Mac's question. "Maybe more, maybe less. Hard to tell sometimes. Three Japanese clients. Big money." He smiled broadly.

Mac left an envelope for Rebecca. He'd sealed a brief note inside, along with the money from the sale of his watch, promising to pay the balance by the end of February. Mac had big plans for February, and if everything worked out, he'd have more than enough to pay off his debts and buy more dog food. Feeling pretty good about things in general—better than he'd felt in more than a month—he returned to Sam and Ellin's place and harnessed a team of dogs for a training run. Sam came out of the hangar to watch him take off. "You might try the trail that leads down to the river," Sam shouted over the frenzied barking of the dogs. "The Mazey Creek trail. The river's frozen solid and it's fine traveling right now—you can make a lot of miles on it. Good training!"

Mac nodded, pulled the release knot on the snub line, and the team shot down the trail at warp speed. Mac loved the takeoffs best of all, the wild, blind explosion

of power and speed that catapulted the sled—with him
hanging on for dear life—down the narrow twisting path
that led from the Dodges' cabin out onto the main trail,
which, in turn, led to the river. He'd avoided running
the river before because of the rough pack ice. But Sam
was right. If he was going to make good in February,
he'd need to start putting longer miles on his team.

When he reached the main trail, he gave Merlin the
command to turn to the right. "Gee, Merlin!" He
grinned, as the big, handsome, blue-eyed, black-and-
white husky veered unerringly to the right. "Good
dog!" The idea that one could steer sled dogs with mere
voice commands was still novel enough to astound him.
Driving a big team of dogs was like driving a freight
train from the rear of the caboose without the benefit of
rails to keep the train on track, and without a steering
wheel to make the turns. A good lead dog like Merlin
made the job easy. A simple verbal command and the
entire train turned smoothly to the right or the left.

The trail veered suddenly and Merlin disappeared
from sight, followed by five pairs of dogs, all running
hard. The sled whipped around the corner, and Mac had
a split second to assimilate several facts: One, he was
airborne; two, his team was below him, descending an
extremely steep bank that dropped onto the pack ice of
the river; and three, when his sled came down to earth,
there was going to be quite a spectacular crash.

And there was. He heard a high-pitched scream and
thought for a moment that it had come from him, although it sounded like a woman's scream.

"Son of a bitch!" he roared just to hear his own
voice, which to his relief sounded normal. "Whoa!" The
dogs were still running. In fact, they were running faster
than they ever had before, even though the sled was on

its side and he was being dragged along behind it, gripping the driving bow with all his strength. "Whoa! Merlin, whoa!"

He heard another scream, closer this time, and definitely not coming from him. The scream was followed by a steady stream of excited babbling in a foreign language.

"Kanemoto! Hold your team!" another voice, a woman's, firm and familiar, shouted in English. "Hideka! Run up and take your lead dogs! Hold them steady! No, Kanemoto, don't get off the sled! Stay on the brake! The brake! That's right! I'm going to try to catch that team!"

Oh, no, you're not, Rebecca Reed, Mac thought grimly as he struggled to right the capsized sled. He got one knee onto the bottom runner, ignoring the pain of the foot board digging into his kneecap. He got his second knee on it, and then both knees were jolted off and he was being dragged face down again. The ice hook was bouncing wildly beside his head, having flipped out of the sled bag when the sled capsized. He seized it with one mittened hand and in the same motion jammed the pointed tips into the ice. The sled stopped so suddenly that his head smashed into the driving bow. He jumped to his feet, jerked the sled back onto its runners and barely had time to get on again before his team lunged forward, ripping the ice hook loose, and galloping madly toward two oncoming teams.

There were screams from the passengers in the other sleds, snarls, barks and growls from the dogs on all three teams, and Rebecca's voice clashing with his own as they both shouted, "On by! On by!" to their leaders.

"Kanemoto!" Rebecca shouted. "Run with your sled! Don't let your team stop! Keep them moving!"

Rebecca was driving the first team, which passed Mac's flawlessly. As she came abreast of him, she gave him a brief up and down, an even briefer smile and a curt, "Hello, Mac. Nice recovery!" Then she turned her head and shouted encouragement to the three clients struggling with the team and sled behind her. The Japanese clients managed to keep their team moving, and soon Mac had the trail to himself again. He looked back to see that Rebecca's team was charging up the river-bank. Her clients' team followed close on her heels. When she reached the top, she raised her arm to him in a slow farewell wave. Her action startled him so much he didn't have time to wave back before she was gone.

REBECCA STOOD under the hot, powerful, therapeutic stream of water in the Dodges' shower and let her muscles relax for the first time in more than a week. She was tired but she felt great. It had been a good trip, a profitable trip, and she couldn't wait to tell Ellin about the unexpected bonus she'd gotten. Rebecca squeezed more shampoo from the bottle and lathered her hair for the third time. The tension between her shoulder blades was beginning to ease as the forceful stream of hot water worked its magic.

She exited the bathroom in a huge cloud of steam dressed in clean clothes top to bottom, thick wool socks and expedition-weight fleece. She padded into the warm kitchen with the towel still wrapped in a thick, white turban around her wet hair. "Thank you, Ellin. Once again, you've saved my life."

Ellin poured a second cup of tea and set it on the table. "Sit down and tell me what's gotten you so excited. You've been hopping up and down since you got here this morning."

Rebecca dropped into a chair and pulled the tea toward her. "I can't believe it myself. It's a dream come true for me! Ellin, Kanemoto's coming back here in February."

"That's wonderful! Two trips in one winter! He must be some kind of nut, but so long as he's rich, who cares!"

"No, Ellin, he's not coming back for another trip. He wants to be my handler for the Yukon Quest! We talked about the race a lot this past week. He's always wanted to be here for the running of it. He said how much fun it would be if he personally knew a team and driver. Then we began to discuss the possibility of *my* running the race!"

Ellin's eyes widened with surprise. She blinked rapidly and sat up straighter. "My dear, you never said anything about running the Quest this season."

"I hadn't planned to. It's way too expensive. But Kanemoto has paid my entry fee, and Ellin, you know he usually gives me a tip at the end of each trip, a couple hundred dollars or so. But yesterday? Yesterday he writes me a check for five thousand dollars. Five *thousand* dollars! He hands it to me and says, 'You get ready to run that race, Miss Reed. I'll be back to handle for you one week from race start!' Can you believe it!" Rebecca leaned forward, eyes sparkling. "I have my first official sponsor!" Then, after a brief pause, she said, "What's wrong, Ellin? I thought for sure you'd be excited for me."

"Well!" Ellin said, composing herself quickly. "I am, my dear, I'm just surprised, that's all. That's something, all right!" Ellin took a sip of tea. "The Yukon Quest is a very tough race, Rebecca," she cautioned.

"I've already talked to Donny about taking care of

the kennel for the two weeks I'll be gone. Oh, Ellin, I can't believe it!'' Rebecca jumped out of her chair and paced to the woodstove and back. ''I'll need to get my toboggan sled fixed—one of the rear stanchions is cracked and the bed plastic really needs to be replaced—and I'll have to buy some new harnesses. I think I have enough booties, but I'll have to check. Bruce has all the right gear—'' She stopped suddenly and raised a hand to the towel wrapping her head. ''Bruce *had* all the right gear,'' she corrected slowly. ''And I'm sure it's all still there, stashed out in the barn. His lightweight aluminum cooker, the training notebooks, those are important. I'll have to find them. Meat. I'll have to order some good ground meat in Whitehorse and feed the dogs really well. Then there are the food drops to organize. Oh Lord, the food drops! Ellin, you can't imagine the sleepless nights spent calculating how much dog food, people food and extra supplies needs to be shipped to each checkpoint before the race starts. Fortunately, all that information should be in Bruce's notebooks. He kept notes on everything. He…'' She turned and looked at Ellin. ''I wish I could tell him about this. He'd be so excited at the idea of his dogs running the Quest again.''

''I'm sure he would,'' Ellin said quietly.

Rebecca returned to the table and sat down again with a happy sigh. ''I can't wait!'' She took a sip of tea. ''I wonder if Mac's still planning on winning the Percy DeWolf.''

''He's been training,'' Ellin said vaguely.

''Yes, I know. I met him on the river yesterday. He was dragging along quite nicely behind his sled.''

''Dragging?''

''Yes. On his face. Oh, Ellin, you should have seen it.'' Rebecca couldn't stop the laugh that burst from her.

"His dogs came tearing over that steep bank by the Mazey Creek trail, and they were flying! Next comes his sled and it's airborne. I mean to say, it shoots out over the top of the riverbank at about twenty-five miles an hour, straight into the air, with Mac standing on the runners holding on for dear life!"

"And then what happened?" Ellin said.

"He crashed!" Rebecca said. "It was the most spectacular crash I've ever seen! I don't know what held that sled of his together or what kept him attached to it. But I'll say this much for him, he didn't let go. Slamming over that pack ice must have been brutal on his poor beat-up body, but he didn't let go of that sled."

"I wondered why he was limping around this morning," Ellin mused.

"Limping! I'm surprised he can even walk." Rebecca wiped her eyes. "I'm sorry," she said. "I know it's not the least bit funny, but I can't help it."

"But, my dear, what did you do?"

"What do you mean?"

"I mean, didn't you try to help him?"

"I didn't have to. He got the sled stopped using his snow hook and managed to climb back onto the runners. I said hello when we passed." Rebecca grinned and took a deep breath. "I think he was in a state of shock. He never said a word."

Ellin regarded her for a silent moment and then shook her head. "Rebecca Reed, I do believe you have a cruel streak in you."

"I guess I must have," Rebecca confessed. "I haven't had such a good laugh in a long, long time. He's all right, isn't he?"

"If he were dying, he wouldn't say so."

"Maybe we should call Sadie to come have a look at him."

Ellin frowned. "There's little need of that. Sadie's been looking him over every day this week. She's after him, mark my words. She shows up every afternoon around feeding time, because she knows he'll be taking care of his dogs."

"He's in good hands, then. I won't worry about him."

"I should think you should. My dear girl, it's not Sadie he's interested in."

"Ellin!" Rebecca warned.

"He's a good man, Rebecca," Ellin said staunchly.

"Well, I don't know about that," Rebecca said, standing up and stretching stiff muscles. "But if he keeps on the way he's going, he might make a good musher someday. He didn't let go of his sled."

"I certainly hope you're right," Ellin said, looking directly at her. "Because there's something you should know. Sam has fronted him the money to enter the Yukon Quest this year. Rebecca, Mac will be sharing the race trail with you all the way from Whitehorse to Fairbanks."

Rebecca froze in midstretch. "You're kidding, right? Oh, Ellin, please tell me you're kidding!"

Ellin shook her head. "I wish I could, because I don't believe he's got the experience to run a thousand-mile race. But he believes he can. He also thinks he can finish in the money and win enough to pay you what he owes you."

"Is that what this is all about? The money he owes me? Does he realize how tough a race the Quest is? Does he realize he'd be lucky just to finish it? And what about the expense of running it? Does he know how much that would set him back?" Rebecca slumped back into her chair. "I can't believe it," she said, shaking her head. "Mac actually thinks he's going to run the Yukon Quest. Well, he's in for a rude awakening. The race officials will never let him enter. He's not qualified!"

"SO WHAT DO YOU THINK of our Sadie Hedda?" Sam asked, leaning against the Stearman's fuselage.

"Sadie? Oh, she's a real good medic and a nice woman," Mac replied, his voice deliberately noncommittal. His upper body was awkwardly wedged headfirst into the rear cockpit of the old plane. His legs were draped over the back of the pilot's seat, and he rested the heels of his stocking feet on top of the fuselage. He was silent for a moment, trying to decide whether to carry on this personal discussion. "Well, the truth is, Sam, she's coming on to me like a freight train, and I'm afraid if I stop running, she'll just mow me down." Embarrassed, Mac coughed. "Could you hand me the safety wire pliers? Thanks."

"Sadie's the kind of woman who sees what she likes and goes after it," Sam explained slowly.

"I don't have a problem with women going after things. I just don't want to be gotten by her, that's all. And I don't know how to discourage her without hurting her feelings, but I guess there's no avoiding that. Ah! All done! I think that'll be just fine. You better check it over, though. Let's see what else I can play with while I'm in here..." Mac took a deep breath. "Sam, Sadie's a great girl, but the thing is, there's Rebecca."

"I see." Now Sam's voice was neutral. Mac waited for him to speak again. When he did, his tone was gruff with emotion. "Rebecca's like a daughter to us, Mac. I don't know what we'd do without her." He glanced into the open cockpit and shook his head cautiously. "She and Bruce were real close."

"Yup," Mac said heavily. "I got that part."

"Sometimes, I think it's harder for a woman to cope with grief when the death is unexpected," Sam said. "For a long time after Bruce died, Rebecca shut herself away from everyone and everything. Didn't eat, wouldn't speak, just sat in that lonely cabin and stared at the wall. For two whole weeks that went on, and then one day she just got up, went outside, and started running the dogs."

"She's real good with the dogs."

"Yes, she is. She loves those dogs," Sam said. "In some ways, I think they saved her life."

"WELL, THESE SWEET ROLLS are done," Ellin said, sliding the pan out of the oven. Why don't you go and fetch Sam? He's out in the hangar working on that plane of his. I swear he thinks more of that old thing than he does of me!"

"I doubt it," Rebecca said, reaching for her parka. "But that antique flying machine definitely comes a close second."

She had combed out her hair, but it was still damp, and in the frigid air the dampness crystallized as she walked across the packed snow of the yard toward the big Quonset hut. Sam always kept the old double-barrel stove roaring when he was working inside the hut, and the hangar was surprisingly comfortable even on the bitterest of days. Rebecca opened the door and slipped quickly inside, surprised to see Mac's dogs still tethered on their picket lines. She had assumed he'd be out training.

"I don't know, Sam," she heard Mac saying as she

pulled the door shut behind her. His voice sounded strangely muffled, as if it was coming from inside a deep well. "I'd like to think you're right, but I just don't know. What I do know is that I have to pay her back what I owe her, and the sooner the better."

Rebecca could see Mac's legs sticking out of the rear cockpit of the huge yellow Stearman. She could also see Sam standing near the top of the stepladder on the plane's off side, but neither man had noticed her. "I'd like to start all over again without that big debt hanging over my head," came Mac's voice. "And who knows, maybe that won't help. Maybe nothing will change her opinion of me. I seem to be in competition with a dead man and I'm losing. Do you have any idea what that does to a man's ego?"

Rebecca felt her face flush. She reached back, opened the door again and slammed it hard behind her.

"Sam? You in here?"

"Over here, Rebecca," came Sam's slow, mellow voice.

"Ellin's made a batch of her cinnamon rolls and she's just taking them out of the oven." Rebecca walked toward the old plane. She saw Mac's legs writhe about wildly as he wriggled, twisted and levered his body out of the cockpit.

Rebecca waited until he'd extricated himself and was sitting on the back of the pilot's seat. "What are you doing in here?" she asked. "I should think you'd be out running your dogs. If you plan on entering the Quest, you'll need to put at least another thousand miles on them. Better hop to it! Oh, and by the way, that was an interesting technique you employed yesterday coming down the Mazey Creek trail."

"You liked that, did you?" Mac said.

"That was without a doubt the most spectacular crash I've ever witnessed," Rebecca said. "And the most miraculous recovery, I might add."

"Coming from you, I take that as high praise."

Rebecca nodded. Mac was dressed in dark-green wool army pants and a thick red-and-black-plaid flannel shirt with the sleeves rolled back. His arms and hands looked strong and powerful, and she had no doubt that they were. For him to have held on to that sled yesterday had required Herculean strength. She noticed his fancy Rolex watch was missing. "Look, Mac, don't take this the wrong way, but you don't have enough experience to run the Yukon Quest."

"Maybe you think I don't, but the dogs, you have to admit, do," Mac said, narrowing his eyes on her.

"The judges on the race committee don't base their decision on the dogs. They want to be sure the musher is qualified to run a long-distance race, and you have to prove yourself by finishing some shorter races, like the Fireplug and the Percy DeWolf. They won't let you run the Quest."

Mac's grin was irritatingly arrogant. "They've waived that requirement," he said with a casual gesture of the pliers he held in one hand. "Sam told them I'd been trapping up on the Flat with my brother's team of dogs and they figured that was qualification enough. I'm good to go."

"Good to go?" Rebecca stared at him incredulously. "You can't be serious! You have absolutely no idea what you're getting yourself into!"

"Ignorance is bliss," he said.

"Baloney! Ignorance can kill you out there!" she snapped. "Sam, I can't believe you fronted his entry fee knowing how inexperienced he is!"

"Well," Sam said, dusting off his coveralls and avoiding her eyes, "I'd better get inside. Ellin's cinnamon rolls don't like to be kept waiting..."

"Trapping up on Flat!" Rebecca scoffed when the door had closed behind Sam.

Mac eyed her defiantly. "I lived there for four months with the dogs."

"You trapped one fox and you let it go!"

"Would it have made me a better musher if I'd trapped two hundred wild animals and killed them all for their pelts?"

"That's not the point! This race is about being tough, about having tough dogs, about being able to travel across a thousand miles in some of the worst weather and over some of the most gruelling terrain there is. Believe me, it isn't like that Walt Disney movie *Iron Will*. You can't live on a piece of fruitcake for two weeks, never feed your dogs, and end up winning enough money to save the family farm. You can't fake it out there. It's for real, and it can get really, really nasty!"

Mac's eyes narrowed speculatively again. "You don't think I'm tough enough, is that it? You think I'm too much of a greenhorn to go the distance?" He pushed himself off the side of the cockpit and descended the ladder propped beside the plane, stepping off the bottom rung to stand beside her. Even in his stocking feet he stood a good ten inches taller. He braced the palm of his hand against the plane's fuselage and looked down at her with those clear, piercing eyes. The nearness of him scrambled her thoughts. She felt her heart rate accelerate and a curious warmth flush her face.

"I don't think you can get the miles on your team," she said. "You'll need at least a thousand training miles.

Competitive mushers put more than twice that many on their dogs before they run that race."

"I'll put the miles on them." He reached for his boots beneath the tail of the plane. "I've got until February and it's only November now. We'll be ready."

"Good to go, right?" she said caustically. "Look, Mac, if you're running the Quest to finish in the big money, I'll tell you right now, you don't have a snowball's chance in hell."

He paused, boots in hand. His expression was carefully polite. "Why, thank you, Rebecca Reed, for your inspirational vote of confidence. You don't know what it means to me to have your support."

Rebecca pulled an envelope out of her parka pocket and held it out to him. "Here," she said. "Take this. If you're really serious about running the race, you'll need every cent you can get."

Mac recognized the envelope and a muscle in his jaw tightened. "That's your money," he said.

"You pawned your watch to get it, didn't you?"

"That's right. And I'll pay you the rest of what I owe at the end of February. Keep it, Rebecca," he said, and his eyes were steely. "I mean it."

Rebecca dropped her arm and stuffed the envelope angrily into her pocket. "If I were you," she said, glaring at him, "I'd be harnessing my dogs right now." She whirled and stalked out the door into the weakening afternoon light. She stood for a moment, letting the keen-edged air cool her temper. The arrogance of the man! Didn't he understand that it would be his team that suffered from his inexperience on the race trail? She turned back and opened the hangar door, intending to pursue her argument until he came to his senses, but instead, she froze, transfixed by the sight of Mac walking across the hangar to where his dogs were tethered. He held a multicolored mass of harnesses in one hand and he was moving stiffly now, limping in his worn-out pack boots, unaware he was being watched.

"Hey, Merlin," she heard him say to his brother's lead dog, whose ears flattened and entire body wagged in response. "Hey, old man, what do you say? Let's burn some trail. Let's put on some miles." The dog waited until Mac drew near before rearing onto his hind legs and placing his front paws on Mac's chest. Mac, still holding the harnesses in one hand, used the other to rub Merlin's shoulder. They gazed into each others eyes. "You're a good dog, Merlin," he said quietly. "You know that, don't you? You're the best."

Rebecca backed out and closed the door quietly behind her. She was moved by the interaction between man and dog in a way she couldn't have begun to explain, and she felt the hot sting of tears in her eyes. She raised her hands to the sides of her face, overwhelmed by the flood of emotion that threatened to overwhelm her. "Oh, Bruce," she whispered past the tight pain in her throat. "In so many ways, he reminds me of you."

"Rebecca?" Ellin's voice jarred her. She quickly brushed her palms across her face and turned toward the cabin. Ellin waved from the doorway to get her attention. "Hurry up, my dear, these cinnamon rolls are getting cold!"

"Thank you, Ellin, but I don't have time!" Rebecca called back. "I've got to get home and run some dogs!"

CHAPTER FOUR

IT WAS SNOWING heavily on December 10 when Rebecca drove her fourth group of clients to the airport outside Dawson to catch their shuttle back to Whitehorse. She waited for the plane to disappear into the whiteout, then returned to her truck, where Tuffy had taken her usual place on the passenger's seat. It was just past noon. Rebecca would have time to pick up some groceries in town and get home before evening chores if she hurried. The roads in town were protected from the wind by the buildings, but outside town the drifts could get really big, really fast.

She was just passing the Eldorado Hotel when the truck's engine quit. She depressed the clutch and turned the engine over. It sounded fine but wouldn't catch, even with the clutch engaged. "My luck," she muttered, wrenching the steering wheel hard and guiding the truck over to the curb with the last of its fading momentum. She popped the hood and leaned in to check a few of the obvious possibilities, like fuel flow to the carburetor and spark-plug connections.

After ten shivering minutes she went to phone the local garage from the Eldorado's lobby. The mechanic promised to send a tow truck, "but we won't be able to get to it sooner than tomorrow morning," he said. "We're backed up here real good." Her pleading fell on deaf ears. "It's always an emergency, ma'am," he said. "Sorry, but tomorrow's the best we can do. Take it or leave it."

"I'll call you back," Rebecca told him, and hung up. She dialed Ellin's number next, relief flooding through her when Sam answered. He listened to her for a moment while she described what happened, and then another male voice broke onto the line.

"Rebecca? Listen, call that mechanic back and tell him you're all set," Mac said, and the sound of his deep voice caused her heart rate to accelerate.

"But I'm not," she said. "The truck won't start—the engine just died on me. It's getting gas and everything else seems okay, but I have to get it fixed! Someone'll have to feed my dogs tonight, and if you could do that for me, Mac, I'll pay you. Same as I pay Donny. Twenty dollars. I know it's not much, but—"

"Listen to me," Mac interrupted. "I'll take care of things over at your place, and then I'll come into town and fix the truck myself. It'll save you a bundle of money and a lot of time, and it'll only set you back maybe forty, fifty bucks."

"How do you know that?"

"Because that's just about what an ignition module costs."

"But...how do you know?"

"Because I just know," Mac said patiently. "Are you listening to me?"

"Yes," she said.

"It's half-past twelve now. I'm going over to feed your dogs. Go get yourself some lunch, buy some groceries, do some window-shopping. I'll drive my team into Dawson and meet you at the wharf on Front Street, the place where the stern-wheeler ties up, in about three hours. I'll pick up the part we need, and we'll fix your truck. You'll be sleeping in your own bed tonight, and I'll get a good long training run on my dogs.'' Mac sounded smug. He had it all figured out. "You with me?''

"I'm with you,'' Rebecca said reluctantly.

She hung up the phone, called the garage and then wondered how she was going to kill the next three hours. She wandered over to the farmers' market on Second Avenue to pick up her groceries. She loaded them into the cab of the truck, ordered Tuffy to stand guard over them, and then ate a hamburger in the Eldorado's lounge as slowly as she could. With an hour and a half left, she walked up to the Palace Grand Theater, past Diamond Tooth Gerdie's Gambling Hall, and was wandering past Hank's Trading Post when a familiar object in the display window caught her eye. She stopped and stared.

She entered the store and worked her way to the register, where the proprietor was immersed in the local newspaper.

"Hank, you have a watch in your display case,'' Rebecca said.

"Ah, yes,'' the man said, lowering the newspaper and peering at her over the top half of his bifocals. "The Rolex. A beautiful watch, Rebecca. Beautiful!''

"Is it for sale? I didn't see a price tag.''

"Certainly it is! Here, let me get it out of the case for you. I've never seen a finer watch, that's for sure. I'm surprised it doesn't have a color TV built into it,'' he said with a laugh, pulling a tiny key out of his pocket and making his way to the display case. He unlocked it and removed the Rolex, laying it ceremoniously in her hands. "This is a very valuable watch!''

"It may be valuable,'' she said, "but it isn't new, is it?''

"No, it isn't. If you look at the back, you'll see that it's inscribed. The man who sold it to me showed me his ID so I can vouch for the fact that it definitely wasn't stolen. See the inscription?"

Rebecca turned the watch over and read the four tiny lines of neat engraving on the back:

Captain William Kimball MacKenzie
For Outstanding Service
1997-1999
VF92 RAG, Mirimar

"Like I said, he showed me his military ID. It's a real nice watch, and watches like that don't lose value over the years."

"How much?" Rebecca asked, frowning.

"Well, that's real quality, what you're holding in your hands. Real quality."

"How much?"

"New, that watch probably runs well over five thousand dollars. You'll be getting the bargain of a century to pick it up for, oh, say, one-fifth of that."

"One thousand dollars, Hank?" Rebecca was incredulous.

"That's right. And worth every penny."

"But you only paid him three hundred for it, isn't that right?"

Hank blinked his surprise behind his bifocals. "Well, what I paid for it and what I sell it for aren't going to run along the same lines, now, are they? You're a businesswoman. Do you sell dog food to your customers for the same price you paid?"

"Hank, I know this man," Rebecca said, bristling.

"The only reason he sold this watch was to pay back a loan I made him for dog food."

"Well, a man does what he has to do."

"But don't you see? He should never have sold it." Rebecca looked at Hank. "I'll buy it back for what you paid and return it to him," she said.

He raised his eyebrows. "The price is one thousand dollars, Rebecca, and I won't budge on it."

"This man dedicated years of his life to the service of his country!" Rebecca said earnestly. "I think he was a mechanic for his unit, and he deserves to keep this token of their appreciation! It's morally wrong for you to want to make a profit on it!"

"Young lady, I beg to differ. Besides, this is Canada, in case you haven't noticed. I owe no allegiance to ex-soldiers from the United States of America. And another thing," he said with an unpleasantly snide laugh, "there's no way in hell that watch ever belonged to a mechanic!"

IT WAS SNOWING HARD when Mac stopped his team at the wharf. He wrapped the sled's snub line around the nearest piling and waved up at the small figure who stood huddled on the dock above. "Hey!" he said. "We had a great run! The team never dropped out of their lope—they ran the whole way. Twenty-five miles!"

"That's great," Rebecca said, scrambling down the ladder onto the river ice. She helped him run a picket line and snap the dogs onto it, unharnessing them and pulling their booties off. "Do you want to snack them?"

He shook his head. "Don't want to slow them down for the run back. We must have kept up a steady fifteen miles an hour coming down here. What time is it now?"

"Quarter to four."

"Jeez, we made great time. Great time!" He gave Merlin an affectionate rub as he walked past, flashed Rebecca a grin and patted the pocket of his parka. "I have the part for the truck. Sam had a spare. All the tools I need are right here," he said, lifting a sack out of his sled bag. "Where are you parked?"

Thirty minutes later he had finished the repair job and was sitting in the driver's seat turning the key. The engine roared obediently to life. "And that," he said to her with a grin of pure satisfaction, "is how we do that." He patted the passenger seat beside him amd Tuffy sat up and wagged her tail. "Climb aboard, and we'll take her for a test drive. I'm sure Tuffy won't mind riding in the back seat."

Rebecca was suitably impressed and very grateful. "I'll buy you a beer," she offered, and was surprised when he gave his head a rueful shake.

"There's nothing I'd like better, but I can't. I've got to get the team back on the trail, get home and feed my dogs. I'll take a rain check, though."

They drove back to the wharf, and she helped him harness, bootie and hook up his fourteen dogs. "Want me to lead Merlin around and get him pointed in the right direction?" she offered as Mac walked to the sled. The team dogs were jumping, yelping and barking in their eagerness to go.

"No need," Mac said. "Merlin really knows his stuff. Watch this," he said with a proud grin. He pulled the safety knot on the snub line, freeing the sled from the piling. "Merlin!" he snapped to his lead dog. "Come haw! Come haw!"

Rebecca jumped back as Merlin immediately sprang to his left and then quarter-turned again, bringing the entire team—all seventy feet of gang line and thirteen galloping dogs—back toward the sled at about a hundred miles an hour. "Mac, watch out!" she cried just as the sled whipped around behind the dogs, slammed its right runner against the piling and flipped upside down. She caught a glimpse of Mac flying through the air, landing hard behind the sled and making a desperate grab for the trailing snub line as his team and sled took off without him. Moments later his body was bouncing over the rough pack ice as he clung to the line.

"Let go, Mac!" she screamed, cupping her hands around her mouth. "Let go of the line! You'll be killed!"

Mac might have heard her, but he obviously wasn't about to follow her instruction. She knew that just as surely as she knew that she wouldn't have let go, either. She scaled the wharf ladder with frantic haste, leaped into her idling truck and sped down Front Street, focusing her eyes onto the dimly illuminated river ice and marking where the team was. There! There they were, a long dark blur right below her, still running hard, dragging Mac behind.

She gunned the engine and raced through town, hoping to reach the Klondike cutoff before the team did. She parked across from the RCMP building, headlights pointing down at the river, and plunged through the deep snow toward the riverbank. She fell several times in her haste, each time getting up and struggling on. The riverbank dropped her down onto the ice, and in the darkness she paused and listened. Nothing. Had the team already passed?

No, there was something—a noise coming from the direction of town, the musical chime of neckline snaps, a man's muffled voice swearing. She ran out onto the ice, falling several times on the uneven footing. "Mac!"

she shouted. And then she saw the dogs, their dark, wolf-like forms barely discernible in the darkness, coming toward her. She could hear their panting breaths and the muffled drag of the sled through the fresh snow, but there was no reply from Mac.

She turned to run in the same direction as the team. Merlin overtook her, followed by the point dogs, the team dogs, the wheel dogs and, finally, the sled. When she saw the nose of the toboggan out of the corner of her eye, she dove for it, feeling the solid slam of the driver's bow against her shoulder. She reached blindly to grasp it. The sled was still on its side, and she lay on it for a moment, catching her breath, before reaching over the sled bag and fumbling for the snow hook. She felt the cold steel and drew it out with one hand, keeping a death grip on the driver's bow with the other. The sled was pounding over the ice like a bucking bronco. She tried to stab the hook into the ice. For a moment the sharp points just skittered over the surface, then all at once they dug in and held. The sled came to an abrupt stop, jolting the dogs back in their harnesses and nearly dislodging Rebecca. She got off the sled and stood on shaky legs, afraid to let go of the sled in case the dogs pulled the hook loose.

"Mac?" She wished desperately that she had her headlamp! She peered into the darkness. "Mac!" She reached down and gave the snub line a tug. Something was definitely still holding on to it, and she heard a muffled, "Okay, okay." Slowly, with tremendous effort, she began to reel him in like a giant fish, hand over hand, keeping one knee braced against the sled, ready to grab for it if the dogs should pull the ice hook out. "Dammit, Mac, you're a heavy load!" she said, fear giving strength to her arms and shoulders. And suddenly there he was, on his hands and knees with the snub line wrapped around one arm.

"Get up!" she said. "Hurry! The dogs could pull the hook out at any moment!" His dogs were already beginning to move, jumping and barking and raring to go. She stepped on the ice hook with one booted foot to keep it secure as the dogs put more and more pressure on the gang line. "Hurry!" She tugged on the snub line again, jerking his arm, and he crawled the last few feet. "I'm going to tip the sled onto its runners. Do you understand?" In the darkness she thought she saw him nod. "When I get it upright, I want you to sit on top of it and hold on. I'm going to drive the team to the Klondike cutoff and turn them around." She took her pocketknife out of her parka and cut the knotted snub line away from his arm. The last thing he needed was to be dragged again. "Ready?"

"I'm okay. I can drive," he said, his voice sounding very faint. "I can drive them back home."

"Sure, Mac," Rebecca said. "Just get on when I tell you to."

She heaved on the driver's bow and tipped the sled back onto its runners. "Get on!" she said as the dogs renewed their forward lunging.

"I'm okay," he said. "You go on back to your truck."

"Climb on, dammit, and shut up!" There was an edge of hysteria in her voice that must have compelled him to obey, and he had no sooner deposited himself atop the bag when the dogs, in a frenzy to get going, ripped the ice hook free and continued their wild run down the frozen river toward home. She hung on tight and kept both feet on the section of snow-machine track between the runners, hoping to slow the dogs enough to tire them before the Klondike cutoff, but her weight proved an ineffectual drag. When the time came to turn around, they were traveling way too fast. She cursed as the opportunity blurred past. She was bareheaded and barehanded, and the cold was beginning to get a firm grip on her. Where could she turn the team around? She had to get back to her truck. She'd left the headlights on, and Tuffy was sitting in the front seat waiting for her.

Her parka had a hood with a good fur ruff, and she pulled it over her head with one hand, cinching it tightly against the stiff wind. She checked the pockets for a spare pair of gloves and came up with a thin pair of polypropylene liners. They wouldn't help much but were better than nothing. She pulled them on. "Think," she said to herself. "Where can I turn this team around?"

"I can drive them home," Mac mumbled.

She ignored him and tucked one hand inside a pocket. The fresh snow had slowed the trail some, but the dogs were still loping. "Mac, where's your headlamp?"

"Gone," he said. "Lost it while I was dragging."

"I don't suppose you carry a spare."

"Sorry."

"What about spare gloves?"

"Check the glove compartment," he said, and then laughed or coughed, she couldn't tell which. But after a few moments she felt something hit her leg, and it was Mac, flapping one of his big mitts against it. "Wear mine," he said. "I can keep my hands in my pockets."

She pulled them on gratefully. Her fingers were completely numb, and even wearing Mac's prewarmed mitts it took a while before any feeling returned. She hunkered down inside of her parka and peered ahead into the snowy darkness. Turning the team around was no longer an option. They were running home for their supper and wouldn't stop until they reached Sam and Ellin's.

MAC WAS IN AGONY, but it wasn't only his bruised body that was causing him pain, it was his wounded pride. Once again he'd made a fool of himself in front of Rebecca. He had completely blown any chance of impressing her. If he'd been a weaker man, he might have given up. Instead, he levered himself out of the sled bag and swung his upper body around until he was sharing the runners with Rebecca and standing closer to her than he ever had before, which was a very pleasant experience.

"My turn," he said before she could speak. "Climb into the sled bag and take a break. I've warmed it up for you."

"I don't know if I trust you to drive," she said. "What if you go into shock and fall off the sled?"

"Look!" he said in the sternest voice he could manage. "This is *my* team and *my* sled. These dogs are used to running for me. They'll run faster and we'll get home quicker if I drive."

"A little while ago you were practically unconscious!"

"Not true. I had the wind knocked out of me, that's all. You should know by now that I'm pretty resilient. Now get inside the sled bag."

He was relieved when she finally did. "Comfortable?" he asked.

"Yes, thanks. You take the mitts. I'll use my pockets."

She passed him his mitts. They were still warm from her hands. Her lovely, strong, capable hands. "I know a shortcut we can take that'll shave five or six miles off the run," he told her.

"You'd better stay on the river trail," she cautioned. "It's still snowing pretty hard. The side trails might be drifted in."

"Oh, no, this one's fine. Trust me. I use it all the time." Moments later he gee'd Merlin up over the riverbank. A few miles later, winding their way at a quick trot through the spruce woods, John Campbell's abandoned cabin loomed beside the trail. Merlin, seeing that the door was ajar, made the sudden decision to take the team inside. Before Mac had time to shout a proper curse or step on the sled brake, half of the dogs had scaled the cabin steps and disappeared within.

"Damn you, Merlin!" he growled, hobbling stiffly off the runners and working his way up the snow-covered cabin steps. The floor of the cabin was rotten and his feet broke through twice, banging his shins hard both times. It took all his remaining strength—combined with Rebecca's help—to haul the dogs out of the cabin and get Merlin pointed in the proper direction. He waited for some sarcastic comment from Rebecca, but she remained silent, though once they were moving down the trail again, he could have sworn he heard her laughing softly.

Forty minutes later Merlin led the team up to Sam's hangar. The house was lit up like a palace, the big Wisconsin generator was roaring, and there were several vehicles parked in the cabin yard. Mac barely had time to open the hangar door and drive the team inside before Ellin and Sam confronted him.

"Mac!" Ellin cried out. "Have you seen Rebecca? The police called—they found her truck parked beside the river with the engine running and Tuffy inside... Rebecca! Is that you! Oh, thank God, thank God, you're safe! We were worried to death!" Ellin's hug was so vigorous that she knocked Rebecca back into the sled.

"Mac!" another voice cried, and he froze in the act of unsnapping the dogs' tug lines. "Mac!" Sadie Hedda rushed toward him like a freight train, her face a mask of concern. "What happened to you? Your face! All that blood!"

"I'm fine," he said. "I fell on the ice, that's all. Sadie, please, I need to get the dogs unhooked and fed."

"Son, you'd better sit down," Sam said, taking him by the arm. "Let Sadie have a look at you. Your face is cut up pretty bad."

The warmth inside the hangar had caused the blood to flow. He could feel a warm trickle running down his neck. "It's just a cut, that's all, head wounds bleed a lot. I've got to get the dogs fed. They've had a long day."

"I'll feed your dogs, Mac," Rebecca said. "You better let Sadie look at you." She began walking past him, and he reached out and caught her arm.

"I can take care of my own dogs!" he said, and she turned to look at him, startled.

"I know that," she said. "But the least you can do is let me help you, after you fixed my truck and fed my dogs."

"Mac, your face is a mess," Sadie said. "A couple of those cuts are definitely going to need stitches, and you could have a concussion!"

"Now look!" he said, releasing Rebecca's arm and glaring at Sadie. "Right now, I'm going to take care of my dogs. When I'm done, if you feel it's absolutely necessary, you can examine my cuts, gashes, and lacerations to your heart's content."

Rebecca busied herself unharnessing the dogs and picketing them with the others on the far wall. Mac stepped out, grateful for the cold and darkness, and made his way to the little cabin where he lived, hoping that the big pot of water atop the stove would still be hot enough to mix the dogs' food. He lit the oil lamp, fed some firewood onto the bed of coals that still glowed inside the stove and thrust his fingers into the pot of water. It was plenty warm. He was mixing the food with a long-handled spade when the door opened and Rebecca walked in.

She didn't say anything, just crossed to the sink as if she'd been in his cabin a hundred times before, took a hand towel down from a nail above the washbasin and poured some water from the teakettle into the basin. Mac was astounded. *She* was going to minister to his wounds? He continued mixing the dogs' food, deeply moved by this action of Rebecca's and struggling with something inside he couldn't begin to verbalize. Then, just when he thought that maybe he'd found the right words, she turned with the towel and washbasin in hand, cool, brisk and businesslike.

"Mac," she said, "I think the reason Merlin tried to stop at that cabin was because he has a cut on his foot. He must have pulled the bootie off on that first stretch of river trail and cut his pad on some sharp ice. I'm going to clean and wrap it. It's not that bad, but you probably shouldn't run him for a week or so." Mac looked at her, nodding dumbly, the important words he had been about to say remaining unspoken, unheard. "And I really think you'd better let Sadie have a look at you," she added. "You have a couple of pretty deep cuts on your face, and you're bleeding like a stuck pig. Sam's taking me to Dawson to get my truck."

"Merlin's hurt?" he said.

She nodded. "Merlin's hurt. I'm going to wash his paw and bandage it."

He closed his good eye and slumped against the cabin wall. She watched him for a few silent moments and then put a hand on his arm. "You okay?" she said, and he nodded even as he struggled with the mental and physical pandemonium that her touch evoked. "Listen, Mac, if I were you, I'd seriously reconsider my plans to run the Quest. You still have time to drop out of the race and get your entry fee back."

He straightened to face her squarely. "And if I were *you*," he said, "I'd be home harnessing my own team just as soon as I got my truck back, because if you expect to finish that race ahead of me, you've got some serious training to do."

FOR THE NEXT FEW WEEKS, they both trained hard, meeting each other frequently on the trail. Mac's injuries from his wild ride out of Dawson didn't slow him down, nor did his bruised ego. In fact, he seemed determined to flirt with her. Whenever they met, he'd stop to talk, and during the course of these conversations, he would switch the subject from training dogs to things of a more personal nature. "Ellin wanted me to ask you to supper tonight if I saw you out on the trail." To which she would reply, "Really? I talked to Ellin just this morning and she mentioned no such thing. Besides, I have too much work to do. A deadline to meet." He would lean closer. "All work and no play... Say, you owe me a beer. Remember? I could take you to Dawson tonight, and we could tank up on beer and pizza. My treat. I'm a workingman now. Sam lined up a few jobs for me on the side, mostly mechanical stuff for friends of his. Oh, and by the way, before I forget, here's another installment toward the dog food. Go ahead, take it. It won't bite. It's good, honest money. So what do you say? I could pick you up after chores."

She would politely decline, and he would continue his attack the next time they met. "You know," he commented during another such encounter, "I have this wicked craving for Chinese food. Ever get those cravings? Let's hit Dawson after chores tonight. If you won't let me buy, we could go Dutch. That way you wouldn't feel obliged to kiss me good-night."

Finally, unable to face him again, she began changing her training routines, using different trails and training at different times. That didn't work, either, because after a week of playing such wilderness hide-and-seek, he drove his dilapidated truck into her yard just after chore time and jumped out, taking the porch steps two at a time. His hair was carelessly tousled and his face wind-burned from long miles on the trail and still showing the damage from his escapade on the river. There was the bristle of stitches over his right cheekbone, another shorter row above his right eyebrow, tape strips across the bridge of his nose. But his badly bruised eye had opened up, and his gaze was as clear and keen as ever. He grinned unabashedly as she stepped onto the porch. "Hey! Guess what's playing in Dawson tonight? *Iron Will!* It must be fate! What do you say? I'll spring for the popcorn."

Rebecca's heartbeat tripled. "Mac, how many times do I have to say no before you finally get the idea?"

"Oh, I get the idea, all right. You want to be a hermit. A recluse. You want to hide out here in this cabin with your typewriter and your dogs and shut out the rest of the world. I just don't think it's a very good idea, that's all."

"What I do with my time is my business. Maybe it's time you started minding yours."

"Rebecca, you don't have to talk to me, you don't even have to sit next to me in the theater. We don't have to hold hands, kiss good-night, have sex or get married. I'm just asking you to go to town with me. To get away from here for a little while. That's all. Honest."

"No!"

Mac squared off, his countenance darkening with frustration. "You know what you are? You're a living mausoleum. You're the most beautiful mausoleum I've ever seen, but a mausoleum nonetheless. Living for your husband's memory isn't enough, Rebecca. You can't shut yourself away from the world forever."

Anger swept through her in a hot, fierce wave, and she tensed against it, keeping her voice calm. "Did Ellin put you up to this?"

He shook his head. "No. I care about you, that's all. I know you aren't exactly crazy about me, but you've helped me out in so many ways. I just want to return the favor."

"By asking me out to the movies?" Rebecca moaned with frustration and pressed her palms to her temples. "Look, Mac, why don't you ask Sadie? She'd love to go with you. I appreciate your concern for me, but it's completely unwarranted. I like what I do. I like how I live. I don't mind being alone. I honestly don't! I just wish you'd let me be!"

Mac was silent, then he shoved his hands into his parka pockets, stared at his boots for a moment, nodded and turned to go. He paused at the bottom of the steps and glanced back at her, his sudden grin brash and unexpected. "I guess you're telling me to get lost, right? You'll be glad to hear I almost got good and lost today, trying to find you out on the trails. We must've covered close to a hundred miles. I got so turned around that if it weren't for Merlin, we'd probably still be out there.'' He took two steps toward his truck and glanced back, still grinning at her in a way that caused butterflies in her stomach. ''I guess there might be worse reasons for getting lost than looking for you, Rebecca Reed, but I don't know if there could ever be a better one.

CHAPTER FIVE

IN THE YUKON TERRITORY on December 24 there were three-point-eight hours of daylight, the temperature was minus thirty degrees Fahrenheit, and it was snowing. Rebecca was running her team and had been out since 8 a.m. It was noon now, and in another hour she would be home. The dogs were moving well, trotting steadily, eating up the miles. She was pleased with their progress, pleased with Raven and Cookie's strengthening leadership abilities, pleased with the number of dogs that could still make her A-team. December was the hardest training month. The days were short and the miles were long. The instinct was to hibernate next to a woodstove with a good book, but she knew she had to run the dogs farther and longer in spite of the bitter cold and the endless dark.

She hadn't seen Mac since that last awkward encounter at her cabin, though no doubt he'd be at the Dodges' tonight for their traditional Christmas Eve supper. Rebecca had wrapped all her presents the night before. She was also taking a Christmas stollen she had baked, a vegetable casserole and three bottles of reasonably good wine. Unexciting fare but not bad for the bush. Ellin was baking a big ham and some Yukon Gold potatoes, and Sam, the man with the sweet tooth, would probably contribute his delicious homemade fudge to the feast. Rebecca was looking forward to it, even though Sadie

Hedda would be there. Ellin had invited her on a sympathetic impulse when Sadie had shown up bearing glad tidings of great joy—and the giant ham Ellin was baking for their supper.

Rebecca hopped up and down on the runners to keep her toes warm. It wasn't that she didn't like Sadie, because she did. She just didn't feel like watching Sadie fuss over Mac, though she couldn't for the life of her explain why. Sadie and Mac would make a perfect couple. Mac was seriously accident-prone and could do with a qualified emergency medical technician in attendance at all times. Sadie just plain needed to be needed, and she enjoyed playing doctor—especially with Mac.

Suddenly Cookie and Raven's pace quickened, and an accelerating surge swept through the team. The lead dogs' ears were pricked and their heads were both pointing to the right. For a moment Rebecca couldn't see what they were looking at through the swirling snow. When she did, she immediately stepped on the sled brake with both feet, grabbed the snow hook and, crouching down, rammed it into the snow beside the sled runner. Ahead, barely visible through the veil of snow and grouped near the inside curve of the next bend in the river, stood three wolves. They were upwind with their backs to the team, standing like statues and watching something Rebecca couldn't see. She'd seen wolves before, but never quite as close as this, and she'd never spotted a wolf before it spotted her. One of the wolves was black, two were gray.

"Wow," she breathed, thrilled by the sight and hoping that her dogs didn't give full voice to the low growls they were emitting. Hackles raised, her sled dogs watched the wolves and sniffed the snow-laden air. Cookie whined and looked back. Raven shivered. Thor and Seal, in point, lowered their heads and peered around the leaders. Her team dogs could surely smell the wolves but not see them very well, which was fine with her. The black wolf moved suddenly, trotting to one side of the gray pair, its entire body focusing on whatever was coming up the river. The gray wolves half-circled around the black, and the three stood abreast a few moments more before wheeling as a single entity and loping up the riverbank and into the forest.

Gone in the space of a few heartbeats, vanishing into the wilderness from which they came. Rebecca let her breath out slowly. "Wow," she said again, smiling. Unbelievable! Cookie let out a yelp as she spied movement up at the river bend, an oncoming team of sled dogs. No wonder the wolves had fled! The approaching dog team was moving briskly. Rebecca reached down and pulled her snow hook out of the snow. If they were going to pass head-on, it was better if both were moving. "All right!" she said, and her dog team dug in and pulled. The two teams began to pass flawlessly, but Rebecca stood on her brake when she saw the other driver gesturing to stop. It didn't surprise her that the driver was Mac.

"Did you see them?" Mac said. "The wolves! Did you see them?"

The teams had stopped so that the sleds were standing side by side but facing in opposite directions.

"Yes, I did," Rebecca said. "They were magnificent, weren't they?"

Mac was grinning, clearly exhilarated. "They were out on the ice in front of my dogs when we came around a corner about a mile back. They ran ahead of us but didn't seem to be afraid. They kept stopping and looking back. I wish I'd had a camera. What a picture that would have made!''

Rebecca felt a tender surge toward him as he related his experience. "Most men around these parts wish they had a high-powered rifle when they sight a wolf.''

"I guess I'm not like most men," Mac said. "I hope that doesn't weigh too heavily against me.''

Rebecca fiddled with the cuff of her parka sleeve, cinching it tighter against the cold. "No," she said, dropping her eyes to the task.

"Good." Mac leaned toward her, resting one hand on her driver's bow. "Can I ask you a question?''

She fiddled with the other cuff. "Go ahead," she said.

"Would your husband have been one of those men who wished he had a high-powered rifle?''

The question startled her, and she lifted her eyes to his. "Yes," she said quietly.

"Can I ask you another question?" he said.

"As long as it's not personal.''

"What would you do if I kissed you right now?''

"Why, I'd slap your—" She never had time to finish the sentence before he leaned over and kissed her on the mouth. It was not a long kiss, just a tender, tentative touch of his lips to hers. She drew her head back, too shocked to speak, and stared into his eyes. She struggled to catch her breath. Her lips tingled as if from an electric shock.

"You didn't slap me," he said.

Oh, God! He was too close! Too close! Panic surged through her. She eased her foot off the sled's brake and called up her dogs. "All right, Cookie! Raven! Get up!''

Her team exploded forward, and Rebecca didn't dare look back as they rounded the curve in the river.

ELLIN DODGE WAS in a terrible state. Rebecca was as dear to her as her own daughter might have been, and she desperately wanted to see her happy. In Ellin's opinion, Bill MacKenzie was as good a man as Rebecca would ever stumble across in this wild and lonely land, or anywhere else on earth, for that matter. If only Rebecca would come to her senses and fall in love with him, but instead, Sadie Hedda had decided to set her cap for the rookie musher.

Sadie wasn't beautiful the way Rebecca was, but she was a woman, a very warm and willing woman in a land where warm and willing women were few and far between. And Bill MacKenzie was a red-blooded man, no doubt about it.

Ellin had invited Sadie to share their traditional Christmas Eve supper. If she hadn't invited her, it would have been just the four of them. Mac and Rebecca, she and Sam. It would have been a perfect Christmas Eve! But Ellin had had no choice. Sadie had as much as invited herself by going on and on about how lonely Christmas Eve was for her...and then to cap it all off she had produced this gigantic Virginia cured ham!

How could Ellin not have invited her?

Moot point, now. Sadie would be here in another hour, as well as Rebecca and Mac. She'd heard Mac return from his training run a while ago. He had snuck cat-footed into the kitchen where Ellin was putting together a simple salad and asked humbly if he might shower, to which she had replied matter-of-factly, without looking up from the vegetables she was slicing, "William MacKenzie, if you don't take a shower and shave, and if you don't put those doggy-smelling clothes of yours into the laundry hamper, you won't be the least little bit welcome here for supper!"

He had emerged from the shower all spruced up and freshly shaved, smartly dressed in a black-watch flannel shirt and his best blue jeans, and to her surprise had taken over her kitchen, finishing the salad, pinning bright yellow rounds of pineapple to the ham with whole cloves, and sprinkling brown sugar over the ham before sliding it into the oven. While she'd watched from the sidelines, he'd cleaned the pots, pans and dishes in the sink, wiped down the counters, scrubbed the potatoes, set the table for supper and then he'd turned to her and said, "I kissed her today, Ellin. I shouldn't have done it but I did, and I guess she's mad enough at me now that she might not even come over tonight."

He looked so dejected standing there that for a moment Ellin didn't know whether to laugh or cry. In the end she just patted his arm. "She'll come, Mac. Rebecca will come."

It never even occurred to her that Mac might have been talking about Sadie, because Ellin knew full well who Mac was in love with.

REBECCA LOOKED at her reflection in the tiny mirror above her sink and made a face. No doubt about it, she was homely. The fact that Mac had actually kissed her was an unexpected, unexplainable, and unnatural phenomenon. It would probably never happen again, and that was just as well. Kissing was a pointless pursuit, when it couldn't possibly lead to anything but pain and misery. She lifted her hair up and heaved a discouraged sigh. She would like to sneak over to Ellin and Sam's and take a shower, but that was probably what Mac was doing at this very moment, and after what had happened this afternoon, she didn't see how she could possibly look him in the eye again.

With another heavy sigh, Rebecca let her hair drop back onto her shoulders. Maybe she should call Ellin and tell her she just didn't feel up to a night out. Ellin would understand. Ellin understood all things. She was the wisest woman Rebecca had ever known. She was so lucky to have Ellin and Sam. Without them, she never would have survived after Bruce's death.

Yes, Ellin would sympathize.

Rebecca connected her radio phone to the battery and dialed their number. Ellin answered on the second ring, and before Rebecca could utter a word, the older woman spoke. "My dear girl, if you're going to tell me you can't come over tonight, please don't bother. If you can't come over here, then we'll all just have to come over there. I certainly hope your cabin is spotlessly clean and ready for lots of company!"

"Ellin," Rebecca said, "I just called to tell you I'm on my way."

"Well, hurry up then! There's still time for you to take a nice hot shower before supper."

CHRISTMAS EVE was a rather interesting affair. Rebecca managed to take her shower before Sadie arrived, the ham came out of the oven about the time Mac made his appearance, and the seating arrangements at the table, not prearranged by Ellin, placed Sam between Mac and Sadie, and Rebecca next to Mac. Ellin suspected that Mac and Sam were in cahoots, but that was fine with her. Nonetheless, Sadie was not to be put off.

"I sure hope you like the Christmas present I got you, Mac," she said as soon as she was seated.

Mac, carrying the ham to the table, froze in midstride. He opened his mouth to respond, but no words came forth.

"Boy, am I hungry!" Sam burst out, slamming his fists onto the table and making the silverware dance. "Who's going to carve the beast?"

"Mac will," Ellin said.

"Uh-oh. Better get your medical kit ready, Sadie," Rebecca advised, lifting her wineglass for a sip.

Mac set the giant ham in front of his chair and picked up the carving knife. "Don't worry," he said. "I may be dangerous with a dog team, but I'm pretty good with a knife."

"Not as good as I hope to become," Sadie interjected, twirling the stem of her wineglass. "I've been thinking about going back to school. Medical school."

"You don't say!" Ellin smiled. "I think that's a wonderful idea."

"Well, the Territory needs more doctors, and the way I see it, two or three more years of study will give it a darn good one."

"Here, here!" Sam said, lifting his wineglass in salute.

Mac waved the carving knife and grinned his brash, handsome grin. "That's great, Sadie. Medical school! You were born to be a doctor."

Rebecca took a sip of her wine and suddenly found herself resenting Sadie. Sadie was smart, pretty, accomplished. Sadie already had a good career and now she was going to make it better. Sadie was motivated. Sadie... Sadie wanted Mac and she was in a perfect position to grab him.

Not that Rebecca cared.

She took another sip of her wine and watched Mac carve the ham. His shirtsleeves were rolled back, and she glanced covertly at the play of muscle and tendon in his powerful hands and arms. Raised her eyes briefly to his face and was startled to see that he was looking at her. She felt the heat come into her cheeks.

He kissed me! she thought, her cheeks burning. *What a nerve that man has!*

"Thank you, Mac," Ellin said as he handed her the platter of sliced ham. "A masterful job!"

The meal was delicious, the wine and conversation flowed freely, and over dessert—a chocolate cream pie Sadie had made that surpassed Sam's fudge—Rebecca found herself listening with one ear to a somewhat strange and one-sided dialogue between Mac and Sadie, while keeping the other ear tuned to an argument between Ellin and Sam. The conversation between Mac and Sadie involved reincarnation.

"Oh, yes, I am quite sure," Sadie was saying as she leaned back in her chair and gazed across the table at Mac, "that I've been reincarnated several times, the latest as a horse in the Civil War. In fact, I'm absolutely certain that I was killed on a battlefield there!"

"A horse?" Mac said, elbows on the table and wineglass in hand. Rebecca found his nearness unsettling, and she jerked her leg away involuntarily when his knee nudged hers beneath the table. She felt her cheeks warm again.

"Yes. A black horse with one white stocking and a snip on my nose. I honestly believe I could take you to the exact spot where I was killed."

"You have spent *thousands* on that plane, Sam," Ellin was saying to her husband. "Thousands! And I'm not even considering the enormous amount of money you squandered on purchasing it in the first place!"

"Oh, now, Ellin..."

"I believe I was in the Seventh Cavalry," Sadie continued, "being ridden by a man named Captain Richard

Randolph Allen. He used to stroke my neck and call me Stump.''

"Stump?'' Mac said, lifting his glass and draining it in one deep swallow. His booted foot shifted and touched Rebecca's. She moved hers away.

"Over fifty thousand dollars when all is said and done! You can't deny it! That's what you'll have spent on that dratted hunk of scrap metal. I've kept records!''

"Yes, but, Ellin, when it's finished it will be worth five times that,'' Sam said weakly.

"I believe it was a minnie ball that killed me,'' Sadie reflected, gazing sadly into some distant place. "It was quite sudden, and I could hear Dickie saying, 'Oh, my God, Stump, they've killed you!' And there was such noise as I've never heard, explosions and gunfire and men crying out in pain and horses screaming, but I never screamed. I never did!''

"You were obviously very brave,'' Mac said, eyeing the wine bottle and then reaching for it decisively. His foot nudged Rebecca's again under the table, and she kicked it away with a vengeance.

"Five times that? Five *times* that? Good heavens, Sam, who's going to reap the rewards?'' Ellin asked. "We'll both be dead and buried long before you ever get that decrepit old thing into the air!''

"Well, with Mac's help…'' Sam began.

"We'll definitely have her flying by spring,'' Mac said, abandoning Sadie's conversation. "That old girl is ready and raring to go. Believe me, ma'am, she'll fly.''

"There. You see?'' Sam said triumphantly.

"I don't believe it!'' Ellin said with a wave of her hand. "I've heard these stories too many times before, and that plane has been sitting in the hangar for over two years now. That's two years too long, as far as I'm concerned.''

"Why, Ellin Dodge," Mac said, sitting back in his chair with a look of hurt disbelief. ''I always figured you for a romantic.''

"A romantic!" Ellin snorted derisively. "Hah!''

"Ellin," Rebecca said, pushing her dessert plate away. "That was without a doubt the best Christmas Eve supper I've ever eaten."

"Amen," Mac said.

"My dear girl—" Ellin peered at Rebecca with concern "—your cheeks are quite flushed. Are you feeling all right?''

Mac leaned over in an exaggerated study of Rebecca's face, and she glared back at him. "She'll be fine, Ellin," Mac said, delivering his prognosis with a slow, maddening grin. "Too much wine!" Still holding the wine bottle, he refilled first Rebecca's glass, then all the others. Ellin looked at them both with a certain smug satisfaction as she stood and began reaching for the dessert plates. Mac rose and took her hand in both of his. "There's an old tradition in my family," he said. "The hostess never washes the dishes. Allow me."

Ellin looked up at him, surprised. "You know, for a man, you're not a bad sort," she said. And to Rebecca she added, "He's washed them once already today! Prepared most of the meal, too, truth be known."

Sadie jumped out of her seat. "I'll help you, Mac," she volunteered. "Between the two of us we'll make short work of it!" She bent to the task of gathering the dishes from the table, and Rebecca stared at the sight of Mac and Sadie engaged in the very domestic task of cleaning up. There was no doubt in her mind that Mac and Sadie were perfect for each other. She took another sip of wine, unaware that she was wearing a troubled frown but very aware that she was unsettled by the thought of Mac and Sadie setting up house together.

THEY OPENED the presents next, Sam playing Santa Claus. Rebecca had given Ellin an Icelandic sweater, Sam a book on tail draggers in which the Stearman figured prominently, Mac a comprehensive first-aid kit he could pack in his sled to deal with any medical emergency, and Sadie a selection of hand-milled soaps. From Sam and Ellin, Rebecca received a new arctic headlamp, thirty-six D-cell alkaline batteries to power it, and a pair of deluxe musher's mitts. They gave Mac the same things, and Mac and Rebecca exchanged pleased grins, realizing how useful these gifts were.

Mac, though virtually penniless, was not without his talents. In his spare time, sitting beside the woodstove in his little cabin, he had whittled small figurines out of odd pieces of wood. He presented Sam with a fox, Ellin with a raven, Rebecca with a wolf, and Sadie with a rabbit. Rebecca wondered briefly at the symbolism but didn't dwell on it. Sadie gave Ellin a wool scarf, Sam a pair of wool mittens, Rebecca a fleece hat, and Mac a brand-new dazzlingly high-tech yellow, black and red musher's parka with a wolverine ruff. It must have set her back at least six hundred dollars.

Mac was flabbergasted when he unwrapped the enormous gift. He stood up from his chair, bringing the parka with him and turning to Sadie with an expression that bordered on panic.

"What a beautiful parka!" Rebecca said. "Sadie, you sure hit the nail on the head with that one. I don't know of anyone who needs a decent parka more than Mac does."

Sadie blushed prettily. "I sure hope you like it," she said to Mac.

"Oh, yes!" Mac blurted, staring down at the bright colors. "Thank you."

"You'll be lit up like a neon sign on the race trail," Rebecca said. "You probably won't even need to use your headlamp."

Sam was filling his pipe, and Ellin was gathering the gift wrappings when Mac suddenly announced that it was his bedtime. "Have to run a team bright and early," he said, rolling the parka in his hands like a sleeping bag and gathering up his other gifts. "Thank you all for these great presents, and for one of the best Christmas Eves I can remember."

Sadie stood. "I'll walk you out," she said. "It's time I was going, too." She made the round of hugs and kisses, and just as she was slipping her arm possessively through Mac's, the phone rang. Ellin answered, spoke briefly, then hung up and turned to Sadie.

"That was for you, dear," she said. "There's been an accident up near the Inuvik road. Single vehicle, driver and three passengers, possible injuries."

Sadie's face fell. She gazed up at Mac wistfully. "I've got to go," she said. Mac nodded, so clearly relieved that Rebecca was amazed Sadie didn't see it. Love was indeed blind. Sadie gathered her things and rapidly departed, leaving Mac standing near the door with the look of a man who had been granted a reprieve moments before his execution. Sam lit his pipe and chuckled audibly. Ellin patted her husband's shoulder as she passed behind him and shook her head with a faint smile.

Rebecca stood and gathered her things. "Ellin, Sam, you're the greatest. It's been a wonderful evening."

"I was wondering," Mac said, as she shrugged into

her parka, "could you take a quick look at Merlin's foot before you go?"

Rebecca hesitated. "You've been running him for a while. I assumed his foot was healed enough to warrant that."

"I think it is. He seems fine on it, no lameness at all. But he's my ace in the hole, and you have a lot more experience than I do. I'd appreciate your opinion." He looked at her hopefully. "It won't take long."

She followed him out to the hangar and waited while he lit the propane lights. The dogs, curled on their beds of straw, stood and stretched and yawned. Merlin wagged his body and gave a mellow howl as Mac singled him out for individual attention. Freed from his picket line, Merlin whirled and raced from one end of the hangar to the other, causing a ripple of excitement to pass through the other dogs. He spun and jumped in ecstasy, circled the Stearman several times at full speed and came instantly to Mac when summoned.

Mac and Rebecca knelt to examine Merlin's paw. Mac switched on his brand-new headlight and illuminated the injury, which had healed so well that Rebecca could scarcely find the place where the pad had been cut. "It looks great," Rebecca said. "Just keep him bootied and watch him for any signs of soreness."

"I always do," he said, rubbing Merlin's shoulder. He glanced up at her suddenly, his eyes unreadable. "Rebecca, I—"

Rebecca stood abruptly. "I've got to go. It's getting late."

Mac stood with her. "Thanks for the first-aid kit."

She nodded. "Thanks for the wolf."

"Thanks for the kiss."

She drew her breath in sharply. "I didn't give you that. You took it."

"Thanks for not slapping me."

"I should have. You deserved it."

He hunched his shoulders and ducked his head. "My apologies if I offended you, but I'd be lying if I said I was sorry. I'm not." He reached impulsively for her hand. "Come outside. I want to show you something." He led her into the stillness of the night, and they stood side by side in the darkness. The cold was keen and crystalline, and the sky was brilliant with stars. "I saw them earlier, just before supper," he said. "I was hoping we might see them again."

"What?" she asked. His hand still held hers, strong and warm. It felt good to her, so good that she drew it away and moved to put some distance between them. Her inner voices were at war with one another. Emotions fought with intellect. She would not allow herself to feel good with him, to fall in love with him. She could not. Would not! No! Yet her heart raced as she struggled to steady her breathing. "See what?" she asked again.

"The northern lights. They were spectacular! Purples and greens and yellows, broad bands of light shimmering and moving across the sky." The night was so quiet Rebecca could hear trees snapping with the cold along the river. "You know, when I first came to this land," he murmured, "I didn't care whether or not I lived or died. I thought this would be a good place to just disappear. Vanish off the face of the earth. And then something happened that changed all that."

Rebecca, startled by this unexpected revelation, changed her focus from the stars to the profile of his face. She found it hard to imagine him depressed. Hard to picture him as anything other than brash, arrogant and irrepressible. "Look!" he said suddenly, startling her again. She turned her gaze back to the sky to watch the beautiful and mysterious light show known as the aurora borealis. As many times as Rebecca had seen the phenomenon, it never failed to take her breath away. "We're so insignificant in the grand scheme of things," Mac marveled as the streamers of light gradually faded from the sky. "There's so much we don't know."

Rebecca smiled in spite of herself. "That's how it makes me feel, too."

"This is a great land."

"Yes," she agreed. "It grows on you and in you, and in many ways, living in it becomes the very best part of your life. Sometimes I think if I were taken away from this place, I'd die."

"Why did you come here?"

"Bruce thought it would be the ultimate proving ground. He thought if he could survive here, he could somehow justify his existence in a very crazy world. I came because Bruce came, but I stayed because I grew to love it." She paused and then asked, "Obviously you didn't come here just because you wanted to run your brother's dog team."

"Not exactly," he admitted. "I was running away from everything. My failed marriage, my failed career, my failed life. I'd hit rock bottom. I was drowning, and my brother threw me a lifeline. I didn't know whether I should bother grabbing it or not, but in the end I did."

"I can't imagine you failing at anything, Mac."

He was quiet for a few minutes, and then she heard him sigh. "My ex-wife, my father and my commanding officer would all disagree," he said. "But that's all in the past. I've tried hard to put it all behind me. Being here has helped." He looked directly at Rebecca, and she sensed that he didn't want to discuss what had happened.

"Living in the wilderness is good medicine," she said.

"Yes. But it was more than the wilderness that changed things for me, Rebecca," he said, turning to face her in the darkness and reaching out to clasp her shoulders. "I know you don't have a very high regard for me and I don't blame you one bit, but from the moment I first laid eyes on you I felt that maybe there was something left to live for, after all. No, wait." He raised his finger briefly to quell her rebuke. "Let me say this! I promise I won't kiss you again, not until you ask me to. And I promise I won't chase after you like a lovesick pup. I just want you to know that this has been one of the most perfect days of my life. I saw a sun dog this morning just before it snowed, three wolves at noon, the northern lights on Christmas Eve, and best of all, I stole a kiss from a truly beautiful woman. As far as I'm concerned, my life will never get any better than this."

He gave her shoulders a gentle squeeze through her thick parka, and she saw the flash of his teeth in the starlight as he grinned. "*Never,*" he repeated, releasing her abruptly and stepping back. Without another word, he turned on his heel and disappeared into the darkness, leaving her feeling very much alone.

THREE WEEKS LATER Mac and Sam were working on the Stearman's brakes when Rebecca stormed into the hangar. She banged the door behind her and stalked directly to where Mac crouched beneath the plane. "Okay, let off!" he called up to Sam, who was sitting in the cockpit working the brake pedals. "Hello, Rebecca," he said, concentrating on his work in order to avoid her obvious bad humor. "Good to see you…I think."

"You've been going into my cabin while I'm out on training runs, haven't you!" she accused. Out of the corner of his eye, he could see that her cheeks were flushed and her eyes were bright with anger. "I want you to stop doing that! That's *my* cabin, *my* private place, and you have no right to be inside it!"

"Okay, step on 'em," he called up to Sam. He reached up to bleed the brake line.

"Are you denying it?" she demanded.

"I haven't said a thing," Mac replied mildly. "But no, I'm not denying it. I went into your cabin. I filled your wood box. I filled your water barrel. I must have done that five, six times now on my way back home. Just swung my team through your yard so's I could lend a hand with your chores. Sorry if I overstepped my bounds. I honestly thought you might like the help. I thought it would give you more time to write."

"Well, I don't need your help, I don't like it, and I want it to stop!"

"Okay, let off!" he said to Sam, and turned his head and looked at her for the first time. "Then it will stop," he said calmly.

"Good!" She whirled and stormed out of the hangar. Sam leaned out over the cockpit to catch Mac's eye and shrugged sympathetically.

"Well, it was worth a try," Mac said. "But I can see my efforts did nothing to win her over. In fact, they seem to have had quite the opposite effect."

"Oh, I don't know," Sam remarked, thoughtfully rubbing his chin. "She waited until you'd been in her cabin doing her chores five or six times before she got around to complaining about it. I'd take that as a real promising sign."

ELLIN WAS PUTTING the finishing touches on a pair of curtains when Rebecca burst into the kitchen, fairly hopping up and down with indignation. "He has one hell of a nerve!"

"Do you mean Mac?" Ellin said, looping the needle.

"He's been going into my cabin when I'm not home, without asking my permission, and I've had enough!"

"My dear," Ellin said, resting the sewing in her lap and raising her eyebrows, "why on earth would Mac be going into your cabin?"

Rebecca flushed. "He's been filling my wood box and my water barrel!"

"Ah. I see," Ellin nodded. "And that offends you?"

"I don't need his help. I didn't ask for it!"

"We don't ask for Mac's help, either, but since he's come here, we haven't had to carry wood once. He spends an hour a day splitting, stacking and lugging firewood, and he does all sorts of odd jobs around the place when he isn't helping Sam or fixing vehicles or training his dogs. I count my blessings for his help. He's worth his weight in gold as far as we're concerned."

Rebecca paced to the stove, held her hands over it a moment, and then spun around. "He's only doing it because he thinks if he helps me out, I might like him better."

"What's wrong with that? If I were you I'd take full advantage. Put him to work. I told you before, that would be the perfect solution."

"Ellin, I wish he'd never come here! I wish I'd never laid eyes on the man!" Rebecca said vehemently.

Ellin stared at her, openly amazed. "No, you don't!" she said. "You don't wish anything of the kind! You're attracted to him, and you feel guilty because you believe that you're betraying Bruce's memory. But, my dear girl, you're not. Bruce was a good man, a good husband, and you loved him and were loyal to him. He was a lucky man to have had you. But it's time for you to take off your widow's weeds and start living again. Life is too short to squander it in mourning.''

Rebecca gazed at Ellin's kindly face and shook her head. Her eyes unexpectedly filled with tears. ''No,'' she said.

Ellin sighed, shook her head and took up her sewing again. ''As you wish,'' she said.

''I can't!'' Rebecca whispered.

Ellin peered at her. ''My dear girl, how would you know? You haven't even tried!''

CHAPTER SIX

MAC TOSSED A FEW MORE STICKS into his wood stove, refilled his mug of coffee and carried it with him to the table, glancing at the calendar pinned to the back of the cabin door as he passed it. He felt a lurch of apprehension. January 20. Only a few short weeks to the start of the Yukon Quest.

Did he have enough miles on his team? He had kept careful records of each run, and the dogs seemed to be doing well, but he had nothing to compare their performance to. Maybe Rebecca was right. Maybe he was foolish to even contemplate running the thousand mile race.

He dropped into his chair and took a sip of the strong black brew.

Rebecca. Try as he might, he couldn't get her out of his thoughts. She'd made it perfectly clear she had no interest in him, yet last night he'd woken up with an overwhelming feeling of panic, filled with the realization that he was in love with her.

He sighed and picked up the pencil lying beside his notebook. He began to write down the names of the dogs he would run that morning. Merlin, Callie, Wally, Jessie, Dozer—Rebecca MacKenzie. He wrote the words slowly and sighed again, tossing the pencil aside. He was behaving like a lovesick pup!

He had nothing to offer her. Nothing she needed or

wanted. He had no money, no respectable job, no mushing skills and his irresistible personality obviously held no sway with her. Worse, once she found out about his past, she'd turn her back on him with a vengeance.

It was hopeless.

And yet, he wasn't ready to give up. What could he do to improve her opinion of him? Why did Sadie chase after him, while Rebecca pushed him away? Just yesterday, Sadie had shown up at chore time. "My truck's running funny again," she'd said. He'd found nothing wrong, but then when he'd taken it for a brief test drive with her sitting beside him, chattering away a mile a minute, who should he pass? Rebecca. It bothered the hell out of him that she'd seen them together, even though Rebecca herself had suggested that he romance Sadie.

Mac dropped his head into his hands and moaned aloud. He'd never felt this way about a woman before. He'd never lost his appetite, his ability to sleep. Suddenly he was unable to focus on anything except how to prove his worth to Rebecca. Dammit, there had to be something he could do.

He pushed out his chair so abruptly that it crashed behind him as he grabbed his parka and shrugged into it. He had a team of dogs to train. And one thing was for certain. He wasn't going to impress anyone—least of all Rebecca—by sitting here feeling sorry for himself.

SOME TIME DURING THE NIGHT the fire went out, and when Rebecca opened her eyes she knew her morning was going to have a very chilly beginning. Tuffy had given up her blanket beside the cold stove and had climbed the steep stairs to the loft, tucking herself into a ball at Rebecca's feet and shivering periodically.

"Tuffy," she murmured, "why can't you make yourself useful and start the fire? Make me a pot of coffee, too, while you're at it."

She lay for a few moments thinking about the coming day, the dogs she would run, the trail she would take, the pace she would try to set. In a few short days she'd have to start organizing her food drops for the race checkpoints. Kanemoto would be arriving next week and he'd be a big help with that. From now on, every waking moment would be focused on the race. Preparing for it, mentally and physically. Already Rebecca was experiencing pre-race jitters, and the starting line was still fourteen days away.

Her team was ready—but was she? Today she'd train in the hills, give her dogs a taste of what lay ahead on the race trail when they would have to climb American and Eagle summits. Bruce had told her tales of scaling those heights, of how the wind had blown his fully loaded sled over, of how his lead dogs had crouched down, refusing to continue. He had tried every dog in lead until finally he hooked Tuffy in, an older team dog he'd never paid much attention. Tuffy had dug in and hauled the rest of the team over the summit. Tuffy was no longer part of the team, but Rebecca had confidence in Thor, Raven and Cookie. They were tough little ladies, no doubt about it.

In the midst of these early-morning thoughts, barging in unwanted and unsummoned, came William "Mac" MacKenzie and all his troubling ways. The troubling way he pierced her soul when he looked at her with those clear, keen eyes of his, as if he could read her innermost thoughts. The troubling way her heart quickened at the sound of his voice. The troubling way she enjoyed being in his company. The troubling memory of that brief kiss they had shared, and the breathless tingling warmth she'd felt afterward. All of it scared her. In fact, *he* scared her! She could never, ever allow herself to love anyone the way she had loved Bruce. She never wanted to suffer that kind of loss again.

There was little chance she would. Her self-imposed isolation and her emotional cowardice had directed Mac's attention elsewhere. Rebecca had seen Sadie's truck just yesterday afternoon heading into Dawson. Mac had been in the driver's seat. Just a glimpse of them she'd had, but Sadie had been laughing at something he'd said. They'd been on their way into Dawson...to catch a movie, perhaps? To go out to dinner? Chinese food? Pizza? Rebecca couldn't have explained why on earth the sight of them had bothered her so, yet there was no denying that it had. In fact, still did. Damn the man! Why did he have to land here, of all places, just when she was starting to get her life in order again?

And why was it so difficult to stop thinking about him? Already she'd missed two deadlines. Instead of writing her column, she been staring out the window wondering about Mac. Wondering what could possibly have happened in his past to give him such a poor self-image. Wondering what kind of woman his ex-wife had been. Wondering...

Rebecca threw off the goose-down coverlet and jumped out of bed, the cold galvanizing her into immediate action. Paper, kindling, a few split pieces of dry spruce, a match, and soon the fire in the stove was roaring, though it would be a while before it threw enough heat to warm the cabin. She set the big pot of half-frozen water on the propane stove and lit the burner beneath it, set the coffeepot over another burner and lit that, as well. She dressed quickly in the usual layers, glancing at the thermometer on her way to the outhouse. Thirty-six below. No wonder she was cold!

The smell of perking coffee buoyed her spirits, and she drank her first cup while mixing the dogs' breakfast. She planned the team's lineup on a scrap of paper while she drank her second cup, and an hour later she was out on the trail. The sky was lightening in the east, the stars still shone in the west. It was the most promising time of the day.

Rebecca relaxed on the runners as the trail unwound before her. It followed the river for several miles before swinging away and climbing into the hills. Then the relaxing was over. On the steepest part, she jumped off and ran alongside the sled, and when she stood on the runners, she pedaled to help the team. It wasn't long before she was exhausted. The muscles in her legs burned, her lungs gasped for air, sweat trickled from her scalp. She ripped off her hat and threw it onto the sled bag, but within moments her sweat-soaked hair had frozen, and she was pulling her hat back onto her head. Hill work was like that. Running uphill was a churning struggle that produced tons of heat, but the downhills that followed had her zipping up her coat, pulling down her hat and looking forward to the next uphill section when she could jump off the sled and run, warming up her toes again.

Three hours later, she stopped to snack her dogs, and she heard the unmistakable sound of another team ahead, yelping and howling. She tossed each of her dogs a chunk of frozen meat and when they had wolfed it down, she pulled the snow hook and continued up the trail. A quarter of a mile farther, the trail dropped suddenly, winding through a thick grove of wind-stunted spruce before leveling off on a high bog. She saw a dog team in front and brought her own to a stop. The man bending over his wheel dog was unmistakable even from a distance in that shabby old parka. William Kimball MacKenzie! Rebecca's heart gladdened even as her brain reminded her that she was Bruce Reed's widow, and Mac was Sadie's man.

"Hey!" she called, and at the sound of her voice he straightened and turned, clearly startled.

"Hey yourself!" he replied. "What are you doing out here? Chasing after me?"

"Same thing you are," she said. "Getting in some hill training. What's wrong? And why aren't you wearing your fancy new parka?"

"Nothing. My wheel dog threw a bootie, and I stopped to replace it. I'm saving my fancy parka for the race. Why don't you go by? Your team is faster than mine."

Rebecca was surprised that he would admit such a thing but relieved that she wouldn't have to travel behind him, staring at his irritatingly broad shoulders and thinking about how happy Sadie had looked in his truck. She nodded. "All right!" she said to Cookie and Raven. "On by. On by!"

Rebecca felt her cheeks burn as she remembered the heated words she'd flung at Mac the last time she'd seen him. She'd treated him poorly, and he hadn't deserved it. He grinned at her as she passed, and she wondered what he was thinking. Probably that she was quite a bitch. Which, come to think of it, wasn't too far off the mark, Rebecca thought. *He has every right to think of me that way!*

"Good dogs," she said as they continued across the muskeg. The trail was drifted in here, and her leaders had to push through chest-deep snow. Rebecca jumped off the runners to help them and felt her feet break through the surface of something hard and brittle. She dropped like a stone into very cold water. She pulled herself back onto the runners of the sled, turned to look behind her and felt the sudden, sickening lurch of the sled itself breaking through the ice. "All right!" she shouted as the sled plunged with a heart-stopping drop while she kept a death grip on the driver's bow. "All right!"

She kept her eyes on her dogs. The sled was still moving but very slowly now because of the increased drag. Her body was immersed in water clear up to her chest. The icy shock of it was overwhelming. She tried to put her feet down but couldn't. Her lower body was being pulled sideways by a surprisingly strong current that ran beneath the ice. What creek was this? She had no recollection of ever crossing one on this particular trail. Had she taken a wrong turn? She was in trouble—in deep, fast-moving water—and there was no time to dwell on whether or not she was on the right trail.

"All right!" she shouted again, fear giving strident shrillness to her words. *Don't let my dogs break through,* she thought. *Don't let my dogs break through!*

They didn't, although the heavy sled kept breaking through the ice as it was hauled forward. The dogs came to an abrupt halt when the front of the sled jammed beneath a lip of solid ice. Rebecca tried to put her feet down again, and this time she felt the solid roll of river gravel beneath her boots. It was difficult to keep her footing in the strong current. She pulled herself alongside the slowly sinking sled and took hold of the brush bow with hands that were completely numb. To free the sled, she needed to pull it back until it was clear of the ice, then lift it up and over the ice shelf. Each time she managed to pull the sled back, the dogs pulled it forward. They didn't know a command for backing up, and the longer they remained stopped, the more excited they were to get going again.

Rebecca heaved mightily and gained two inches. The dogs jumped forward and hauled the sled back underneath the ice. This scenario repeated itself several agonizing times until Rebecca decided to try a different approach. "Whoa, Raven, whoa, Cookie, let's take a break," she said in as calm a voice as she could manage. These were the exact words she used when she stopped the team to snack them.

It worked. The dogs instantly relaxed, turning to look behind in anticipation of a snack. Rebecca didn't waste any time hauling the sled back. When there was just enough slack in the line to free the brush bow, she lifted the front of the sled with all of her strength and called out to her leaders. Her voice had an unfamiliar snap to it that startled them. Cookie and Raven jumped to their feet and sprang ahead, dragging the rest of the team behind them and hauling the sled up onto the solid ice. Rebecca moved her feet woodenly onto the runners. She looked ahead to the safety of the dark line of spruce woods that her dogs were already winding into. When it seemed certain that they were off the ice, she stepped on the sled brake and turned around. Mac would be right behind her. He'd fall through just the way she had. Maybe he'd lose his grip on his sled and be swept beneath the ice.

Within moments of stopping, she saw Merlin coming into view with the rest of Mac's team trotting briskly behind. "Mac!" she shouted, waving one arm wildly above her head. "Bad ice! Turn around! Go back!"

Mac paused his team at the sound of her shouts,

peered ahead at the visible span of dark, turbulent water where her sled had fallen through, and then spoke to his leader. Instead of turning around, they came onward.

"No!" Rebecca shouted again. "Go back! The ice is bad! Go back!"

But he didn't, and even as she watched, Merlin, listening to commands given by Mac, left the trail that her dogs had already broken and veered into deep, unbroken snow. Head down, body taut and finely attuned, that wonderful dog led Mac's team safely across the river.

Mac drove his team up behind hers, threw his snow hook down, stomped it in, and ran through the snow toward her. "God, Rebecca!" he said. "You're soaking wet! We've got to get you dried out in a hurry—it's at least thirty below and the wind's coming up!"

Rebecca's teeth had begun to chatter so hard she couldn't speak. She nodded, pulled her snub line out of the snow with numb fingers and walked to the nearest stalwart spruce to tie off her team. Already ice was forming on her clothing, turning it into an unyielding suit of armor. In a few short moments she would be unable to move.

Mac was snubbing his own team off and grabbing something out of his sled bag. He ran toward her, and she saw that he was pulling his sleeping bag out of its sack. "You've got to get out of those wet clothes!" he snapped. "Hurry up, get them off and get into my sleeping bag."

She nodded stupidly. That was the correct thing to do, of course. Hypothermia was already taking hold and her fingers were frozen, useless, unable to perform the simplest of tasks. Mac's hands were suddenly slapping hers aside, and he was unzipping the frozen zipper of her parka, forcing it down in a shower of brittle ice, stripping it off her, doing the same with her bibs, making her stand on the growing stack of soaked and fast-freezing clothing. "How many damn layers are you wearing?" he said as he attacked yet another layer.

"Mac—" she said.

"This is no time for modesty, woman!" he said, and then finally she was naked. Her skin was cold and very blue. He snatched the sleeping bag and held it while she stepped awkwardly inside, then he zipped it up around her, clear to her neck, and pulled the hood down over her head. He took his parka off and wrapped it around her, as well, then scooped her into his arms and carried her back to his sled where he placed her on top of his sled bag. "I'm going to build a fire," he told her. "We have to get your clothes dried."

She nodded, or thought she did, but her entire body was convulsed with cold. She'd been cold before, plenty of times, but never like this. She watched Mac build the fire not six feet from where she lay. He was crouched over a blue curl of smoke, and she saw the yellow lick of flames. Daylight was waning. In another hour it would be dark. Rebecca closed her eyes, her convulsive shivers slowly ebbing. She wasn't quite as cold now. Warm, almost. And tired. So very tired. She needed to sleep. Needed to close her eyes and—

"Rebecca!" Mac's voice again. What a nuisance that man was! she thought groggily. "Rebecca! I found a thermos in your sled. I want you to take a drink." He hoisted her up and held the steaming cup to her mouth. She swallowed obediently. Orange-spice tea, sweetened with a dollop of honey. She closed her eyes, shuddering again with the cold. "Open your eyes!" Mac ordered. "Take another swallow! That's my girl! The fire's going strong," Mac said. "I'm going to get some more wood and hang your clothes to dry. You keep shivering and you stay awake. You hear me? You stay awake!''

Moments later she heard the sounds of his ax, the sound of crackling flames, and then his arms were lifting her again as if she were weightless. "I'm so cold!" she heard herself say.

"I know, baby, I know," she heard him reply. "I'm going to get you warm."

He had spread a ground cloth near the fire and he lowered her onto it. Then he unloaded his sled, tipped it onto its side so that it opened toward the fire, extended one of the top flaps as a ground cloth and used two sticks to prop the other flap up. An instant lean-to. He picked her up again and placed her inside it. Suddenly the reflected warmth of the fire enveloped her. Moments later she looked out and saw her frozen clothing draped over a thin line of twine strung between two spruce that flanked either side of the fire. She heard a loud chattering noise and wondered for a moment what it was, then realized that it was her teeth. She tried to stop but couldn't.

"My dogs?" she said when he approached with an armful of wood.

"Your dogs are fine. Curled up and sleeping. None of them broke through the ice. Rebecca, drink some more tea." He propped her up and she swallowed again. "Good girl," he said. "We'll get you warmed up." She watched through drowsy eyes as he threw more wood on the blaze and then pulled off his boots, his wool pants, his old wool army sweater. Her eyes opened a bit at the sight of him in his red union suit, and opened wider when he unzipped the bag again and wriggled in beside her.

"Mac!" she chattered.

"Don't worry, this is purely professional. I learned

these techniques in navy survival school. They teach you all kinds of things like how to eat snakes, find water in the desert, elude capture, deal with hypothermia and, of course, how to share a sleeping bag with a beautiful woman. Life and death stuff like that," he said, as he pulled her tightly against him and then rezipped the sleeping bag. "Relax. You're perfectly safe with me. I promised I wouldn't kiss you again until you asked me to, and I won't," he said, his big, rough, strong hands rubbing the icy skin of her back. "But as you'll recall, I never said anything about heavy petting."

BRUCE USED TO CALL HER "Coldfoot Classic" and tease her mercilessly when she cuddled with him in bed. "You only want me for a foot-warmer, girl," he'd say, and flinch when she'd tuck her icy feet between his. "That's true enough," she'd say smiling, "and you're a good one, Bruce Reed."

She'd snuggle into him, into the warm, solid curve of his body, and let his warmth soak into her like a sweet and sensual solution. His fingers would tease the hair at the nape of her neck, and he would breathe into the shell of her ear, his breath moist and hot. "Reeba," he'd whisper with growing passion. "Reeba!"

Rebecca stirred against him, felt the need, the urgent need, to have him close to her, closer to her. She moaned with desire. It had been so long. So long! Why had he stayed away so long? Where had he been? She had missed him so! She slid her feet between his, wondered why he was wearing socks—he never wore socks to bed—wondered why he wasn't stroking her the way she liked to be stroked. She pressed against him, against the long, lovely hard masculine length of him. He felt so good, so solid and so real. He smelled so good, and when she nuzzled her face against his neck, he responded. His hands moved over her willing, pliant body exactly the way they should, and his body moved against hers in a way that made her catch her breath and moan again. His mouth sought hers the way she so desperately wanted it to.

It was electrical, that kiss. Oh, God, it dazzled her! That long, hot, passionate kiss was undoubtedly the best she'd ever had. The raw, powerful voltage of it made every fiber of her body throb. She tightened her fingers in his hair, moaned into his mouth, and when finally she broke away to breathe, she gasped his name aloud, her eyes filling with joyous tears. "Bruce!" she said. "Bruce, oh, Bruce!"

"Rebecca?"

The voice that breathed in her ear was not Bruce's. She opened her eyes and for a moment didn't know where she was or whom she was with—except that it wasn't Bruce. She stiffened as realization struck. With a growing sense of dismay, she realized that she'd fallen asleep and that her limbs were intimately intertwined with those of the man she had tried so desperately to avoid! Bill MacKenzie lay flat on his back, and she lay full-length on top of him, cocooned within the tight confines of his sleeping bag and encircled by his warm, powerful arms. He was breathing as rapidly as she was, and she sensed that this dream had not been hers alone. She lay motionless, stricken with remorse, trying to determine what had just happened. She'd been dreaming of Bruce, but had she…? Had they…? She pushed away from him abruptly as if to bolt from the sleeping bag, but his hands held her close.

"Whoa, now!" he said. "It's a little too cold out there to be running around in your birthday suit."

"Oh, God!" she gasped. "I was dreaming and I thought… I thought…" Her throat closed up and tears stung her eyes.

"It's okay," Mac soothed. "We both fell asleep."

"But I thought… I mean, I dreamt… Did we…?"

"Nothing happened," Mac said. "You spoke his name and started to cry."

The taste of her kiss was still in his mouth, the tender, passionate sweetness of it. He could still feel the sensual movements of her lithe, graceful body against his. For a moment, as he'd awakened, he'd thought that all his wishes were finally coming true, but then she had spoken her dead husband's name and Mac's hopes had been dashed. He felt as if his heart would break for wanting her, but Rebecca Reed still belonged to another man.

"Mac," she said, removing her feet from between his and drawing her weight off him. "It's time to go," she said.

"You okay?" His hand touched her face in the darkness, briefly curved itself to the contour of her cheek and then brushed back to smooth her hair. He wanted her so badly! He would not give up the fight! A curious kind of anger coursed through him, anger channeled toward a dead man. *Let her go!* he raged silently to the husband she still loved. *Let her go! You can't help her now. You can't protect her now. You can't love her now. Let her go!*

REBECCA FELT MAC shift into position, and his hands slid down her back again. "You feel a lot warmer than you did." His fingers expertly kneaded the muscles between her shoulders. "But there's always room for improvement. Your feet are still solid blocks of ice and could definitely use a little more quality cuddle time."

His hands slid lower and closed around her hips as he pulled her gently back down against him. "You know, pretty woman, if you asked me real nice, I just might kiss you in spite of the fact that your feet are so damn cold!"

Rebecca stifled a nervous laugh that came unbidden. The dream had been so real. So real! She laid her cheek against his chest and drew a breath, listening to the strong, rapid cadence of his heartbeat, hoping he couldn't feel how her own was racing. They lay in silence for what seemed like a very long time before she spoke again. "I'm scared of drowning, Mac," she said softly. "I'm afraid of falling through the ice."

Mac's hands moved over her as tenderly as if she were a baby needing comfort. "I didn't think you were afraid of anything," he murmured into her ear. "But I promise I won't hold it against you, and I won't tell anyone else about your weakness, just as long as you ask me to kiss you. Go ahead. I know you want me to. Just say the words, woman. I'm bilingual, in case you didn't know. English, French, either works for me."

This time her laugh was audible, and she was grateful for his humor. "Mac, I have to get home and feed my dogs. It must be late."

Mac groaned. "I'll get your clothes and hand them to you. You can wear my parka. I don't think yours'll be dry yet."

True to his word, he handed over her clothing, giving her time between items to awkwardly dress herself inside the sleeping bag. When she'd put on her undergarments, he threw a few more sticks onto the coals and the flames lit the immediate area. She saw several pairs of eyes glowing in the darkness. "My dogs?" she said.

Mac walked out and checked both teams. "They're

fine," he said, coming back to her. "Still sleeping like babes."

Her clothes, with the exception of her parka, were reasonably dry. Her boot liners were still damp but they warmed up promisingly when she put on her boots and stomped her feet.

"Thank you, Mac," she said quietly as he was stuffing his sleeping bag back into its sack. He paused as if surprised by her words and then nodded.

"My pleasure."

TWO HOURS LATER Rebecca drove her team into her kennel yard. Mac was behind her, and she expected him to continue down the trail to Sam and Ellin's. Instead, he snubbed his team to the post in front of the cabin, and when she looked questioningly at him, he paused in the act of unsnapping his dogs' tug lines. "I know," he said, raising one hand as if to quell her protest. "You don't need my help. You're perfectly capable of taking care of things here, more perfectly capable than the most perfectly capable person on the face of this planet. But just this once you're going to do exactly what I tell you to do, Rebecca Reed. Go inside the cabin and get the woodstove going. Put your big kettle of water on to boil. Stoke up the fire, light all the lamps, heat some water for a pot of coffee, get out of those clothes and into something warm and dry, and bundle yourself into bed."

That said, he continued tending his dogs. She stood for a moment beside her own team and was about to open her mouth to protest when he turned suddenly, walked toward her with a determined step, took her by the arm, marched her up the cabin steps and propelled her through the cabin door, shutting it firmly behind her.

She opened it immediately. "My dogs!" she said.

"I'll take care of them. You do what I told you to do."

"But they haven't been fed!"

"Dammit all, woman, I know how to feed dogs! I've learned that much at least in the past few months. Now shut that door! You're wasting heat!"

He came into the cabin about an hour later, stamping his feet to rid them of snow, pulling off his hat and gloves and holding his hands over the stove to warm them. He looked at her in the lamplight and grinned. "That coffee sure smells good."

"Won't Ellin and Sam be worried about you?" she asked as she poured him a cup.

He shook his head, shrugging out of his parka. "I planned this run as an all-nighter. I was going to run five hours, rest five hours, then run another five. They don't expect me to haul in until one or two in the morning." He took the offered mug with a nod of thanks and cupped his hands around it appreciatively. I figure it must be seven now, or somewhere thereabouts."

"Seven-thirty," Rebecca said.

"I just fed both teams, and if I could just hang here for another hour, I'll take mine down onto the river for another run. I don't have to stay in here with you," he added hastily. "I can wait outside until it's time to go. I just want to give them a little time to digest their supper. If that's okay."

Rebecca lowered her eyes and lifted her coffee for a sip. His words stung and made her feel small. "Mac, I never meant what I said the other day." Her voice was low. "I don't know what came over me. I said things I shouldn't have. I'm sorry." Mac's surprised look made her feel even worse. "I get in moods," she said, her cheeks coloring. "I guess sometimes I can be a real pain in the neck."

"I understand," he said. "My ex-wife was the same way."

Rebecca glanced up at him indignantly. "I beg your pardon?"

"Monthly moods," he explained weakly. "You know…"

"Of course," Rebecca said acidly. "The woman thing."

"This is real good coffee!" he said, changing the subject.

"I'll fix you something to eat."

"No need to bother."

"It's no bother. It's the woman thing. Besides, I'm starving." She busied herself in the kitchen, which was one small corner of the cabin sectioned off by an L-shaped counter. There was a trap door in the kitchen floor that opened into a tiny root cellar. Rebecca opened it and descended the ladder with an oil lamp in one hand, contemplating the food stores that were neatly arranged on the deep shelves. There were two sand-filled wooden boxes on the floor itself, one filled with potatoes, the other with carrots, turnips and beets. She selected four large baking potatoes, pulled a canned ham from the shelf and passed these up the ladder to Mac. "What's your pleasure for a vegetable?" she asked. "I have carrots, canned corn, string beans, beets…"

"I'm not particular," Mac said. "I eat most everything and like it."

She chose corn and climbed the ladder with two cans of it. A big man like Mac, she figured, probably ate like a horse. She put the ham and potatoes into the oven, opened the cans of corn into a saucepan and set it atop the stove.

"I still owe you a beer for fixing my truck, but I have wine, too," she offered.

"I'll have whatever you have."

She retrieved a bottle of cabernet from the cellar. "Look, Mac," she said as she uncorked the bottle. "About today…"

"It was a good run, except for your dunking," Mac said.

"I mean, about what you did out there."

Mac accepted the glass of wine and eyed her warily. "Did I do something wrong?"

"You saved my life! If you hadn't been right there, I'd have frozen to death. I'm trying to thank you!"

"You already did," he said. "And anyway, you underestimate yourself. You would've been fine even if I hadn't been there. You'd have done all the right things."

Rebecca shook her head. "I'd have frozen to death," she repeated simply. "I was in the water too long. I couldn't have gotten out of my wet clothes. I screwed up. I should have known about that creek, but I didn't."

"So you made a mistake." Mac shrugged, then set his glass on the table and threw two more sticks of firewood into the stove. "Still, if I truly did save your life, time-honored tradition dictates that it now belongs to me." He grinned wickedly. "Think about that one too long, Rebecca, and you'll probably jump back into the creek. Meanwhile, I guess I'll fill your wood box." He reached for his parka. "That is, if you don't mind."

Rebecca drew a deep breath. "It's because of Bruce," she said, and Mac froze with his hand on the doorknob. "It's because he used to do those things. He use to split and haul the wood and lug the water up from the spring to fill the water barrel.''

Mac nodded slowly, watching her.

"Those were his chores," Rebecca continued. "Of course, he wasn't always here to do them. Sometimes he'd be gone for days at a time, when he was out running his traplines.''

Mac nodded again.

"I missed him when he was away. He said he never worried about me because he always knew I'd be okay.''

Mac let his hand fall from the doorknob, amazed that she was talking to him about her husband. "And you always were," he said.

Rebecca smiled faintly. "Not really, but I faked it pretty good.''

"What did you do before you came here to live?''

"I was still in school. Bruce had a job as a substitute teacher and he worked part-time for an accounting firm. Hated where his life was heading. One day he showed up at my apartment and told me he had quit everything and was heading north, and if I wanted to come along I'd better be packed and ready to leave in an hour.''

"So you quit school?''

Rebecca nodded. "I packed my bag, went to the registrar's office, phoned my mom in Boston and that afternoon was on my way north with Bruce.''

"Any regrets?''

She lifted a shoulder. "Sometimes I wish I'd finished my degree, but otherwise, no. None. Our first winter was hellacious. We lived in an old school bus camper and damn near froze to death. Bruce bought someone's trapline, dog team and all, and we very nearly starved to death, too, trying to feed those dogs. The next summer we built this cabin and netted enough chum salmon to feed the team through the winter. He did better with the trapline, and he really liked running the dogs. I stayed home and took care of the animals he'd bring back. I'd skin them and stretch the pelts. It was awful work and I hated the whole idea of trapping, but those furs bought food and supplies for us.''

Mac crossed to the table and dropped into a chair across from her. In the lamplight Rebecca's face was very nearly angelic. He picked up his glass of wine and took a sip, but said nothing to interrupt the flow of her thoughts. Her gaze was fixed on the far wall, but he knew she wasn't seeing the tightly fitted, hand-hewn spruce logs.

''The next spring we were married. My mom flew into Dawson to stand with us before the justice of the peace, then came out here and went into an immediate state of shock. I don't think she'd ever been in the woods before, and for sure she'd never used an outhouse. She departed two days later and hasn't returned since.'' Wry smile. ''We built the dog barn in our second summer and started selling dog food. Bruce advertised dog tours in the Whitehorse paper, and we were surprised by the response. And that's how we spent the next four years, trapping, guiding and running races. Things were good and getting better.'' She gave a bitter laugh. ''That's the thing about life, Mac. When things are good and getting better, watch out!'' She met his eyes and smiled again, but it was a bitter smile, full of pain.

Mac leaned back in his chair and twisted the stem of his wineglass between his fingers. Her cabin was still full of Bruce. In addition to his coat on a peg by the door and his boots behind the stove, his pictures cluttered the top of the plain pine bureau and his impressive race trophies glittered on every shelf. This cabin stood like a shrine to his memory. The only thing of Rebecca's was her old Royal typewriter, circa 1860, sitting on the little desk beside the east window.

"That's why I got mad at you," Rebecca explained. "When you took over Bruce's chores, I thought you were trying to take his place."

I was, Mac thought darkly, but he said, "It must have been quite a struggle after he died. You could have left here and gone back to school."

Rebecca was quiet for a while. "I thought about doing that, but the more I thought about leaving, the less I liked the idea. I love the dogs and I've grown to love this country. The wild beauty of it. I don't think I could ever leave here now. It's in my blood."

"But trying to make ends meet..." Mac shook his head. "I don't know how you do it. Why don't you sell some of the dogs?"

"They were Bruce's. It would be like selling a part of him. And I need them, too. The dogsled tours pay very well. Selling food brings in a little bit extra, and the weekly column for the *Whitehorse Star* generates a small but steady income. Every little bit helps."

"I've read every word you ever wrote," Mac said, and at her surprised glance, he added, "Sam and Ellin keep them in a special notebook and they let me borrow it. You're a very good writer. I don't know what they pay you at the *Star,* but whatever it is, it isn't enough. You should consider writing a book."

Rebecca smiled faintly at his compliment. She toyed with the stem of her glass. "It's a matter of finding the time," she said. "There aren't enough hours in the day as it is."

Mac stood and crossed to where her little typewriter sat. He studied the sheet of paper rolled into it. "A Walk in the Woods," he read aloud. He glanced at her. "Well, you've gotten the title written. When is it due?"

Rebecca pulled a face. "Yesterday," she said.

Mac nodded and returned to his chair.

"Maybe it's a matter of having some help around here," Mac said, leaning forward with his elbows braced on the table and the wineglass cradled between his hands. "I'm more than willing and I'm a good worker. I could relieve you of all the mundane chores so you'd have the time to write. Quit shaking your head, you stubborn woman! When I came here and filled your wood box and hauled your water, I was trying to help you, that's all. You helped me when I needed it. Why won't you let me return the favor?"

"Because I'm doing just fine on my own, thanks."

Mac slumped back on his chair and sighed wearily. "I know that. I'm talking about making your life a little easier. I'm talking about making it a little better."

Rebecca lowered her eyes. "We've had this conversation before." She drew a deep breath and released it slowly. She raised her eyes and her gaze was steady. "I appreciate your concern, but you're not Bruce," she said. "You can't just walk in here and sign up to take his place. I'm not looking for another man in my life, Mac, but I could use a good friend."

Mac pushed out of his chair and reached for his parka. He paused by the door and zipped it up. His eyes revealed nothing, but his voice was quiet and this time there was no brash grin. "Okay." He nodded. "If it's friends you want to be, then friends it is. But like it or not, as your good friend, I'm still going to fill your water barrel and your wood box."

RACE DATE APPROACHED with the speed of a forty-five-caliber bullet. Kanemoto had arrived from Japan one week prior, as promised, and was proving himself a great help in organizing Rebecca's gear and preparing her food drops. The start of the race occurred in Whitehorse on even years and in Fairbanks on odd years. This year the thousand-mile race would begin in Whitehorse, which meant they'd be running right onto Lake Leberge, and that could mean losing the trail in the lake's notorious windstorms. Once past Leberge, the teams would run up Chain of Lakes, where there might be nasty overflow. It was 160 miles to the first checkpoint at Carmacks, a long haul with a lot of weight in the sled. But not the longest haul by far, and not the hardest.

Rebecca flew out of Ellin's bathroom and into the kitchen, wrapping her damp hair in a towel and tucking her flannel shirt into her jeans. "Ellin, I can't run the race!" she announced. "There's no way I can run the race!"

Ellin was elbow-deep in a batch of bread dough, and she glanced up and gave Rebecca a quizzical look. "A few short months ago you couldn't wait to run it," she reminded her.

"That was months ago. Somehow it seemed much safer then." Rebecca paced between woodstove and kitchen counter. "There's still so much to do! I make long, important lists in the middle of the night when I can't sleep and then I misplace them. Kanemoto told me this morning that I was driving him crazy. Ellin, what am I going to do!"

"You're going to finish putting all your food drops together, pack up all your gear and all your dogs, and drive down to Whitehorse in time for the drivers' meeting tomorrow night. And then you're going to get on your sled and run the race."

"But I'll never finish it!"

"Nonsense. Of course you will! Once you get out on the trail, everything will be fine. It will be you and your dogs, just the way you like it. Take your time and enjoy yourself. Concentrate on keeping your dogs happy. And Rebecca, when you get so tired and discouraged that you feel like quitting, stop your team, feed your dogs, feed yourself and take a good long nap. When you wake up, things will look much brighter."

Rebecca stopped pacing and stared. "Ellin, how did you learn all that?"

Ellin smiled. "By listening to you."

"I haven't been able to sleep for the past week! By the time we start the race, I'll be falling off the sled runners with exhaustion."

"I don't know why you're so nervous," Ellin said, kneading away. "This won't be your first race."

"I'd be a lot less nervous if it were," Rebecca said. "I know firsthand how awful things can get out there."

"Oh, stop dwelling on the dark side, for heaven's sake! You'll be just fine. I wish we could make it to the race start, but Sam's got a bad cold and it's really dragging him down. We'll see you in Dawson, though. We'll be there with bells on!"

Rebecca sank slowly onto a chair and dropped her head into her hands. She sat for several long moments and then lifted her eyes to Ellin's. "I guess I've just lost my nerve," she said. "You probably heard about what happened last week."

Ellin paused and looked Rebecca in the eye. "Of course, I did, but I would have preferred to hear it from you. All Mac told me was that you got a little wet."

"I was on a training run up in the hills. Mac was running the same trail and I caught up and passed him.

We were crossing a river I didn't even know was there. My sled broke through the ice. I went in clear up to my neck and it took me forever to get out again. If Mac hadn't been right behind me..."

"He rescued you?" Rebecca saw a smile cross the older woman's face as she divided the dough into equal halves and patted each into a greased bread pan.

"I've been so awful to him," Rebecca moaned. "So awful! Oh, Ellin, stop grinning! I'm a nervous wreck about this race. All those river crossings, all those lakes! My biggest fear is falling through the ice and drowning. Mac isn't always going to be right behind me to pull me out!"

"Well, my dear, you never know. As I recall, Mac was out most of the night on that particular training run," she commented, setting a cup of tea in front of Rebecca. "Did the two of you spend it together out on the trail?"

Rebecca shook her head. "He came back to my cabin." Then she glanced sharply at Ellin. "It's not what you think."

"Too bad." Ellin sighed.

"I fed him supper. It was the least I could do. And then he took his dogs for another run on the river." Rebecca paused, and then continued, "Oh, Ellin, I'm so confused. I told him that all I could offer was friendship!"

"My dear girl, as far as I'm concerned, he's brought you back to life again and more power to him! Whatever it is you're feeling, for heaven's sake, give yourself to it! You only live once, and life is pretty darn short!"

Rebecca spun her teacup around and at length she shook her head. "It wouldn't be fair to make him wait.

I'm not ready for another relationship, and I may never feel for him the way he wants me to feel.''

"Baloney!" Ellin said, putting the loaf pans atop the warming shelf on the cookstove and draping them with clean kitchen towels. "You already do. You're so smitten with him you're scared to death, and he's so in love with you he hasn't eaten a decent meal in over a month. I tell you what. Between the two of you, you're driving me crazy! I can't wait till you're out on that race trail together. Fate is bound to take a firm hand with the two of you!''

The sound of a truck door slamming brought Ellin to her feet to peek out the kitchen window. "My goodness, what good timing! It's Mac and Brian! I haven't seen Brian since he left for college! I'd best get more tea brewing!''

Rebecca jumped up and would have hidden in the bathroom, but she was caught in mid-dash, towel falling from her wet hair. She snatched it up and whirled as the door opened, and that was how Mac found her as he walked into the kitchen, followed by his younger brother.

"I TOOK A WEEK OFF from classes to handle for Mac as far as Dawson," Brian MacKenzie explained to Ellin and Rebecca as they sat at the kitchen table drinking tea. "He'll take his thirty-six-hour layover there and I'll handle the team. After he leaves, I'll fly back to Fairbanks and try to be there at the finish. No promises, though," Brian said to Mac. "Depends on when you finish. If it's a Saturday or Sunday between 10 a.m. and 9 p.m., I'll do my best to be there to congratulate you."

"Gee, that's real swell of you," Mac said. "I'll try to time things accordingly."

The MacKenzie brothers were a study in contrasts; Mac's hair was tawny, Brian's was black; Mac's complexion dark and weather-burned, Brian's pale from a winter spent indoors. Mac was tall. Brian wasn't. Brian was boisterous, Mac was quiet. They were both good with dogs, though, something Rebecca could appreciate. "He been treating my dogs right?" Brian asked her, and she looked at Mac and smiled, blood warming her cheeks at the way he returned her gaze.

"He's been spoiling them rotten."

"Are they ready to run?"

"Of course they are," Mac interrupted. "What do you think?"

"I think it would be nice if you placed in the top ten," Brian told him. "I've decided to get my master's after I finish this semester. I'm going to sell the dogs, and they'll sell real easy if you place well with them in the Quest."

Mac's expression was one of shock. "You're selling the team?"

Brian nodded. "There's no point in keeping it. I can't run the dogs, and I might never live back here again once I'm out of school. And feeding them, as I'm sure you've discovered, is a huge financial challenge. So the best thing is to get rid of them."

"Merlin, too?" Mac said.

"Of course. It's pretty near impossible to sell a team without a lead dog. I ought to be able to get ten grand for them. Hell, Merlin alone is worth five."

"But…" Mac slumped back in his chair. He glanced at Rebecca, then stared down at his cup. He shook his head in disbelief. "I just never thought…"

Brian looked at his brother. "You've gone soft on me,

Mac," he said, grinning. "You've gotten attached to the damn pot lickers, haven't you?"

Mac lifted his head, eyes glinting defiantly. "They're good dogs."

"Don't worry, we'll find them a good home. You told me when you came here you wouldn't stay for long. You haven't changed your mind about that, have you?" Brian kicked his brother's leg under the table. "Don't tell me you've gotten soft about something else? Or should I say, someone else? I ran into Sadie Hedda in Dawson yesterday. She certainly rambled on and on about you!"

"Sadie does have a tendency to ramble," Mac commented stonily.

Brian gave Rebecca a wicked grin. "She has a tendency to do other things, too," he said. "Personally I think she's looking to settle down."

"Well, I wouldn't know about that," Mac said, abruptly pushing to his feet. "Ellin, thanks for the tea. Rebecca, guess I'll see you tomorrow night in Whitehorse." Mac's eyes conveyed something that made Rebecca's heart jump.

"Yes," she said. "I guess you will."

"My goal is to beat you across the finish line," he said with the faintest hint of his brash grin, which she was inordinately glad to see.

"Good luck," she coolly replied. "You'll need it."

When the kitchen door had closed behind the MacKenzies, Ellin laughed. "Promise me something," she said, reaching for potholders to take the bread out of the oven. "Promise me the two of you won't get hitched in Fairbanks before Sam and I can get there, all right? I'd sure hate to miss such a monumental event."

"BUT SERIOUSLY, Mac, you can't mean you're in love with Rebecca!" Brian shifted gears and the old truck groaned in protest as they swayed down the Klondike Highway toward Whitehorse. They were fully loaded and then some, with fourteen dogs, two sleds and hundreds of pounds of dog food and gear. "You've got to be kidding me!" He laughed outright at the absurdity of it.

Mac shifted in the passenger seat and glanced out the side-view mirror, reassuring himself that the dog-box doors were all securely shut. His brother's words rankled. "What's so funny about that?"

Brian shook his head. "Nothing," he said hastily. "Well, I mean, it's just that you swore last summer you were never getting involved with another woman. Remember? You mentioned something about becoming a monk."

"That was before I met Rebecca. I didn't set out to fall in love with her," Mac said. "But somewhere along the line I did. I'm hooked."

"Rebecca and Bruce were pretty tight. I guess I just never imagined she'd ever fall in love with anyone else again. She's like a wolf, Rebecca is, bonding with her mate for life. Some wolves wander off and disappear when their mate dies. I just kind of figured she'd become a loner. She's...I don't know, it's hard to describe. She's very quiet, but she's...intense. You know what I mean?" Brian glanced across at him. "I just can't imagine her as being anything but Bruce's grieving widow."

"She's not in love with me," Mac admitted to his brother. "Actually, she thinks I'm a jerk. And I guess I am, kind of. I owe her a lot of money."

"Sam told me that was why you decided to run the race."

Mac stared out the window at the cold white blur of

Yukon winter. "Yeah," he said softly, knowing he wasn't telling his brother the whole truth. Running the race had become much bigger than his debt to Rebecca. It was a personal challenge, an incredible adventure through some of the wildest and most beautiful country he'd ever seen.

"Well, I don't know what to tell you about Rebecca," Brian said. "I've known her for five, six years now. She's a great girl. Beautiful, smart and grittier than an egg rolled in sand. Just don't get your hopes up."

"KANEMOTO, IS THERE any coffee left?" Rebecca asked as she guided the big lumbering dog truck down the highway. "I didn't get much sleep last night and my brain is pretty fuzzy."

Much sleep? That was an understatement. Nighttime had meant lying awake in a cold sweat with her heart pounding in fear, imagining all the catastrophes that could befall her. Sleep was a place she drifted to, off and on, a place of thin ice and overflow, misplaced trail markers and dogs who were too sick to eat or drink. Sleep became the nightmare where she lost her team and wandered in the darkness calling out for her lead dogs while the snow deepened and the cold intensified. In her dreams the ice broke and the strong current sucked her and her team to a cold and watery grave. In her dreams she let Bruce down, over and over again.

"Here," Kanemoto said, handing her a steaming cup poured from her thermos.

"Thanks." Had she remembered to pack everything? Dogs, harnesses, sleds, gang line, booties, mandatory equipment, food drops and a hundred other items too numerous to possibly remember. Why on earth was she doing this? Ellin Dodge was right. All mushers had dog biscuits for brains!

AT THE DRIVERS' MEETING the night before the race, the participants drew bib numbers for their starting order, paid any fees they owed and listened to a long and interminable description of the trail by the race marshal, including rules and regulations. Then came a few comments from the chief veterinarian and another hour of personal testimony from trail crew members and volunteers on the status of the race trail and what would be happening at each of the checkpoints.

By 10 p.m. the lecture was finally drawing to a close. Rebecca sat next to Mac, and when the meeting was done, he turned to her with a wry grin. "Kind of like the military," he murmured. "Ninety-nine percent bullshit."

Rebecca sighed. "They really expect us to remember everything. That's the part that scares me." She glanced down at her notes and made a face.

"Just take it as it comes." Mac yawned and stretched. "Boy, I'll sleep well tonight! Brian kept me up late last night, reaming me with last-minute advise."

"You'll sleep tonight?" Rebecca said, disbelieving.

"Sure. We have a nice hotel room. I'm going to take a two-hour shower and hit the sack. What's the matter? You need a place to hang out?"

"No," Rebecca said. "I won't sleep a wink, and I don't need a place to hang out. And by the way, I hate you for not being the least bit nervous."

"What's to be nervous about? What's going to happen is going to happen. Worrying about it won't help. If I don't win, I don't win, and that's all there is to it."

He grinned at her disarmingly. "Smile, Rebecca," he said. "The worst part's over."

"It is?"

"Sure. Training was hell. The schedule was exhausting. Making up the food drops was one of the biggest logistical nightmares I've ever experienced. The race is going to be easy compared to everything that came before."

Rebecca stared at him, amazed, and then laughed again. "You're probably right," she said.

"So will you sleep tonight?"

"Nope. Sorry. It must be the woman thing." She stood up and waved to Kanemoto, who was waiting patiently by the door. "See you in the morning, Mac. And good luck."

CHAPTER SEVEN

Have you known the Great White Silence, not
   a snow-gemmed twig aquiver?
Have you broken trail on snowshoes? mushed
   your huskies up the river,
Dared the unknown, led the way, and
   clutched the prize?
            Robert Service, from *The Call of The Wild*

RACE DAY. Ten a.m., and the staging area was pandemonium—a wild uproar of noise, chaos and color. Rebecca knelt beside her truck with her arms around
Raven, steadying her lead dog for the veterinarian who
was in the process of drawing blood. "We're doing ran-
dom drug testing," the veterinarian explained as the vial
filled with bright red fluid. "We're also running some
baseline tests to check blood chemistries and monitor
any changes that might occur during the race. We'd like
to test Raven again in Dawson and at the finish in Fairbanks, if you don't mind."

"I don't mind, but Raven probably will," Rebecca
said, rubbing the black dog's ears.

The vet laughed, straightening and handing the sy-
ringe to an assistant. "Your team checks out fine. No
problems that I can see. You'll need to keep this notebook with you and present it to the vets at the checkpoints. This is your first run on the Quest trail, isn't it?"

The vet gave her a pat on the shoulder before departing. "Good luck. See you in Carmacks."

Rebecca's stomach was churning as she harnessed her dogs. Keeping busy helped, but the crowds of curious onlookers kept up a constant barrage of questions, and her dogs were shy with the children who wanted to pet them.

Last night she had drawn bib number fourteen out of twenty-five. The teams would leave the starting line at three-minute intervals, beginning at eleven o'clock, which meant Rebecca had well over an hour before she had to get her team to the line. She was harnessing them up too soon. She took the harnesses off and paced nervously to and fro, answering questions, checking the contents of her sled bag for the hundredth time, patting her dogs and glancing down the line of trucks to where Mac's was parked. He was starting in tenth position, twelve minutes ahead of her. She'd probably overtake his team within an hour and never see him again. Why did that thought trouble her so?

Kanemoto asked her a question, and she stopped pacing to look at him.

"Booties?" he repeated, holding up a nylon bag.

"Yes, we'd better bootie." It was too soon for that, too, but she had to do something or she'd go crazy. She bootied slowly and carefully, checking the dogs feet thoroughly as she did, though there was no need. The veterinarian had found no problems. Her dogs had great feet. She'd used booties on every training run, and the precaution was paying off now.

At quarter to eleven she harnessed her dogs. The noise was deafening. Three hundred dogs were yelping and howling in their excitement to get going. Rebecca lifted a package off the seat of her truck and walked down to where Mac and Brian fussed over their team while Sadie looked on anxiously. "I have a little something for you," Rebecca said, leaning close to Mac so he could hear her over the mind-numbing din. "Ellin made it. Snack food for the trail!"

"Cinnamon rolls?" Mac said hopefully, tucking the package carefully into his sled bag.

"Better than that," Rebecca said. "Fruitcake!"

"Fruitcake!" he exclaimed with exaggerated pleasure. "This sure makes me feel like Iron Will! Guess I'll just have to win the race now, won't I?"

"I guess you have no excuse not to." Rebecca smiled. "Good luck, Mac."

"Same to you." As she turned away, he touched her arm. "Hey," he said with a grin. "If it makes you feel any better, my nerves are pretty bad right now."

HER MOUTH WAS DRY. Swallowing didn't help, so she fumbled for a stick of gum in her pocket, found one, popped it in her mouth and began to chew. Her stomach was doing flip-flops. She checked her watch. Ten minutes to go. "Let's hook them in!" she said to Kanemoto.

Volunteers appeared to help with the hookup, one volunteer standing just behind each pair of frenzied huskies holding on to the gang line. The sled was snubbed to her truck, and Kanemoto was going to ride it into the starting chute while she led Cookie and Raven. The team ahead of them had already gone into the chute.

It was time. She waved an arm to Kanemoto, and he pulled the snub line free. The dogs surged forward, dragging six strong volunteers, heels braced and leaning back, toward the starting chute. She could hear the loudspeaker counting down for the team ahead.

"...three, two, one, GO!"

And then she was leading her dogs into the chute. Lines of spectators stretched as far as the eye could see down Main Street. The voice over the loudspeaker blasted deafeningly. "And here comes musher number fourteen, Rebecca Reed! This is Rebecca's first time on the trail of the Yukon Quest, folks, but she's running a great team of dogs! Most of these dogs finished this race three years ago in second place, driven by her late husband and champion musher Bruce Reed, who, as many of you recall, was tragically killed in an accident not long afterward. Rebecca's lead dogs are Cookie and Raven, and, folks, notice that she's running a twelve-dog team, the smallest in the race, but that's no handicap for this lady! She also runs a very successful dog-tour business out of her home near Dawson and writes a weekly column on the outdoors for our very own *White-horse Star!* Okay, folks, we're coming up on the thirty-second countdown. Good luck out there, Rebecca! We'll be rootin' for you!"

Rebecca had been kneeling beside her leaders. Now she stood and walked slowly back down the length of her team, pausing beside each pair of dogs to give an encouraging pat or straighten a tangled line. Kanemoto relinquished the runners to her as the announcer's voice blasted out,

"...five...four...three...two...one...and GO! Good luck, Rebecca Reed!"

The volunteers holding her sled jumped back. She took her foot off the brake, put it down firmly on the section of snowmobile track between the runners, and called out an unnecessary, "All right!" for her dogs were already pulling for all they were worth. There was no stopping them now. They were as anxious as she was to get away from the crowds, the blaring loudspeakers, the chaos of the city, and onto the familiar quiet of a wilderness trail. The spectators passed in a blur of color and sound and soon were left far behind. Rebecca heaved a sigh of relief and felt her body relax.

It was approximately a twenty-mile run to Lake Leberge. She checked her watch as soon as they were out of town. By 2 p.m. at the latest they'd reach the lake. More than likely it would be pitch-dark before they were off it, and, as she'd learned at the meeting last night, long sections of lake trail had been blown clean of snow. Yes, there were trail markers—tall bitch-pole tripods with reflectors nailed to them—but Rebecca had little faith in markers, especially at night. The trail crew tended to space them too far apart to be spotted in the beam of a headlamp, which at best gave the musher only a hundred feet of visibility. Rebecca enjoyed night runs when the moon was full, but other than that she could do without them, especially on an unfamiliar trail.

Within the first hour she passed four dog teams, making up as much as fifteen minutes on some of the slower contestants, but none of them was Mac's. By the end of the second hour her dogs were still loping, showing no signs of tiring, and still no sign of Mac. She was beginning to think she had underestimated the average traveling speed of his team, or perhaps overestimated hers.

And then came Lake Leberge, famous for its fickle winds and whiteouts. Ahead of her by at least half a mile she could see another team moving along, and knew that as long as she could keep it in sight she'd be okay. She wouldn't mind closing the gap a bit and trailing behind that other musher until they were off the lake. Already daylight was leaning toward darkness, and it was cold. She cinched up her hood to thwart the stiff breeze that blew across the lake, lifting streamers of snow over the backs of her dogs.

Could that be Mac's team up ahead? Were his dogs finally beginning to slow down after the excitement of the start? Should she pass him? Or should she trail after him like a scared pup? What was the matter with her? She was far more experienced than he was. He should be the one who had spent all those sleepless nights tossing and turning and imagining the worst!

It was dark before she finally caught up with the musher ahead of her, and she was greatly disappointed to discover that it wasn't Mac. The musher wore bib number eight, which meant Mac had to have passed him.

"Bib number ten? Hell, yes! He passed me a couple of miles before we came onto the lake. Damn good-looking team he was driving, by the way, cruising right along. Passed my team like it was standing still. Do you want to pass, too?"

"No, I'm fine right where I am, if you don't mind me tagging along behind."

"Glad for the company." He grinned over his shoulder. "I don't care much for this lake." He faced front again and was quiet for at least another hour before he turned around again. "There's a poem about this lake. *The Cremation of Sam McGee*, by Robert Service. You know it?"

"Yes, I know it. It's a great poem."

"Would you mind if I recited it to my dogs? I sing to them quite a bit, and sometimes I recite poetry. This seems a fitting place to recall those immortal lines."

"Please do," Rebecca said, and so he did. In a boisterous voice that carried back to her clearly, he launched into a dramatic rendition. Head thrown back, one arm gesturing, he gave life to the lines written so long ago by an English immigrant living in the Yukon. Up one verse and down the next, he never missed a beat.

There are strange things done in the midnight sun
    By the men who moil for gold;
The arctic trails have their secret tales
    That would make your blood run cold…

Rebecca shivered and jumped up and down on the sled runners to warm herself as her dogs trotted on, mesmerized by the deep, dramatic voice of musher number eight.

…The Northern Lights have seen queer sights,
    But the queerest they ever did see,
Was that night on the marge of Lake Lebarge
    I cremated Sam McGee.

Another gust of wind spiraled up the lake, whipping the snow into a whirling vortex, blinding them temporarily. Rebecca was relieved when they made it off the legendary lake without mishap. When number eight stopped his team to check his dogs, Rebecca bade him farewell and ordered her leaders on by. She was going to try to keep to her planned schedule of six-hour runs followed by six-hour rest breaks. By her calculations she still had another hour and thirty-five minutes to go. She had programmed the alarm on her watch to alert her at six-hour intervals. Time lost all its familiar dimensions out on the trail. The days had no beginning and no end. It was just the team running and running and the trail leading on and on until it all became one long, endless blur. No matter where she was, when the alarm went off, Rebecca was going to keep to her strict regimen. The only exception would be when they arrived in Dawson for their thirty-six-hour layover.

When her alarm sounded, she found a good place to pull off the trail. She snubbed the sled to a spruce, pulled out the cooler and feed pans and immediately fed her dogs the thick meaty soup she had prepared for them in Whitehorse. This was probably one of the easiest meals she'd feed them during the race. They wolfed it down with great enthusiasm, and she dished out a chunk of frozen liver to each dog for dessert. Then she pulled forty-eight booties off forty-eight feet, unsnapped tug lines and gave each animal a brief rubdown before slogging back to the sled, reloading the cooler and feed pans, and pulling out the sack that held her own meal. She sat on the sled bag, leaned back against the driver's bow and began to eat her peanut-butter-and-jelly sandwich. She poured herself a cup of hot tea and switched off her headlamp to save the batteries.

"Where's Mac?" she pondered aloud, chewing the stiff, icy peanut butter. Her dogs were curled up and sleeping soundly, which was good. They'd get six hours of rest and be more than ready to go again by midnight. Rebecca ate her sandwich, sipped her tea. She was tired. It would be nice to take a nap, but if she fell asleep, would she wake up when the alarm went off? She eased her body into a more comfortable position, zipped up her parka to her chin and snugged the hood down over her hat. Warm and toasty. The temperature wasn't too bad, maybe thirty below. Farther along the trail, it would drop to fifty, fifty-five below. There were cold spots along certain sections of the Yukon River that froze the very thoughts in a musher's head.

Rebecca closed her burning eyes. A short nap. She

needed a nap. Just a short one…but this nagging thought kept surfacing—where was Mac?

MAC WAS LOST. He'd taken a wrong turn somewhere and hadn't seen a trail marker in more than thirty minutes, which was about twenty minutes too long. The trail he was following had steadily narrowed and worsened. He stopped his team and walked ahead of it, scanning the path with his headlamp, searching for some sign that other teams had passed this way. But there was nothing to indicate the presence of another team. No paw prints, no parallel tracks of sled runners. Only a snow-machine trail that probably led to some trapper's shack. Mac rubbed his mittened hand over the bridge of his nose to warm it. No telling where he'd gone wrong. He'd just have to turn the team around and hope that Merlin would pick up the correct trail.

His confidence in his lead dog was badly shaken. Merlin had failed to keep them on track. Mac was gruff when he gave the "come haw!" command, and he made sure before he did that there was nothing the sled could get hung up on. The team trotted past at a reasonable speed, and he maneuvered the sled into the right direction before the dogs took up the slack in the gang line.

Mac had lost thirty minutes at least and would have to push to make up that time. His team was tiring. They had stopped loping two hours ago, and when he turned them around their speed diminished to what he figured had to be a plodding ten-mile-an-hour trot. He checked the watch his brother had lent him and swore softly. To keep to his game plan he'd have to stop and feed his dogs in less than half an hour. What if they hadn't made it back onto the race trail by then?

Anxiety took hold as he peered through the dark,

searching for the intersection. If Merlin reached it and swung the team the wrong way, they'd be on their way back to Whitehorse, not a pleasant thought. He leaned over the driver's bow and finally he saw the junction. He slowed the team as they approached it. Which way should they turn? He thought frantically about what the crew had said about markers. When approaching a turn, there would be a reflective marker on the side of the trail in which the turn should be made. If no turn was to be made, there would be reflectors beyond the side trail, signaling to the musher that he or she was on track.

Mac stopped the team just shy of the intersection and once again walked to the front. He walked far enough ahead to see the other trail, and he scrutinized it carefully. He saw pawprints, lots of them, all pointing to his right. When he panned his light along the right fork, he saw reflective material nailed to a tree some fifty or sixty feet distant. Relief flooded through him. He turned to retrace his steps to the sled, but he hadn't figured on his team being so anxious to follow him. Merlin had generated enough get-up-and-go attitude that the team had pulled the hook loose and was already bounding toward him. He held out his arms in a futile gesture. "Whoa! Merlin, Whoa!"

If he had thought his command would slow or stop the dogs, he should have known better. He had learned some time ago that dogs had selective hearing. If they heard a command and wanted to obey it, they did. If they didn't want to obey, they simply didn't hear the order. "Dogs don't make mistakes," Rebecca had told him on more than one occasion. "Mushers make mistakes."

No time to dwell on his mistake—neglecting to snub his team to a tree. He leaped out of the path of his charging huskies and hurled himself across his sled as it blurred past, holding on for dear life.

"Gee, Merlin," he shouted while he was still upside down and facing backward, knowing that Merlin must have already reached the intersection. Merlin geed. The team followed. The sled, by some unfathomable piece of luck, didn't tip over. Mac regained the runners, thoroughly shaken and wildly relieved. He let out a whoop of exhilaration. They were back on the trail, and he hadn't lost his team! "Good dogs!" he praised as they loped along. Shortly after, Merlin put on the brakes so hard that the rest of team accordioned into a ball of fourteen dogs all trying to stand in the same spot. "Hey!" Mac shouted angrily, jamming on the sled brake. "Get up! Merlin, get up! Go ahead! All right! Goddammit! Go ahead!"

Instead, Merlin veered off the trail, uncoiling the team but leading it into deep, unpacked snow. The stubborn husky forged along until he came to a second stop, and just as Mac was getting ready to jump off the sled and give his leader a verbal thrashing, a headlamp flashed on in front of Merlin and slowly panned his team, eventually coming to rest on him.

"Merlin?" a very familiar voice said. "Mac, is that you?"

"Rebecca?" Hope surged wildly through him.

"I thought you were ahead of me!" Her voice was surprised and sleepy.

"I got lost." He grinned foolishly as he snubbed his sled to the nearest tree. He walked up the length of his team and when he got to Merlin, he knelt down and put his arms around the dog's neck. "Sorry, old man. You're a good dog," he murmured quietly into Merlin's ear.

"You're the greatest dog in the whole wide world! Thank you, thank you, thank you!"

MAC FED AND CARED FOR his team, and when he had finished, he walked toward Merlin on the pretense of checking the dog out, but what he was really doing was seeing if Rebecca was asleep. Her headlamp was off and she was lying on her sled. Her eyes were closed, but the minute he knelt down beside Merlin, she said—without opening her eyes—"Did you have a nice run?"

"Sure. You?"

"Yes." She opened her eyes. "Have you eaten yet?"

"No, not yet."

She sat up and swung her legs over the side of her sled. "I have some tea if you'd like a cup."

"I don't want to interrupt your rest."

She switched on her headlamp and reached her thermos out of her sled bag. "I wasn't really sleeping," she said. "I'm just semi-comatose."

"How long have you been here?"

"Not more than an hour. I plan to stay until midnight and then move along."

"I might follow you," Mac said. "Even though my dogs are tired, I don't think they're going to rest very well yet. They're still pretty wired from the race start."

"It'll take them a couple of days to settle in," Rebecca agreed, uncapping her thermos and pouring him a cup of hot, strong tea. "My dogs are so used to taking clients on camp-outs that they're a pretty mellow bunch. Whenever I stop, they curl up and sleep."

They both switched off their headlamps. Mac sat on the edge of Rebecca's sled, up near the nose, and sipped the delicious tea. He reached into his pocket for a handful of gorp and stuffed it into his mouth. Not even eight hours into the race and he was already sick of the high-energy snack. From another pocket he pulled out a stick of greasy smoked salmon. "I'd kill for a pizza," he said.

"What kind?" Rebecca murmured.

"Huge," he rhapsodized, "loaded with everything but anchovies."

"Mushrooms?"

"I can tell by the tone of your voice that I should omit them. Fine by me, I can live without 'em. I'll call it in. Domino's delivers!"

She laughed softly, and Mac thought her laughter a warm, lovely sound in the cold darkness. They heard another noise, and moments later a dog team was running by. It was musher number eight. He was singing a ballad to his dogs in a fine, strong baritone, and when he spotted them in the beam of his headlamp, he waved one mittened hand to them cheerfully. His team passed quickly, and soon the dark became quiet again.

"Tell me about your tours," Mac prompted. "You've had a busy winter. Ellin says it's the best one yet for you."

"I've taken out eight groups since November. It's been busy."

"Must be tough on you, doing it by yourself." Mac ripped off another piece of smoked salmon with his teeth and forced it down. "I'm sure you're perfectly capable," he added hastily. "But the logistics of it..."

"Where did you learn to fix airplanes?" Rebecca asked.

Mac took a swallow of tea. "My uncle. He used to work for United, and then he found a job at a little airstrip near where we lived at the time. I spent every spare moment tagging along behind him, soaking it all up. He was so good at what he did that folks would fly their planes in from hundreds of miles away. My uncle was a great guy. Never married. Shy as hell. Three words in a row was a long sentence for him.'' Mac drained his cup. ''I must have driven him crazy, but he never let on, just fed me sticks of Big Red gum and peanut-butter sandwiches and let me think I was being a help to him.''

''He sounds nice,'' Rebecca said. ''But somehow I thought you learned all that airplane stuff in the military.''

Mac gave an abrupt laugh. ''Hell, no,'' he said. ''The only thing I learned in the military is how to land on my feet running.''

Ah, Rebecca thought. A paratrooper, not a mechanic.

Mac pulled a handful of jerked moose meat from another pocket and chewed away. ''You suppose there's a good pizza joint in Carmacks?'' he asked hopefully.

Rebecca racked her memory. Two years ago she'd driven to all of the accessible checkpoints to monitor Bruce's progress. Pizza in Carmacks? Her brow furrowed.

''I'm not sure,'' she said. ''It's a small town. You may have to wait for Dawson.''

''I don't know if I can survive that long.''

''You don't have much choice. Would you like a peanut-butter sandwich?''

''Thanks, but no thanks. Could I offer you some moose jerky, smoked salmon, gorp?''

''Ugh,'' she said.

''You'll change your tune when you get hungry enough.''

''So will you.'' She yawned.

''Fruitcake?''

''Pardon?''

''Would you care for a piece of fruitcake? Remember?

You gave it to me this morning. Ellin made it and no doubt it's damn good, even though I'm not a fruitcake fan.''

"Save the cake for later. Try to get some sleep.''

"I'm not sleepy. It's only nine o'clock.''

"Try. Come 4 a.m. you'll wish you had.''

Mac stood up, taking the hint. "Thanks for the tea,'' he said.

"Welcome.''

"See you in a few hours.''

"Right.'' She heard him walk back down the long length of his team and arrange his sled bag before sprawling on top of it. She heard one of his dogs whine restlessly, and she heard his deep, resonant voice calming it. She lay back and looked up at the dark sky. No stars. Overcast. Could snow before morning. Might snow before midnight. Hard to tell. She closed her eyes. Tried to relax. Wiggled her toes to warm them. Tucked her mittened hands beneath her armpits. Tried to think about her race strategy, but could think of only one thing, one thing in the entire universe.

Mac.

HE DIDN'T SLEEP. How could he when Rebecca Reed lay scarcely seventy feet from him? He closed his eyes and willed himself to relax and found himself listening intently to the huge silence of the Yukon night and remembering the night the two of them had been cocooned inside his sleeping bag...

Remembering Ellin grasping his wrist two days ago with her strong fingers and saying, "Look out for her, Mac! She's very dear to us.''

Remembering Rebecca handing him that fruitcake just before the start when he was so damn nervous he wasn't sure if he was going to puke or pass out. Her mere presence had settled him.

Was she sleeping? Would she hear him if he was to sneak a piece of that cake now? He was still hungry. Ravenous, in fact. In lieu of a pizza, perhaps a chunk of fruitcake would do the trick.

Mac slid one mittened hand into his sled bag. The sound he made seemed loud to him, but only because the night was so still. If she was sleeping, she wouldn't hear. Couldn't, separated from him by seventy feet and fourteen sleeping huskies. Hah! His fingers closed clumsily around the firm object of his quest. In his hands now. Wrapped in a plastic bag, wrapped in foil. He pulled his mitts off to get at the cake. The cold wasn't too bad. Dry cold, he thought wryly as he fumbled with the brittle plastic, was like dry heat. Wasn't really cold. Wasn't really hot.

Yeah, right.

He had the plastic off, was working on the foil. The cake was certainly a lumpy thing. His fingers touched something that came apart from the package. Something wrapped separately in paper. Curious, he switched on his headlamp, keeping his head bent to avoid casting light ahead and disturbing Rebecca. Brown wrapping paper. Tape. He stared at it for a moment, wondering why it was inside the fruitcake packaging. He frowned, moved his stiffening fingers to break open the paper. For a long moment, long enough for his hands to become completely numb, he sat and stared at the object he held in his hands.

His Rolex watch. Still ticking.

A note had been wrapped around it. He unfolded it. Read it. Brief, terse and to the point. Totally Rebecca.

"If you want to keep to your race schedule, you'll need a good watch. Hope this one is good enough. R.''

He closed his hand around the watch and raised his head, inadvertently sweeping his headlight beam across her sled. She lay still, asleep. He lowered his head abruptly, switched off his lamp and sat in silence, his heart beating a strange cadence. Then he swung his legs over the side of his sled with a moan of frustration. She'd spent her hard-earned money to buy the watch back. Anger warmed his blood, warmed his fingers. Shame and humiliation left a bitter taste in his mouth. How was he ever going to repay her?

Merlin whined and Mac lifted his head. Several of his dogs were on their feet, looking around in the darkness, wondering why they were stopped for so long when the night was perfect for running.

Why, indeed? His dogs weren't resting and neither was he. If he cut this break short, he'd make Braeburn in an hour at most and then be headed for Carmacks. He could give them a real break in another six hours, and by then they'd be ready for it. If this was a young team, he might not make such a rash move, but these dogs were tough and experienced. And they sure weren't going to win any race money standing around and waiting for him to get his act together.

Mac put the watch around his wrist and pulled his parka cuff over it. He stood quietly, stuffing the fruitcake back into his sled bag. Instantly all his dogs were on their feet and a ripple of excitement ran through them, as if they were saying, "Hey, the boss is finally up! Let's get going!" Mac began the tedious task of booting. Four booties per dog, fourteen dogs. It took him thirty minutes to finish the job. He snapped the tug lines back into the dogs harnesses, and they were all dressed up and ready to go.

Rebecca, of course, had awoken. She was sitting up, watching him work. "Hey," she said. "What about your schedule?"

"My dogs aren't resting and neither am I," Mac replied curtly, angry with her for some reason he couldn't explain, and even angrier with himself. "We're heading for Braeburn."

"Oh," she said, small-voiced. "Okay."

He stomped back to his sled and stepped onto the runners, reaching for the snub line's safety knot. She was still watching him. "Well," he said loudly over the din of his team, "if you hurry up, you could come along!"

She shook her head. "I'm keeping to my schedule. I'll leave at midnight."

"Suit yourself." Mac pulled the knot and released the sled. "Haw over, Merlin!" he snapped, then, "On by!" as his leader veered around Rebecca's sled and lead the team back onto the packed trail. "See you in Carmacks, maybe," he said as he passed her, and he thought he saw her nod.

For a long time after that he was grumpier than a hungry grizzly in spring, and he couldn't for the life of him explain why.

REBECCA WATCHED until the light of Mac's headlamp faded from view, and then she stood in the darkness, adrift with uncertainty. She checked her watch. The luminous dials read 10 p.m. Her team had been resting for four hours. They were all on their feet now. Mac's departure had stirred them back to life. They were stretching and yawning and wagging their tails. She checked her watch again and it was still 10 p.m., two hours shy of her departure time. Her team looked good. Well rested and alert. Ready to go.

Mac was gone. He had pulled foot and left her behind, and every moment that passed widened the gap between them.

To hell with her schedule!

It took her thirty minutes to snack her dogs with more of the premixed soup, bootie them and get back onto the race trail. They jumped into an easy lope, one they would maintain for an hour or so before settling into their brisk trot. She might not like these night runs, but her dogs definitely did. They ran faster at night, for longer distances and with less fatigue. No stars tonight. No northern lights. No moon.

Just the tracks of Mac's team on the trail ahead, leading them toward Braeburn. "Catch Mac," Rebecca whispered silently to her lead dogs, willing them to set a faster pace. "Catch Mac!"

BRAEBURN LODGE wasn't a designated race checkpoint, but mushers were allowed to drop any injured, sick or tired dogs there, if necessary. This early into the race very few mushers opted to do so, and not many spent much time there. Rebecca was in and out of Braeburn in less than fifteen minutes, doing nothing more than signing in, filling one of her coolers with water and signing out. Mac was ten minutes ahead of her and she had no intention of letting him get away.

She checked her watch—11:30 p.m. To get back on schedule she'd need to stop and feed her team at 5:30 a.m., giving them a six-hour layover. She had no idea what Mac's routine would be or why he'd become suddenly so abrupt. Low blood sugar? Lack of sleep?

By midnight Cookie and Raven had closed the gap.

She could see another musher's headlamp bobbing up ahead, flickering off trees, team dogs and snowy trail. It had to be Mac. And it was. When he spotted the beam of her headlamp, he swung around on his sled runners. "Took you long enough to catch up," he said gruffly.

"What do you mean? I waited until midnight, just like I planned," she replied, and he laughed in a way that made the heat come into her face. "My dogs weren't resting either," she said in her defense.

"Admit it. You missed me," he said, and she caught a flash of that brash grin of his. "And you didn't want to travel up Chain of Lakes by yourself."

"Whatever you say," she replied coolly.

Mac turned to the front again and that was the last they spoke for a long while as they picked up the Chain of Lakes beyond Coughlan. The trail breakers had been right. There was overflow, and Rebecca was relieved that wise old Merlin was ahead of her, feeling out the good trail, avoiding the bad. Cookie and Raven were excellent leaders, but young, and they hadn't the experience Merlin had. Perhaps they would learn a thing or two by following in his footsteps.

At 1:30 a.m. both teams stopped. Mac and Rebecca snacked their dogs, checked their feet, and replaced any booties that were wearing thin or had gotten wet. It had started to snow, a fine snow that blew out of the west and created poor visibility.

"How far to Carmacks?" Mac asked, as they shared a hot cup of tea that Rebecca had carried to his sled.

"Another sixty miles."

"Could we push straight through? Give our teams a longer break there, eight or ten hours?"

Rebecca shook her head. "We've been running since 10 p.m. We should stop in another couple of hours and feed, rest the dogs for six hours, and then make the thirty, forty mile run into Carmacks. There's a two-hour mandatory layover there, but we'll take another six hours. That will give us time to feed the teams, unpack our food drops, organize our gear and supplies for the next leg of the race to Pelly Crossing.''

Mac swallowed hot tea and listened. She could see the impatient flash in his eyes and waited for the protest.

"That's too long to rest!" he said. "The front runners will be in Dawson before we reach Pelly at that rate!"

"Mac, trust me. Run your team easy right now. It's a long race and this is just the beginning." She took the cup from him and finished the tea.

Moments later they were on the move again. It was snowing harder and the trail was getting punchy. It was slow going for the dogs, and by the looks of things it would get worse. At 4 a.m. Mac voluntarily stopped his team, which surprised Rebecca. He put on his snowshoes and cleared a turnoff long enough for both teams. Then he and Rebecca snubbed their sleds to trees before setting about cooking food for their dogs.

Rebecca's food cooker was alcohol-fired. Within twenty minutes a three-gallon pot of water was boiling. She dropped a seal-a-meal pouch containing her own meal into the water to heat, then poured half of the boiling water into one of the coolers, to which she had already added the chopped, frozen meat mix. In short minutes the meat mix would be thawed. She would add the kibble, stir and serve up a nice warm meal to her deserving huskies. Meanwhile, she pulled off dog booties, stuffing them into a sack, which she tossed into the sled bag. At Carmacks she would sort through all of the used dog booties to rescue and dry those that were still serviceable. She took the feed pans out of the sled and distributed them among her team and soon after was dishing up their supper.

It was gratifying to watch the huskies eat. They ate with great enthusiasm, licked the bowls clean and caught frozen chunks of liver out of midair with a loud snapping of jaws. Nothing wrong with their appetites! Once fed, they immediately dug into the snow and curled up. Because it was snowing, Rebecca covered each of them with a blanket. She gathered up the dishes and stashed them in the sled. She picked her seal-a-meal packet out of the remaining water, filled her empty thermos, and to the cooler, which still held a couple of quarts of the dogs' supper mix, she added the remainder of the hot water. In five hours she'd water them with this rich broth before setting out on the trail again.

Now it was time for her own supper. Or was it breakfast? Mac was still laboriously cooking his dogs' meal, and from the looks of things his dogs were going to have to wait a while for their chow.

"I didn't get water at Braeburn," he explained sheepishly when she walked up to see what was taking him so long. "I was in such a hurry I completely forgot." Mac was melting snow to make the water, and melting snow was a time-consuming process. His dogs gradually gave up their anxious wait and made their beds, curling up to sleep. Rebecca sighed. Mac was learning, but he had chosen a tough race to learn in.

"How about a cup of tea and some hot chili?"

He glanced up from stirring the water pot. "Chili?"

"Homemade. No guarantees. Ellin let me use her seal-a-meal machine, and I prepared a lot of my race meals so I could heat them in the dogs' water."

Mac yawned hugely and then grinned. "No thanks.

My pockets are stuffed with gorp, smoked salmon and Ellin's fruitcake. What more could a musher ask for?''

Rebecca left him to his struggles and sat down on her sled, cutting her meal packet open with her pocketknife. No fork, no spoon. She squeezed the chili into her mouth, chewed and swallowed. Not the best she'd ever eaten, but it was hot, it was food, it was filling, and she was hungry. To hell with Mac if he didn't want to share it with her. Did he think she couldn't cook? Rebecca glared at him. Let him suffer! Let him starve! Bumbling idiot!

She finished her meal in a bad mood and poured herself a cup of tea. She sipped it, relishing the warmth, the spicy orange fragrance, the sweetness of the honey. Let Mac eat snow, she thought as she swallowed. Let him eat snow!

He was dishing his dogs' meal out now. Her dogs had been asleep for nearly an hour, and he was just beginning to feed. His dogs woke up grudgingly. Some of them turned their noses up at his offering, others stood and shook the snow off and bent their heads to the feed bowls. It was still snowing—another inch had fallen since they had stopped and showed no signs of letting up. By the time their rest break was up, there could be six inches of fresh snow to contend with. It would slow them down, but it would slow everyone else down, too. "Mac," she heard herself say, "come have a cup of tea."

He was standing and watching his dogs eat, and at the sound of her voice he turned as if surprised to see her there. "All right," he said, and when she had poured him a cup, he said, "Thanks," and drank from it with such gratitude that she felt a twinge of guilt. "Rebecca," he said, lowering the cup, "you shouldn't have done what you did." She had turned off her headlamp, but his was still on, and she could see fatigue in the lines of his face. "The watch," he said. "You should have just let it be."

Rebecca could think of no good reply. She watched the snow fall in the beam of his headlamp. He looked so damn handsome standing there in the swirling white that she wouldn't have been able to speak even if she could have thought of something to say.

"I owe you," he said, lowering the cup, "and I don't like it." He handed her the empty cup. "I've never lived like this before, hand-to-mouth, relying on other people's kindness."

He paused as if waiting for a response. Rebecca just stared.

"And I can tell you right now that things are going to change. I'm going to pay you back for everything. Sam and Ellin, too. No matter what any of you might think."

He turned on his heel without another word and walked back to his sled. Rebecca watched as he lay down and pulled the top flap of the sled bag over himself, and prepared to take a much-needed three-hour nap.

CHAPTER EIGHT

THE ONLY TROUBLE WAS, Mac couldn't sleep. What he wanted to do was leap up, march back to where Rebecca lay, lift her to her feet and kiss her. Rebecca needed kissing, and lots of it. He was just the man to oblige. So why didn't he? What kept him glued here to his own sled while the snow fell silently and his dogs slept? What kept him away from the woman he felt so passionately about that he couldn't fall asleep in her presence?

Fear. He was scared to death of being rejected by her.

"This isn't going to work," he muttered to himself. "We can't travel together. It just won't work."

But there was no denying that Rebecca knew the ropes. She'd forgotten more than he'd ever know about driving dogs. For the past three months he'd watched her, listened to her, picked her brain. She was driving a good team, as good as or better than his own. Traveling together made sense. They could look out for each other, help each other out over the rough spots.

Mac shifted, drawing his hood closer about his head. Cold! This was cold country, all right. He wondered if a person ever got to the point where they didn't notice it. Didn't shrink up and shiver when thirty below bit to the bone and a stiff wind blew the ice straight through the soul. Beautiful country in spite of the killing cold. Untamed and wild and far-flung. Yukon. The very word conjured up images of the frozen North, of huskies running hard, of breath frosting and snow falling and silence, unimaginably vast silence.

Rebecca belonged here. She was a survivor. She may not believe it, but she could take any situation the north could throw at her. Sure, that fall through the river ice had shaken her. And maybe if he hadn't been there, she would have been in trouble. But maybe not. She was a sharp-minded lady, loaded with common sense. She knew what to do.

Still… Mac shifted again. Even the best of the best could run into trouble. Sometimes circumstances conspired to strike down the finest. Ellin had implored him to watch out for her. "She means the world to us…"

She meant the world to *him!* Mac thought. If anything ever happened to Rebecca…

The snow was falling harder. The wind had picked up, too, and was blowing through the darkness with a soft moan as it worked through the trees. Mac drew a deep, cold breath. Oh, to be in a warm cabin with Rebecca in his arms. Let it snow, let the cold wind blow. Let the wolves and the huskies howl. Just give him Rebecca and the night and a warm cabin and he, too, would know exactly what to do…

In spite of her exhaustion, sleep eluded Rebecca. The fact of the matter was that Mac's presence disturbed her, that the very nearness of him caused her heartbeat to accelerate. She was torn between feeling glad for his company and guilty that she felt so glad. This wouldn't work. She couldn't continue to travel with him. It was too emotionally stressful, and the toughness of the race demanded total focus. If she wanted to do well, she would have to part company with Bill MacKenzie.

She shifted, tried to find a more comfortable position

on her sled. Mac. Oh, God. She felt herself being drawn into something too powerful to resist. She felt herself weakening. She felt herself becoming vulnerable in ways too dangerous to contemplate.

She tried to sleep. Couldn't. The darkness was dizzying, her muscles cramped with cold. But still she tried. She needed sleep... She needed...

Hands. Hands on her arms, squeezing firmly, and a man's voice saying, "Rebecca?"

She struggled out of the black abyss and into the snowy night. A bright headlamp blazed. She squinted and turned her head away. "What time is it?"

"Time for us to be moving along. It's still snowing and there's got to be six inches of fresh powder on the ground."

Rebecca stood up slowly. She felt awful. Her muscles ached and her eyes burned from lack of sleep. The dogs. She must care for them. A thick, white blanket of freshly fallen snow covered them. They slept beneath it, warm and content. She retrieved the feed pans and the cooler from the sled and at the sound of the pans, her dogs awoke, eager for their next meal. They stood and shook the snow from their thick coats. They wagged their tails and whined anxiously. Enthusiastic hunger was a good sign. She dished out a soupy snack and they devoured it while she gathered their blankets and stashed them in the sled bag. This snow would slow their travel time considerably, but she wasn't too alarmed by that. Some runs were fast and some weren't. That's just the way it was.

To her surprise, Mac was ready to go before she was. "C'mon, Turtle Woman!" he called impatiently from the back of his sled while she finished booting her dogs. "Hurry it up! Let's rock and roll! Let's burn some trail!'' And moments later, when she pulled her snub line and released her team, she heard Mac's voice behind her, deep and resonant, and it made her feel dangerously glad. ''Carmacks, here we come!''

TWELVE HOURS LATER Carmacks had come and gone. Another twelve and Pelly Crossing was behind them. The trail, the checkpoints, the rest stops, the catnaps, the ever-present cold, the constant fatigue—these things became so much the norm that Rebecca could hardly recall living any other way.

''Where are we?'' Mac asked when she stopped to throw a snack to each of her dogs and check their booties. It was nearing noon, and the sun felt good.

''I figure we're two hundred miles shy of Dawson,'' Rebecca said.

''That far?''

''It's 235 miles from Pelly Crossing to Dawson, and we've only been on the trail for four hours since leaving Pelly. What did you expect?''

Mac grabbed his snack sack out of his sled and commenced to dole out fist-sized chunks of frozen fish to his dogs. ''I was kind of hoping you'd say we were almost there.''

''Not quite.''

They ran for three more hours before stopping to feed and rest their teams. Mac, Rebecca noticed, was becoming much more proficient in his role as a canine chef. He was dishing up his dogs' meal within minutes of her feeding her own team. He came up and sat beside her on her sled bag when he'd finished. ''Smoked salmon?'' he offered, holding out a slab of the dark, greasy fish.

''Thanks,'' Rebecca said, accepting it. ''Homemade

chili?'' She held out the sealed bag, and he took it from her without hesitation.

"Homemade chili!" he said. "My favorite!"

They shared their meal in companionable silence, and when they were sipping their hot tea, Mac said, "We're in fifth and sixth place right now. The way I figure it, you're three seconds ahead of me."

"That could change in the blink of an eye," she said.

"I've been thinking about our race strategy."

"Oh?"

"Well, since we're traveling together, we might as well devise a strategy that takes into account both our teams. Your team is slightly faster than mine, so on the good sections of trail it makes sense for you to be in the lead and for my dogs to be drafting off your team. On the bad stretches, it makes sense for Merlin to be up front blazing the way. And another thing. I think we should start making longer runs and giving them longer rests, snacking them every hour or so on the trail."

"Every hour?"

"Just small snacks. Bite-size snacks. To keep their blood sugar levels constant."

Rebecca stared at him, amazed. "Do you have enough snacks?"

"Sure. So do you. You can use fat snacks, pieces of frozen liver, scoops of soaked kibble and meat mix, anything they want to eat. That way when you stop, you don't have to bother cooking a big heavy meal. All you really need to do is give them a quart or so of hearty soup and they can curl right up and go to sleep."

"Huh," Rebecca said.

"I think it'll work. It'll keep them fitter. Keep them happier."

"I don't know…"

"Why don't we try it from here to Dawson? See how it works."

Rebecca sipped her tea, then glanced sideways at him. He was three days unshaven and had never looked better. "I suppose we could," she said, still unsure.

"Good," Mac said, nodding. "Good!" He stood and checked his watch. "We'll plan to get rolling around 2100 hours. We'll run until 0500, rest until 1300 hours, run till 2100, rest till 05, and be in Dawson by 1100 hours on day five."

Rebecca stared blankly at him. "Right," she said.

"That's the halfway point of the race, right?"

"Right."

"We'll take our thirty-six-hour layover there, and our handlers can take care of the teams while we rest, right?"

"Right."

"Then, somehow, in the next four or five days, we've got to pass the four guys in front of us and hope to hell no one else overtakes us."

"Right."

"Now, when it comes down to the finish line, this is my suggestion. If we're still running together, let's make it a photo finish. Let's put the noses of our lead dogs over the line at exactly the same moment. What do you say?"

"Dramatic," Rebecca said, "but if you think I'd let you do that, you're out of your mind. If we're still running together, my team will cross the finish line first. You can count on that."

Mac's eyes narrowed. "You told me once that you weren't competitive," he said.

"I'm not," Rebecca replied. "I just don't like to lose."

MAC'S STRATEGY WORKED. They stopped their teams every hour, religiously, for five to ten minutes. They snacked and checked the dogs, then continued for another hour. The difference in the huskies was remarkable. They'd been cheerful enough before, but now they were also quicker. Rebecca thought that the new routine increased their overall speed by as much as two miles an hour. On the long rest break, they fed their teams a soupy mix, and in less than an hour their chores were completed, the dogs were sleeping soundly, and she and Mac were sitting side by side on her sled, sharing their meal.

"Smoked salmon?" Mac said, making his greasy offering. Rebecca took the strip of salmon and automatically handed him the remaining half of her seal-a-meal. Mac held it in the light of his headlamp for a closer scrutiny. "Why, it's Rebecca Reed's homemade chili!" he enthused. "My favorite!"

When they were finished, they both agreed that it was the best meal they'd ever eaten. They shared a thermos of hot tea, and Mac produced Ellin's fruit cake, or what remained of it, from the depths of his parka pocket. He handed it to her. "Try it. You'll like it."

Rebecca took it and stared at it with distaste. "Looks like some wild animal has been gnawing on it," she said.

"Don't worry, no matter what kind of deadly diseases I might carry, nothing would survive on that fruitcake. I only wish she'd made twenty more of 'em."

Rebecca bit off a chunk of the frozen cake and chewed. She swallowed. Blinked her eyes. Stared at the cake. Lifted it for another bite. "My God," she said. "It's pure rum!"

"Good, huh?"

"Alcoholic beverages are prohibited on the race

trail," Rebecca said. "But I guess a fruitcake doesn't count." She took another bite.

"Careful. You'll get drunk."

She laughed and handed him the cake. "It's delicious. And you're right. Any more of it and I'd be tipsy."

"Tipsy enough for me to take advantage of you?"

She laughed again and bumped him gently with her shoulder. "Get some sleep, Mac." Reluctantly Mac repaired to his own sled for a four-hour snooze. Rebecca lay back on her sled and closed her eyes. She was dizzy with exhaustion and the insides of her eyelids felt like sandpaper, yet she wasn't the least bit miserable. She wondered if that one bite of rum-soaked fruitcake had actually made her a little bit drunk, because as strange as it seemed, she was actually beginning to enjoy the Yukon Quest…and the company of her traveling companion.

THEY REACHED Dawson City at 7 a.m. on day five, a full four hours earlier than Mac had predicted. Ellin, Sam, and Brian were awaiting their arrival, and Kanemoto was so excited that his English was unintelligible.

"I think he's trying to tell you that you and Mac are only six hours behind the leaders at the halfway point," Ellin interpreted, giving Rebecca a warm, welcoming hug. "My dear girl, you look as though you've just run five hundred miles without stopping or sleeping!"

"I take that to mean I look awful." Rebecca grinned. "Well, Ellin, the strange thing is, I feel just fine! It's good to be here!"

"Did your dogs try to take you home when they recognized the trail?" Sam asked, because they had all discussed that possibility. Mac and Rebecca both shook their heads.

"Raven and Cookie might have dragged me back to my cabin, but when Merlin went right on by the turnoff, they just followed," Rebecca explained. "Merlin's an incredible leader."

"Yes, he is." Brian nodded. "Which reminds me. Mac, there's someone here who might be interested in the team. I mean, a seriously interested buyer."

"Can't it wait until after the race?" Mac said, his voice terse. The checker was looking through Mac's sled bag, making sure he was carrying all the mandatory gear, and a veterinarian had already begun looking over the dogs. Mac turned his back on his brother to help the veterinarian. The sooner these procedures were attended to, the sooner he could feed and bed down his team. He glanced over to where Rebecca's team was parked.

She was like a drill sergeant whenever she stopped for a rest break. This was done immediately, then this was done after that, and then this and this and this, just so! She had a strict, regimented routine from which she never varied, and that was undoubtedly one of the reasons her dogs got more rest at each checkpoint than probably any other musher's. Mac heard her politely but firmly ask the veterinarian to please return after she'd had a chance to feed and straw her dogs, and damned if the veterinarian didn't back right off! Mac turned around and tried the same tactic with his own veterinarian.

"Hey, if it's okay with you, I'd really like to feed and straw my dogs. Then you can finish checking them over."

"Well, all right, I guess," the vet said, deferring to Mac's request.

Dawson City was the only checkpoint where handlers were allowed to help the mushers with feeding and caring for the teams. Brian was ready to pitch in and take over completely, but Mac had no intention of letting him. "I'm okay," he told his brother. "I'll take care of them and then you can stand guard while I catch some shut-eye."

"I've got the tent set up—you could go right in and sack out. I do know how to take care of a team of sled dogs." Brian was clearly miffed that Mac didn't want his help, but Mac was thinking about Brian selling the team, and the thought disturbed him more than he cared to admit.

"How were the Black Hills and King Solomon's Dome?" Brian asked, referring to some of the hardest stretches Mac had covered.

"No problems," Mac said, pouring the boiling water into the cooler and giving the frozen meat mix a stir. "The dogs are running great."

"How about Merlin?"

"He only steered me wrong once, and that was on the first day. He turned off the race trail and led us up this long, winding stretch—"

"That leads to Joe Willard's cabin?" Brian interrupted, laughing. "We took a rest break there last year. Merlin must have thought you wanted to visit with Joe, too."

"Well, I'll be damned," Mac said, looking at Merlin. "He's a terrific dog."

"Well, I have to tell you, they all look terrific. You must be doing something right. Rebecca's team looks pretty solid, too."

"She has a real nice team."

"Look, Mac, if you're mad about something..."

"I'm not mad. I'm just tired." Mac poked at the hot water and meat mix. The meat had thawed, so he added the premeasured sack of dry kibble and stirred some more.

"I fixed you some food," Brian said. "It's waiting for you inside the tent. A big pot of chili, guaranteed to stick to your ribs! There's a little propane heater in there, too, so it's nice and warm. You should sleep like a baby."

"Thanks." Mac dished the food out to his hungry dogs, and only after they had cleaned their bowls did he unhook and unharness them, and allow them to curl up on their deep beds of straw. The picket line ran right alongside the tent, so he'd be able to hear what was going on with his team, and Brian had picked a good spot, on the outer edge of the checkpoint where foot traffic and disruptions would be minimal. He wanted the dogs to get a good long rest here, and being stared at and petted by spectators was not what they needed.

He glanced over to where Rebecca stood. Having already fed and bedded down her team, she was talking to the Dodges and Kanemoto. She caught his eye, smiled and held up her hand. She was dangling something enticingly, and he walked toward her to see what it was.

"Sam and Ellin rented a hotel room so we could take a shower," she said as he approached. "We both get a key." She tossed him the key she was holding. "Pretty good, huh?"

"A shower?" he said, staring at the key. The number 22 was stamped in white, below the hotel's name.

"That's right. It's this metal apparatus attached to the bathroom wall from which hot water bursts forth in a strong, steamy spray," Rebecca said. "As soon as I'm finished with the vet, it's mine. For at least two hours."

"Okay, you got it." Mac grinned, then nodded to Sam and Ellin. "Thanks. You have no idea…"

"Oh, we can guess." Ellin laughed. "There's everything you need in the room. Soap, shampoo, razors, shaving cream, comb, hairbrush, toothbrushes…"

Mac rubbed his face. He glanced at Rebecca. "Suddenly it doesn't feel much like a race, does it?"

"For the next thirty-six hours, it isn't," she said. "Enjoy them."

HOT WATER. Lovely, steamy, hot water. Good pressure. Great shower. The water needled, pierced, sluiced. Rebecca had long since finished washing, soaping, scrubbing, and was now simply standing beneath the powerful spray, almost asleep on her feet. For the past thirty minutes she had been standing with her eyes closed, feeling her muscles slowly unbind and the ice in the marrow of her bones thaw. She had used up four hours of her thirty-six-hour layover since arriving in Dawson City, and a full forty-five minutes had been spent in the shower. She guessed it was probably the longest shower she'd taken in her entire life, and she blessed the hotel's robust water-heating system.

She turned off the shower when she realized her body was weaving. Ellin had also provided, bless her thoughtful heart, a brand-new set of underwear. A pair of white cotton bikini briefs, size five, and a white cotton camisole with a tiny pink rose embroidered on it. Rebecca dried off, slipped into the new undergarments and began to comb out her towel-dried hair. She sat on the edge of the king-size bed and worked patiently through her long locks, and when that was done she picked up her watch. Eleven a.m. She glanced at the window. Daylight glowed through the sheers. She thought about her dogs. They'd be fine with Kanemoto watching them, and if anything seemed wrong, he'd promised to tell her right away.

Rebecca lay back on the bed with a blissful sigh. Her eyes closed. It would be very easy to fall asleep. Very easy to curl up on this wonderfully firm mattress in this lovely warm room and just sleep and sleep and sleep... Her stomach growled but she ignored it. Hunger could wait. Sleep...sleep was what she needed. Sleep... But that pleasure would have to wait. First she had to get dressed, go back out into the cold. Mac would be coming to use the shower very soon. Mac in the shower...hmmm. Mac naked in the shower...

She'd have to wait for him to leave before sneaking back here and ensconcing herself in the bed. She had to get up right now and get dressed... She'd better do it soon, better open her eyes and move or else...she might... just...fall...asleep....

MAC HAD THE HOTEL-ROOM KEY in one hand and a huge overloaded pizza in the other. He bounded up the hotel stairs three at a time, counting the seconds until he could stand in the hot shower, counting the minutes until he could devour the pizza. Sleep? Sleep could wait. There were far more important things to attend to!

He shoved the key into the lock and turned it. The door swung inward, and he had taken two big strides into the room before he saw her. Rebecca. Lying on the bed sound asleep. He stopped so abruptly that he almost lost his grip on the pizza box. What to do? He stood in silence, the door still open, Rebecca was curled on her side, no blanket over her, no coverlet, clad in white bikini briefs and a white camisole top. Her hands were clasped, childlike, beneath her cheek, and her long, dark, beautiful hair fanned across the pillow.

He took one step backward, one hand on the door-knob, one hand gripping the pizza box. His heart raced. He swallowed. For the moment the shower and the pizza were forgotten and the only thing in his universe was the woman lying on the bed. The woman he had come to admire so greatly. The woman he loved.

A door banged down the hallway and there was the sound of approaching footsteps. Mac hesitated, then stepped inside and closed the door firmly enough to wake her. She didn't stir. Her breathing was slow and steady. He reconsidered. If he slunk quietly into the bathroom, chances were she'd never hear him in the shower. He could be out of the room in ten minutes and she'd never even know he'd been there.

Mac set the pizza on the desktop. He opened the closet door quietly, and yes, there was a spare blanket, which he shook out and very gently laid over her. He needn't have worried. He could probably have shouted into her ear and not woken her. He stood over her for a moment, feasting his eyes on her the way he never quite dared when she was awake. He toyed with the idea of kissing her cheek, but the idea brought the heat to his face and left him feeling embarrassed. He dragged himself away, turning for one last look before he closed the bathroom door behind him.

Five minutes later he was sure he had died and gone to heaven.

Twenty minutes later he reemerged amidst a billowing cloud of steam and reached for the pizza box, surprised to find it so light. He opened the top. Three pieces were missing. He glanced at Rebecca still lying on the bed. "Hey," he said.

She opened her eyes slowly. "Sorry," she said with a guilty smile. "I had a dream about this giant pizza, and all of a sudden I woke up and there it was, right beside the bed, still hot.'' She smiled again and stretched languorously. ''Thanks, Mac. Once again you saved my life.'' She looked him up and down with her sleepy eyes. ''I see you found the shower. Nice boxer shorts. Isn't that a Mickey Mouse design?''

He grinned unabashedly. ''There was a package in the bathroom with my name on it and I—''

''I know. I had one of those packages, too, and I'm wearing it.''

''Sam and Ellin are amazing,'' Mac said, lifting a piece of pizza out of the box and stuffing the tip of it unceremoniously into his mouth. He sat down on the edge of the bed and didn't stop chewing until the last piece, refused by Rebecca, was devoured, and then he stared forlornly at the empty box.

''I'm sorry,'' Rebecca said. ''You're still hungry.''

''I could get us another one,'' Mac offered.

''Why don't you take a nap first? By eight o'clock we'll both be starving again. You could get two more pizzas. One for each of us. And a six-pack of beer.''

Mac looked at her, his expression cautiously optimistic. ''Are you inviting me to stay?''

''It would be cruel of me to deny you what by right is your half of this bed. You need it as much as I do. But no hanky-panky. Race rules prohibit it.''

Mac didn't have to think very long about Rebecca's proposal. The alternative, sleeping in a two-person tent on the edge of the noisy checkpoint while his brother Brian prodded him about the race and brought prospective buyers to view the team, was infinitely less desirable. He crushed the pizza box, stuffed it into the wastebasket and climbed into his side of the bed. ''I'd better warn you in advance,'' he said as he pulled the covers over him. "There's a possibility that I might snore like a lumberjack."

Rebecca opened her eyes. "How strong a possibility?"

"I'm pretty damn tired."

"Well, we've been sleeping within earshot of each other for the past five days and I've never heard you snore. Don't lose any sleep over it. I know I won't."

He shifted his shoulders and drew a deep breath. "Are you sure about no hanky-panky? I don't remember reading about that in the race rules."

Rebecca curled onto her side, her back toward him and drew the blanket up over her shoulder. "Positive," she said, but in fact, she wasn't. The only thing she was truly positive about was that she wanted him beside her in that bed. She wished that he would move closer, that he would roll over and put his arms around her and draw her into his strong, warm embrace. She was losing the struggle to keep herself aloof and apart from him, and she feared that if Mac ever suspected how she felt, they'd never finish the race.

REBECCA, IN SPITE OF her emotional torment, finally slept, and her sleep was deep and blissfully dreamless. When she awoke there was a moment of disorientation. She didn't know where she was or why she was there. She rolled over and looked at the other half of the bed.

Empty. She sat up, pushing her hair away from her face. "Mac?"

The bathroom door was ajar and the light was on, faintly illuminating the dark room, but no reply came from within.

Mac was gone.

Rebecca reached for her watch on the bedside table.

The luminous dials read 9 p.m. She flopped back onto the bed with a moan. Eight hours! She'd slept eight hours straight without twitching a muscle! She could have slept longer, truth be known, except that she was hungry. Starving! She sat up again. She'd get dressed, walk down and check on her team, find some food. A lot of food. Tons and tons of edibles she could stuff into her mouth to satiate the lions that roared in her stomach.

She pushed out of bed, washed her face in the bathroom with lovely warm water, brushed her teeth, finger-combed her hair and contemplated leaving it loose. Looked in the corner of the bathroom for her stack of arctic clothing and did a double take. Gone! Her long underwear, her fleece pullover, her bibs, her parka—all gone! She made a quick search of the bedroom, thinking she might have stashed all of it elsewhere in her previously catatonic state, but there wasn't a trace. Even her hat and gloves were gone. Her mitts and boots were the only two items remaining to remind her that she was a musher driving a team of dogs in the Yukon Quest.

She was standing in the middle of the room in a state of confusion when a key turned in the lock and the door opened. Mac entered, shrinking the room, filling it with his energy. He had a huge duffel slung over one shoulder and a large brown paper bag cradled in one arm. He grinned when he saw her, slung the duffel onto the bed and held up the paper bag in both hands as if it were a religious icon. "Chinese food!" he announced.

"Where are my clothes?" she asked, snatching the spare blanket off the bed and wrapping it around her.

"In the duffel, all clean. Ellin took them to the Laundromat. Jeez, that woman thinks of everything. C'mon, let's eat. I've got enough food here to patch hell forty miles. Hope you like Szechuan chicken, egg rolls, fried rice, wonton soup, beef with broccoli, barbecued pork ribs and Guinness stout.'' Mac began unloading the bag's contents onto the desk, paper carton after bulging paper carton. The smell of Chinese food permeated the room. He pulled a bottle of beer out of the six-pack, flipped the top off with his jackknife and handed it to her.

"Okay, here's the scoop,'' he said. "I've checked on the teams. They're fine. Kanemoto is following your instructions to the letter. He's feeding them every six hours, massaging them, smearing that special liniment of yours on their muscles, giving them the vitamin supplements, putting neoprene sweats on the six dogs you specified, walking each dog for ten minutes after each meal and letting them sleep the rest of the time. Here's a fork and spoon. We can eat our soup first and use the containers as a plate.'' Rebecca took the offered plastic cutlery and the container of hot wonton soup. "I checked out the other teams, too. I'd like to tell you that the front-runners' dogs were tuckered out, lame and off their feed, but, lady, they looked good. We'll have our work cut out for us, catching up to them.'' Mac began spooning the soup into his mouth and then impatiently lifted the container and drank from it directly. He was finished in less than a minute. "God, that was good!'' He began breaking open the boxes with the frantic motions of a starving man.

Rebecca watched him, holding her soup untasted in her hands. How had she missed it? she marveled. How had she ever overlooked the fact that Mac was such a good man? He was solid and calm and dependable. He was always in good humor, even when exhausted. And she'd been wrong about him. He was loaded with common sense. He could think his way out of any problem, and he was so damn magnetic that she was finding it difficult to look away from him long enough to pry the cover off her soup. He had shaved, and his face was lean and masculine and dark with windburn. His eyes were the most beautiful eyes she'd ever seen on a man. Clear gray and thick-lashed.

He glanced up at her, his mouth full of something, and tried to grin with his mouth closed. He lifted his bottle of beer to her, washed the food down with a generous swig and then laughed. "I feel like a barbarian, but I'm so hungry. Eat, woman! You need to put on about twenty pounds in—" he glanced at his Rolex "—a mere twenty-one hours. That's a pound an hour. Eat!"

Rebecca obediently dipped her spoon into the soup. It was hot, salty and delicious. Once she began eating, her physical hunger forced her to concentrate on the task. Mac kept heaping food into her container and she kept eating it. They devoured every last scrap and then sprawled on the bed, shoulders propped against pillows and headboard, gnawing on the last of the pork ribs and drinking beer. "If anyone ever taped that feeding frenzy on video, I'm afraid I'd be forced to kill myself," Rebecca said. "We are truly disgusting animals."

"Truly," Mac agreed amiably. "I think I could go for seconds."

Rebecca laughed. "How did Ellin get hold of my clothes?"

"She headed me off at the checkpoint and gave me the duffel bag. I came back to the hotel room and got them. I have to tell you, she sure was tickled pink when she saw me. She has this idea that we should fall in love and live happily ever after, and she knew that I'd gone to the hotel room for a shower and I hadn't been sleeping in Brian's tent. When I told her that I left you sleeping peacefully in the room, I thought she was going to shake my hand and congratulate me." Mac laughed, remembering.

"Naturally you told her there was nothing going on."

"I did no such thing," Mac said, raising his beer for another swallow. "I have my reputation to consider. What would folks think of a guy who spent the night in bed with a beautiful woman and never laid a hand on her?" He lowered the bottle, staring at the label with a bemused grin. "No, let them think what they will. It'll give 'em something to talk about."

"Mac," Rebecca said carefully, "what about Sadie?"

"Sadie?" Mac turned his head to look at her as if he had absolutely no idea what she was talking about. "What about her?"

"Sadie Hedda's in love with you. I'm surprised she's not in town!"

Mac rubbed his shoulders against the headboard and slouched a little lower. "Well, she was, just before we got here. But she got called out for some medical emergency. That's what Ellin told me."

"Oh," Rebecca said.

"Rebecca, you should know that I never encouraged Sadie. Never," Mac said. "I wish she hadn't given me that damn parka."

"It's a beautiful parka, and Sadie's a nice woman."

Mac studied his beer bottle, resting it on one of his knees. "Well, the thing is, I'm not in love with her," he said.

Rebecca stared at her own beer bottle. She felt the familiar wave of heat coming up into her face, and all of a sudden it seemed as though she and Mac were sitting awfully close together on the big bed. They were close enough that she could feel the sexual energy radiating from his powerful body, and she could certainly feel the answering response in her own. She swung her legs over the side and stood, acutely aware that she was wearing hardly anything at all beneath the blanket she clasped about her. Moments ago it hadn't seemed the least bit important, but now her heart was beating so loudly she was sure Mac could hear it.

"Mac," she said, forcing herself to look at him, forcing her voice to sound normal, forcing herself to be cool and aloof when she felt anything but. "I'm…you're… we're…" She stopped, glanced down at her bare toes, then back into those incredible eyes. She felt that curious flutter at the base of her diaphragm that she had felt too often in his presence. "We have a race to run. And please, don't waste your time on me. You'd be much better off with Sadie, and she cares a great deal for you."

She set her beer bottle on the desk, grabbed the duffel from the foot of the bed and dragged it into the bathroom, closing the door firmly behind her. She washed her hands and face, brushed her teeth, brushed and braided her hair, and dressed in her clean but definitely sexless bulky arctic wear. When she emerged from the bathroom, she was no longer a scantily clad young woman who'd shared a bed with an extremely virile and handsome man. She was a musher from head to toe, competing in one of the toughest sled dog races in the world.

"Well, I guess the party's over," Mac said, looking her up and down.

"I'm going down to check on my dogs," she said, and he looked back at her, tipped his head back against the headboard in a gesture of reluctant defeat and nodded.

"Okay," he said. "If you see Brian, tell him I'm on my way. Tell him to fire up the propane heater in the tent and get my sleeping bag out. I think I'm ready for another long nap."

"HEY RAVEN, COOKIE, my little girls, how're you doing?" Rebecca sat cross-legged on the big bed of straw that her two leaders shared and gave back the affection she received. Her team was very glad to see her. They had just been fed and were awake and on their feet when she returned to the checkpoint. Kanemoto was applying ointment to Seal's feet, and a quick glance showed her that he'd cared for her team superbly. He was looking a little tired and frayed around the edges, but he was still highly enthusiastic, giving her a nonstop verbal replay of everything he'd done and of every dog's reaction to everything he'd done. He'd even made notes in a special race diary he was keeping. The dogs looked great. They were already anticipating getting back out onto the trail, and they still had another nineteen hours of rest coming to them. By the time they left Dawson City, they would be a pack of screaming demons and would probably gallop clear to Eagle without stopping. "We're halfway there, Raven," she said, scratching beneath the dog's collar. "Another five days."

Five more days of traveling with Mac. And then what?

Brian wandered casually over, hands in his parka pockets. "Hey, Becky," he said. "Your dogs look terrific."

"So do Mac's," she replied.

"They're still my dogs," he corrected her with a grin. "But I must admit, Mac's doing a good job driving them. Better than I thought he would."

"He enjoys it," Rebecca said. "He's a quick study,

and the dogs really like him. It's too bad you're selling the team."

Brian hunched his shoulders in self-defense. "Look, Becky, you don't know Mac like I do. He's not the kind of guy who's going to stick around for very long. I mean, he's here now, sure, but it's just a temporary diversion for him. He's way too ambitious to stay out here in the boonies. Know what I mean? He's mad at me because I'm selling the team, but he won't be around to run them next winter. He'll be raking in big bucks at some high-tech engineering firm in Silicon Valley or flying a Concorde for British Airways."

Rebecca stared up at Brian, fighting down the surge of blind panic his words triggered. "What exactly did Mac do in the military?"

Brian frowned. "You mean you don't know? I thought the two of you were friends."

"We are. I just never thought it was my business to ask. I figured he'd tell me when and if he wanted me to know."

"Maybe he thought you already did. Through me or Bruce, you know?"

"Maybe. All I know is that something bad happened to him and he came out here to get away."

Brian nodded. "That's why I know he's not going to stick around. Mac was running away from things when he came out here, but once he comes to grips with what happened, he'll get back out in the big world. Jeez, Becky, don't you read the papers? You remember that big blowup in the Middle East a year or so ago? The navy pilot who shot down two Iranian fighters over the no-fly zone?"

"Mac's a navy pilot?"

"Was," Brian corrected. He rubbed his chin and hunkered down beside her. "See, he was a navy fighter pilot flying cover for a search-and-rescue mission to find a carrier pilot who'd had to bail out over the no-fly zone. Two fighters showed up on the scene. Mac assumed they were Iraqi and he testified at his trial that they had a radar missile lock on him and were about to shoot. He had no choice but to shoot first. Turned out the planes were from Iran, and the whole thing blew up into this nasty and embarrassing international incident."

"And Mac got kicked out of the navy?"

"Congress put the pressure on the admiral in charge of the board of inquiry to find a scapegoat to appease the Iranians."

"But didn't Mac have a defense attorney?"

"Sure, for all the good it did. The court found Mac guilty of dereliction of duty. They court-martialed him, fined him a bunch of money and gave him sixty days' confinement, suspended. They took his wings away and ordered him off the ship on administrative leave pending discharge. Congress got their scapegoat."

"And Mac came out here."

Brian shrugged. "Yes. He lost everything, even his wife, who served him with divorce papers right after the court martial. Told him she couldn't live with a civilian husband and a man who had disgraced his country. He didn't contest it. He gave her everything. The house, the savings account, the car."

"Does he have any children?"

Brian shook his head. "Married three years, no kids."

Rebecca was silent for a long moment, thinking about

all Mac had been through in the past year. "Did they rescue the downed pilot?"

"The rescue mission he was flying cover for was a success, but ironically that same pilot was killed less than six months later in a plane crash. He was Mac's best friend."

"Was his name Mouse?"

Brian looked at her, surprised. "I thought you said he never talked about it."

"He didn't. He had a nightmare and talked in his sleep."

"I imagine my brother has a lot of nightmares. You know, the worst part of that whole mess was how my father reacted. For all intents and purposes, he disowned Mac."

"How could he, after all Mac had been through!"

"My father's a navy man himself. Mac's behavior cast a dark shadow on his reputation and jeopardized his climb to the top."

"What about your mother?"

"Died five years ago." Brian sighed. "Jeez, Rebecca. I really thought you knew. Like I said, I thought you would have read about it in the papers, heard it on the radio."

"Or been told by his brother, perhaps?" Rebecca said.

"Well, I didn't run around advertising it," Brian admitted.

Rebecca shook her head and sat in silence, her arm wrapped around Raven. She was stunned by Brian's revelation. She let her fingers drift through the dog's soft fur and looked up at Mac's brother.

"After Bruce died, I kind of tuned out the rest of the

world. But if Mac said that those Iranian jets were about to open fire, I believe him. There has to be a way to prove his innocence!''

Brian uttered a bitter laugh. ''You don't know how the military operates. Once they've killed you off, you can never come back to life. You're dead.''

Rebecca shook her head again. ''It isn't fair,'' she said softly. ''Poor Mac.''

Brian nodded, standing with his hands shoved deep in his pockets. He started to turn away, but then he paused. ''Becky? I love my brother and I think he's innocent, same as you. He was too damn good at what he did to make that kind of mistake. He got a bum rap and he's hiding out right now nursing a big hurt, but I don't want to see you get hurt, too. Just don't count on him sticking around, okay? And don't be mad at me for selling my dog team. It's not something I want to do. I just don't have any choice.''

''I'm not mad at you, Brian,'' Rebecca said, slowly, still trying to assimilate what she'd just heard. ''Thanks for telling me the details.'' She gave him what she hoped was a believable smile and added, ''And don't worry about me. Mac and I are just friends.''

After Brian had left, she repeated softly, ''Mac and I are just friends.'' She pulled Raven into her arms, rested her chin atop the dog's head and closed her eyes.

MAC CHECKED HIS TEAM before heading into the tent. He was standing in the soft light cast by gas lanterns when he heard Sadie's voice behind him.

''Mac!''

He turned. She was striding purposefully toward him,

grinning from ear to ear. "Oh, Mac, I'm so proud of
you!" she said. She threw her arms around him and gave
him a hug. He raised his hands and closed them on her
upper arms, gently pushing her away. She seemed oblivi-
ous to his need for distance and raised her face to his,
her eyes shining. "I'm so sorry I'm late! I wanted to be
here when you arrived, but I got called out!"

"I know. Ellin told me." Mac kept her at arm's
length. "Listen, Sadie—"

"Are you hungry? I brought some food with me—it's
in my truck. I made a huge pot of homemade chili!"

"Thanks, but I've already eaten. Sadie, can we talk?"

Sadie's eyes flickered. Her sunny expression clouded.
"What's wrong? Are you feeling okay?"

"Come inside." Mac led her into the dimly lit tent.
He sat beside her on one of the cots and drew a deep
breath. "Sadie, I think you're a really special person
and—"

"Okay, stop! Whoa! Not another word!" Sadie said,
raising one hand. "I can tell by your tone of voice and
your expression where this is going." She looked at him
and sighed. "I guess I expected it. I'm not blind. I guess
I just hoped... I mean, Rebecca told me she wasn't interested in you, and so I just thought that maybe..." She
lifted her shoulders and sighed again. "I guess it wasn't
meant to be. Oh, don't look at me like that, Mac. I'll
survive. And I don't blame you at all. Any man with
half a brain would fall in love with her. And you know
what? The only thing I have to say about all this is, she's
absolutely crazy for not loving you the way you love
her!"

Mac stared at Sadie. "She doesn't care about me and

she probably never will, but I can't help the way I feel about her.''

"I know that." Sadie reached for his hand and squeezed it. ''Just promise me something, Mac. Promise me that if Rebecca never comes to her senses and you ever get tired of chasing her, you'll give me a call.'' She rose to her feet, and he followed her outside the tent, still holding her hand. She turned into him and put her arms around him. ''Because as a matter of fact, I happen to think you're some kind of wonderful,'' she said. ''And if you don't mind very much, I'd really like to be there to see you finish this race.''

Mac put his arms around her and bent to kiss her gratefully on the cheek. ''I'd like that, Sadie,'' he said. ''Very much.''

REBECCA WAS FETCHING a bucket of water when she saw Mac and Sadie come out of Mac's tent, saw them standing in the lamplight with their arms around each other, saw Mac bend his head, kiss Sadie. She saw all these things out of the corner of her eye as she hastened toward the checker's cabin, and she felt as if she'd been struck in the solar plexus. Her breath squeezed from her lungs and her stomach lurched. Breathless, she staggered into the cabin and closed the door behind her, standing there long enough for one of the checkers to ask if she was all right.

''What?'' She gazed at him as if he were an alien from another planet.

''You look kind of pale. You feeling okay?''

''Sure. Fine!'' Rebecca took the bucket of water from him and turned back into the cold darkness. She avoided walking past Mac's tent on her way to her dogs. She couldn't bear the thought of him with Sadie, and yet she knew she could never give Mac what he needed. At least with Sadie he stood half a chance of finding happiness. He was doing what she had told him to do. She should be glad for both of them. She should be *glad!*

But by the time she reached her own campsite, the hot salty tears had frozen on her cheeks.

CHAPTER NINE

MAC WAS DREAMING. It was a good dream. Hell, it was a fine dream. Rebecca was in it and she was glad to see him, he could tell by the way she smiled. She was cooking something on the stove when he came into the cabin and it smelled good. He wrapped his arms around her from behind and kissed that tender, ticklish place on her neck that drove her crazy. "What's for supper, Rebecca?" he growled in her ear. "I could eat a whole moose, horns and all."

"Cooked or raw?"

"Either way. I ain't particularly particular."

"I'll serve it up raw, then. It'll save on firewood, and I'm tired of slaving over a hot stove."

"In that case, forget supper. I'd much rather have you. Let's see if we can make this cabin rock and roll."

Rebecca laughed and elbowed him. "Go feed the dogs. I'll finish getting supper ready." Mac grudgingly loosened his arms, but he let his hands slide over her stomach and he cradled her there. "How's my little one doing?"

"Your little one has been kicking like a mule all day long. I wouldn't be surprised if she were born with four legs."

"She? You mean Mac Junior, don't you?"

"Sarah," Rebecca corrected him. "Sarah Elizabeth

MacKenzie. Only a baby girl could have that much stamina. Now let go of me so I can get my work done.''

Mac released her and walked slowly to the cabin door. He paused for a moment to watch her slicing carrots into the stew pot, and such a feeling of protective tenderness came over him that his throat closed and his eyes stung. His life had never been so good. Never been so full. Lord, how he loved that stubborn and fiercely independent woman! He opened the door and stepped out into the cold darkness, but when he turned to take one last look before closing the door, he was shocked to see that the lamp had gone out. The door was gone. The cabin was gone. Rebecca was gone.

''Rebecca?'' he said. ''Rebecca!''

''Mac? What is it? I'm right here! I'm right behind you!'' A light flashed on, strong and blinding, and Mac came fully awake. He was standing on the runners of his sled, gripping the driver's bow, and his team was trotting steadily into the darkness. ''You all right?'' Rebecca called. Her lead dogs' noses were practically at his feet.

''Sure,'' he called back, wiping a mittened hand over his face. ''I'm fine.''

''I thought I heard you shout my name.''

''No, I was just talking to my dogs.'' Mac turned to face front, feeling foolish. Dawson City seemed like a hundred years ago. Why was he so tired? They were headed for Eagle and had turned off the Yukon River, taking a westerly tack up the Fortymile. Two hours ago they had stopped at a trapper's cabin five miles from the mouth of the Fortymile and been offered a bowl of some kind of stew. The stew had been very hot, but Mac had no idea what was in it, nor did it seem polite to ask. He had never tasted anything quite like it before, and he was still tasting it now.

The night was really cold. It had to be close to fifty below. Rebecca had given him some of her chemical warmers, and he'd put one in each of his boots, one in each mitt and one in his battery pack. They helped, but nothing could truly thwart cold that intense. Maybe it was the cold that was making him sleepy. He could easily close his eyes and drift off again. He switched on his headlamp and checked his team. The dogs all looked good. Their faces and shoulders were frosted white from their breath. All fourteen were still going strong, and this was a source of great pride to him. Brian had dropped two dogs by the time he'd reached Dawson last year. Mac wanted to finish the race with all fourteen, all of them healthy and happy. And, of course, it went without saying that he wanted to finish in first place.

He and Rebecca were still running in fifth and sixth position, but they had closed the gap on the teams ahead. At the trapper's cabin they learned that just four hours separated them from the two teams in first and second place, and the third- and fourth-place teams were only an hour or so ahead. He and Rebecca were slowly gaining ground. Their running and resting routine, combined with the hourly snacks, seemed to be working. Mac switched his headlamp off to save the batteries, which didn't function well in extreme cold. "Lithium batteries are the way to go," Rebecca had told him earlier when he had complained about short battery life. "They work much better in the cold. But they're very expensive. I can't afford them."

Money. Everything boiled down to money. Life was all about getting by, making do and doing without, all of which related to how much money one made. Mac had never been wealthy, but he'd never been destitute, either. He didn't like living this way. A man had to be able to provide for a woman before he could even consider asking her...

Asking her what? What would he ask Rebecca? He let his imagination take over. She'd be fussing over her dogs, and he'd stride up and say, "Excuse me, Rebecca, but I'd like to ask you something, if you don't mind."

If he was lucky, she'd stop what she was doing and look at him, but she probably wouldn't. She'd keep on with her task, stirring dog food, smearing ointment on paws, rubbing liniment on tired muscles, following her strict routine. "What is it?" she'd say.

He would draw a deep breath to fortify his courage. "Well, I was kind of hoping you might seriously consider marrying me. Wait! Before you reply, hear me out. I may be penniless now, but in another year or so I plan to be a rich man. That's right. Rich. Wealthy. Dripping with money! On the cover of Forbes magazine dressed in a designer suit."

"Oh, really?" She might glance up at him but maybe not. "What's your financial strategy?"

"I've been offered a job flying for British Airways. Huge salary. I'm going to fly with them for two years and invest all my earnings in the stock market."

"British Airways? But you're an American."

"They don't care. They've forgiven us for the Boston Tea Party."

"What about the Revolutionary War and the War of 1812?"

"They like the way I fly. I'm not going to argue with them. It was either flying Concordes or signing on with Delta. I kind of liked the idea of supersonic. So what do you say? Will you marry me?"

She would stand up and wipe her hands on her bibs. "Marriage, Mac? Why on earth would I want to marry you?"

That was the clincher. That was the killer question she was bound to ask. How would he answer? "Because it would work out perfectly. I'd be off flying and most of the time you'd be rid of me, but I'd send you a big money order every two weeks so you could live like a princess. What could be better than that? The only thing I'd ask is periodic visitation rights. The right to look at you in person. Hold your hand. Maybe indulge in some heavy petting."

"Kissing?"

"I made a promise to you about that, Rebecca. Remember?"

"A promise made is a debt unpaid," she said.

Hmm. What did she mean by that? "Will you at least think about it?"

"Absolutely not. Mac, I don't love you. It's Bruce I love and I always will."

"Bruce is dead! Rebecca, can't you see that I'm crazy about you?"

"Crazy? Yes, you're definitely crazy. But not about me."

"Rebecca…"

"The answer's no, Mac. How much clearer can I be?"

Mac slumped. It was hopeless. Rebecca was not in love with him. She would never be in love with him. His brother had been right. Rebecca would always be a lone wolf, gazing behind her into the past and remembering the love of another man.

Cold! Had he ever been this cold before? Not even close. It was clear, so clear he could see enough stars in one small patch of sky to spend the rest of his life counting them. And now the moon was rising, paling the heavens, dimming the stars, bathing the snow in an unearthly glow. So quiet, just the huffing of his dogs, the dry squeak of the sled runners, the musical jingle of harness snaps. Small sounds in a vast and silent wilderness. He looked behind. Rebecca's leaders were still right on his heels. "Do you want to pass?" he called back.

"No, I'm fine. Unless you want me to."

"Not unless you want to."

"Well, let me know if you do."

"Okay." Mac faced front again. Why couldn't he talk more intelligently when he spoke to her? Why did he have to sound like a damn Neanderthal? He blinked his eyes, wiggled his toes inside of his boots. Had to stay awake. Count the stars in the Yukon sky. One, two...

A flash of light ahead startled him. His grip tightened on the driver's bow, and he stared up the river trail, transfixed. He squinted, leaning forward. "My God!" he breathed, unable to believe his eyes. It was incredible! Unbelievable! A huge paddle wheeler was coming down the frozen Fortymile right at them! "Gee over, Merlin!" he shouted urgently. "Gee over!" Merlin swerved to the right, dragging the entire team off the packed trail. "Gee, gee, gee!" Mac jumped off the sled and frantically pushed it through the deep snow. Son of a bitch! The monstrous thing was going to run them down! "Get off the trail!" he shouted behind to Rebecca, who had stopped her team dead in the middle of it. What was the matter with her? Was she blind? "Hurry up!" he waved his arm wildly at her. "Get off the trail!"

"Mac!" she said. "What are you doing? It's not time to snack the dogs yet!"

"Can't you see it?" he said, then swung to look back up the trail—and to his astonishment, the trail was empty! He blinked and switched on his headlamp, panning slowly back and forth in disbelief that such an apparition could just vanish. But he had seen it! Bigger than life! Every minute detail of it had been vividly shadowed and delineated in the moonlight! He turned back toward Rebecca. "There was a huge boat coming down the river toward us," he explained, realizing the moment he spoke how foolish he sounded. "A sternwheeler," he added weakly.

There was a moment's pause and then Rebecca's laugh came clearly to his burning ears. "Mac, you're hallucinating. The only thing you might have seen was the flash of a headlamp. It looks to me like we're catching up to some teams."

Mac looked up the river. He shook his head. "Maybe you'd better lead for a while," he called back to her, an unnecessary suggestion since her team was already moving ahead. He spoke to Merlin, and the dog swung the team back onto the trail. They fell in behind Rebecca and resettled into their brisk, steady trot. He burped and the taste of that strange stew came back up. "I wish I could just puke and get it over with," he moaned aloud.

It was going to be a very long night.

AT THE TOP OF Fortymile River there was a cabin, and parked outside were four teams. While Mac and Rebecca tethered their dogs, the cabin door opened and a man walked out to greet them. His boots squeaked loudly in the dry snow.

"Well, hello," he said to Rebecca. "Never seen you here before."

"Never been here before. I'm Rebecca Reed, this is

my friend Bill MacKenzie. Is it all right if we camp here?''

''You folks get your dogs settled and come on in. The cabin's crowded but it's warm. Warmer than it is out here. Right now I'd guess it's running fifty-six below, but I could be wrong. I'll have to check my thermometer. Last time I looked it was only fifty-five below, but I'm sure it's dropped since then.''

''Thanks,'' Rebecca said. ''We'll be up as soon as we've fed and bedded down our dogs.''

They had to melt snow, and tending their teams took much longer than normal in the intense cold. Two hours later the dogs were curled up and sleeping in their fleece-lined dog coats. Rebecca and Mac made their weary way up to the cabin carrying their own supper and a sack of dog booties that needed to be dried.

The cabin was very crowded. Both bunks were occupied, a third musher slumped at the table, head pillowed on his arms, and the fourth lay on the floor against the far wall, his feet propped up on an empty chair. The sound of four men snoring lustily filled the cabin. Mac and Rebecca stood for a moment inside the doorway looking around, and then Mac took Rebecca's sack of booties out of her hand. ''I'll hang them up,'' he said. ''You sit down. Eat.'' Rebecca sank into the only empty chair. The heat inside the cabin was overwhelming after the cold outside. Her face was burning. She stripped off her mitts, her hat, her parka. She took a slurp of her chili, then put the bag and thermos atop the table. The elderly man who had come out to greet them was sitting in a rocking chair next to the stove, reading a book by lamplight and smoking a pipe, perfectly content. He paid no attention to them at all until Mac had finished hanging up the booties, and then he folded over the page of his book and glanced up.

"It's fifty-seven degrees below zero," he said. "I checked just before you came in. I bet it drops another degree before dawn. It's always the coldest then, and that's another two hours away. I bet it gets down to fifty-eight below. I've seen it hit sixty below a couple of times, but not yet this winter. Sixty below. Now that's cold, I want to tell you! You really feel it when it's sixty below." He nodded at his own words, stuck his pipe back in his mouth, picked up his book, opened it to the folded page and continued reading.

"Smoked salmon?" Mac said, pulling yet another strip of the endless greasy fish from his pocket. Rebecca took it and stuffed it into her mouth.

"Homemade chili?" she mumbled around the mouthful of fish, handing Mac the half-eaten meal of the endless homemade chili. She moved over on the chair and he sat down beside her. They leaned against each other in fatigue. Rebecca melted into the welcome warmth and strength of him.

"Homemade chili. My favorite," he said, taking it from her and squeezing the contents into his mouth. He chewed and swallowed. "You remember that stew we ate back at the last cabin?"

"How could I ever forget?" Rebecca said, chewing on the hard, greasy fish.

"I think it just about did me in."

"I think it was very nice of him to offer it," she said tactfully.

A loud belch from a sleeping musher punctuated the background of snores and was followed by a moan of pure misery. "Another victim," Mac said. "Tell me something. Why do people do this? Why do people race sled dogs?"

"I'm still trying to figure that one out," she replied. "I'll let you know when and if I ever do. In the meantime, you might ask Ellin. She has her own opinion."

They sat for a while after eating, drinking their hot, strong tea and listening to the chorus of snoring. "Do you realize that right now," Mac said, "we're all tied for first place?"

Rebecca took a sip of tea and looked at him, bleary-eyed. "Not really. They got here a few hours before we did. They'll leave here before we do."

"I know. But right at this very moment, we're all in the same place at the same time. It's a six-way tie." He looked around calculatingly at the sprawl of sleeping mushers. "I just wonder…which one of us is going to finish first?"

"Maybe it'll be someone who isn't even here yet," Rebecca said. "We still have a ways to go, Mac. Don't count your chickens before they hatch."

The proprietor of the cabin pushed out of his rocking chair to put another stick of wood in the stove. He hitched up his suspenders and walked over to the door, opening it briefly and then slamming it shut again. "Well!" he announced as he turned back toward the stove. "It is now officially fifty-eight degrees below zero. Dropped a whole degree in less than an hour. We could see sixty below tonight. Yessiree, it's been known to happen! Sixty degrees below zero!"

COOKIE WOULDN'T EAT her breakfast. Rebecca offered it to her in several different variations and each was politely refused. "C'mon, Cook. I need you, baby. Don't give up on me now. I know it's cold and I know you're tired, but you're one of my main ladies. One of my main brains. I need you, Cookie. Oh, honey, please eat. Please eat just a little bit for me.'' Rebecca knelt beside her, enticing her with a chunk of beaver meat, one of the few offerings that almost any dog will eat no matter how tired or ill they might be. Cookie sniffed it briefly and then lifted her dark, apologetic eyes to Rebecca's face. She wagged her tail and licked Rebecca's hand. Rebecca laid the piece of beaver meat in front of her and ran her hands over Cookie's small form. ''You're such a little thing, Cookie. Such a tiny girl. Such a toughie.'' She could feel nothing wrong. There was no abdominal stiffness or pain. No visible lameness, no diarrhea, no temperature. She simply wouldn't eat.

''Maybe she's just not hungry,'' Mac said. He had fed his team and they had all wolfed their food with their usual enthusiasm.

''No,'' Rebecca shook her head, ''it's more than that. There's something wrong. I'm not going to run her. I'll load her into the sled and let her ride to Eagle.''

''That means carrying her over American Summit. That's going to be a tough haul, Rebecca. Carrying Cookie will slow you down.''

Rebecca stood and sighed. ''Look, you don't have to wait for me. You can run at your own speed, Mac. In fact, I suggest you do. Right now you stand a good chance of keeping up with those boys. They're only a couple of hours ahead of us.'' Mac stood silently while she packed her dogs' food bowls into her sled. He watched while she began the long task of booting her dogs. Finally she stopped and looked at him. ''Well, what are you waiting for?'' she snapped.

''You,'' he answered simply. ''I'm waiting for you.''

THE RUN UP American Summit was grueling. Mac's team led the way, Merlin in front, his trot blazing the trail. He never wavered, never shirked. His tug line was always tight, his ears always alert, his blue eyes bright, his demeanor intense. He took his job very seriously and it showed. The extraordinary thing about Merlin was that he never wanted to run anywhere but in lead. When Mac switched him into point or swing to give him a break, he dragged off his neckline, sulked and depressed the entire team. Up front was where Merlin wanted to be, so up front was where Mac ran him.

Rebecca was glad that Mac's team was in the lead as they climbed the treeless summit. Although it was broad daylight, the trail markers were obscured by blowing snow and deep drifts. With Cookie out of commission, her leaders might not have had the savvy to feel out the trail, but Merlin certainly did. He led both teams up and over the windblown summit and then down into Eagle, the first American checkpoint in the race. After Rebecca had fed and strawed her dogs, the veterinarian checked out her team, including Cookie, whom Rebecca had carried in her sled bag for the entire run. The veterinarian could find nothing at all wrong with the little huskie.

"She looks fine to me," he said, stuffing his stethoscope into his parka pocket. "Everything checks out. But she won't eat? Nothing at all?"

"She ate a little bit of her soup just now," Rebecca said. "But normally Cookie's a great eater and drinker. Scarfs it all down." Rebecca knelt beside her leader and ran her hand over Cookie's head. Cookie gazed up at her adoringly and fanned her tail in the snow.

"This may be way off base, but when was she last in heat? Is there a chance she could be pregnant?"

Rebecca's eyes widened. The thought had never occurred to her, and yet the symptoms fit. She looked down at Cookie. "It was around the Christmas holidays," she said with dismay. "But I didn't think... I mean, as far as I know, there was no hanky-panky, but..." But litters of puppies had appeared mysteriously before and probably would again. And the timing was right for Cookie to be experiencing a bit of morning sickness as the pups, if she was indeed pregnant, began to crowd her uterus. The veterinarian palpated her abdomen. "It's possible," he said.

Rebecca made the reluctant decision to drop Cookie at the Eagle checkpoint. Kanemoto would take care of her until the race was over and they could all go back home. The veterinarian left and Rebecca slumped in the straw at the head of her team with Raven curled up in her lap. It was quite a blow to lose Cookie, whose inexhaustible good cheer and buoyant personality kept the entire team in good spirits even when they were tired.

"You look like you just lost your best friend," Mac said, walking up and squatting beside her. "What's wrong?"

She told him and he nodded slowly. "Pregnant? Huh! I'll be damned!" He rubbed his chin, thinking. "You remember that day your truck broke down in Dawson and I fed your dogs before I came to pick you up?"

Rebecca looked at him with growing suspicion. "Why do you ask?"

"Well, I forgot to mention it in all the chaos that happened afterward, but there was a dog loose in the yard when I fed them. I hooked him back up, and that was that."

Anger surged through her. "The very least you could have done was tell me about it! Cookie was in heat! I could have given her a mismate shot and I'd still have her right now! You probably don't even know which dog was loose, do you!"

Mac hesitated. "It was a male Alaskan husky," he said.

"Great. Thanks a lot for nothing, Mac! I've just lost my main leader."

Mac rubbed the bridge of his nose. "I'm sorry, Rebecca. But don't worry. We're traveling together. Merlin'll take us to Fairbanks, no sweat."

Rebecca gave him a stony stare. "I don't need to travel with you, Mac. I'm perfectly capable of traveling on my own. Maybe I should just do that."

"I hope you plan to grab a little rest first. Can I bring you a cup of coffee?"

"I don't drink coffee on a race. The caffeine gives me too many…"

"Yes, I know. Caffeine gives you wicked highs and lows. But I'll take the highs whenever and wherever I can get them." Mac glanced around. "This is a pretty nice checkpoint, isn't it?"

"Yeah."

"I'll bring you a bowl of caribou stew. They're dishing it out in the checker's cabin."

"No thanks, I'm not hungry," she said, feeling very discouraged. Mac disappeared but returned within minutes, carrying two steaming bowls of stew. He dropped into the straw beside her and sat crossed-legged, handing her one of the bowls. She took it from him and prodded it with the spoon.

"Eat," Mac ordered, "before it freezes solid. It's good. I've already had two bowls."

Rebecca dipped and raised her spoon. He was right. The stew was delicious. "How far ahead of us are the other teams?"

"They're all still here," Mac said around a mouthful of stew. "Number one and two teams came in three hours ahead of us. And you saw the third and fourth teams when we were coming down that last stretch. They can't have more than a five-minute lead. We'll leave them in the dust in the next stretch, Rebecca. The checker said that the closest teams behind us are still fifty miles back. We've got a huge jump on them." Mac finished his third bowl of caribou stew and sighed contentedly. "The bad news is, there's a storm brewing and it looks like a whopper. They're predicting it'll hit in the next day or so, just in time to blow us all off Eagle Summit."

Rebecca moaned.

"No sweat," Mac said. "We'll rest our teams well when we get to the checkpoint at Central and take the summit one step at a time. Listen, I've staked a couple of bunks out for us in one of the cabins. Let's go get some sleep."

"You go ahead. I'm not tired," Rebecca said. "I'm going to sit here with the dogs for a while."

"Your dogs are fine. They're all sound asleep and they'll stay like that for another six hours. In the meantime, you're going to get some sleep." Mac pushed to his feet and reached a hand down to pull her up.

"I'm not tired!" Rebecca said, glaring.

"I don't care. You're going to lie down and take a nap. Come on."

"Where do you get off, ordering me around?"

Mac squared to face her. He took the empty bowl from her hand and stacked it on top of his. "Rebecca, when this race is over, you can hate me all you want. You can ignore me, you can yell at me, you can give me the cold shoulder. But as long as we're traveling partners, we have to stick to the same schedule of running and resting. Everyone else is resting. They're going to be blowing out of this checkpoint in a few hours. We need to rest, too. The next leg is 175 miles, and we've got to catch the front-runners before we reach Central.''

"Why?"

"Because I don't want them coasting on our heels going over Eagle Summit. This storm will work in our favor. I want to get far enough ahead of those other teams so that our trail is stone cold and snowed in. I want them to bog right down when that wind hits them on the Summit because I know that Merlin won't. He'll forge right up and over. Nothing will stop that dog. Once we're over the Summit, we're home free. Rebecca, we can win this race if we don't blow our strategy. How's that sound?''

"You're crazy, Mac," Rebecca said wearily. "Stark, raving mad."

He grinned his brash grin and nodded. "You bet I am. But then again, so are you. Would either of us be here if we weren't?''

MAC LAY ON HIS SIDE and watched Rebecca sleep. She was lying flat on her back on the bunk across from him with a gray wool army blanket pulled up to her chin and her feet poking out the bottom. Her eyes were closed and her breathing was slow and even, so quiet he could barely hear it. Her hair was still braided but mussed from her hat, and several unruly wisps had escaped the confines of the braid. They softened the contours of her face. Her arms were beneath the cover, her slender fingers curling over the upper edge of it. She had been sleeping like that for three hours, and Mac had been watching her for almost as long. He knew he should try to get some sleep himself, but he was afraid that if he closed his eyes she might disappear. After all, she had threatened to leave the checkpoint without him.

He couldn't imagine her not being there with him. Most of the racers traveled in pairs, and he could understand why. For the front-runners it was probably to keep a close eye on each other, but for others it was perhaps more for safety reasons than anything else. Mushers could look out for each other, help each other through the tough spots, bolster flagging spirits.

Mac studied Rebecca. She was undoubtedly one of the strongest people he'd ever known. Never once had she complained about the cold or about being exhausted, or hungry, or lame and sore. He'd heard plenty of moaning from the other mushers, but not a word from Rebecca. She was one of only two women who had entered the race. The second one had dropped out—scratched— along with several other mushers back in Dawson.

He was in love with her, no doubt about it. He'd willingly lay down his life for her. He longed to touch her, to take her into his arms, to feel the smooth skin of her face beneath his fingertips, to trace the outline of her lips, to taste the tender sweetness of her kiss. If he hadn't been so exhausted, he might really have gone stark, raving mad with this painfully unrequited love. Instead, he leaned on his elbow, head propped on his hand, and studied her in the dim light.

They had the bunk room to themselves, courtesy of one of Eagle's many generous and warmhearted residents. In the cabin's main room, soft voices droned in conversation. He heard someone open the woodstove and then a heavy thump as another log was fed into the fire. A squeak, a clank, and the stove was closed again.

Rebecca opened her eyes. She lay for a moment staring up at the ceiling and then she turned her head and looked directly at Mac. Her eyes widened, startled. "What are you doing?" she whispered, raising a hand to brush the strands of hair away from her forehead.

"Watching you sleep," Mac said. "Just making sure you followed orders."

"What time is it? Have the other racers gone?"

"Almost midnight. Beech and Wilton have checked out. Gurney and Kinney are still here. Go back to sleep. You have two more hours."

She pushed herself up onto her elbows. "Why are you awake?"

"Just woke up," Mac lied. "Must be getting hungry again. Go back to sleep."

"How long have our teams been resting?"

"We got into Eagle around 6 p.m."

Rebecca rubbed a hand across her face, wiping the sleep from her eyes. "I'm starving," she said.

"Salmon?" Mac offered, reaching for his parka, laid across the foot of his bunk. By leaning and stretching they passed the smoked salmon without leaving their bunks. She pulled a bag from the foot of her bunk and unzipped it, drawing forth the thermos of tea. She poured two cups and handed one to Mac.

"What would happen," she said, chewing on the awful dried fish, "if we were to cut our team's rest a little short here?"

"How short?"

"Oh, say, one hour."

Mac chewed contemplatively. "There's a shelter cabin forty miles from here. Then there's Biederman's cabin another forty miles beyond that, and Slaven's. There are plenty of shelter cabins on the next stretch.

We could take a break at all of them if we wanted. Rest the dogs a lot. I think they'd be okay.''

Rebecca took a sip of tea and swallowed. ''What if we left right now?'' she said.

Mac glanced at her. ''Getting a little anxious, are we?''

''We could snack our teams, get them ready to go and be out of here in thirty minutes. We run to Trout Creek and give them a break there, maybe two hours. Run to Biederman's, rest another two hours. Run to Slaven's and rest four. Then run on into Circle. It's downriver all the way.''

''You make it sound so easy,'' Mac said.

''I'm thinking about that storm,'' she said. ''When that hits, it'll slow us down to a crawl. The farther along we are before that happens, the better off we'll be. Maybe we could even make it over Eagle Summit before it gets too bad.''

''Maybe,'' Mac said. ''But I doubt it.''

FORTY MINUTES LATER they were signing out of the Eagle checkpoint in third and fourth place and dropping down onto the Yukon River for the long run to Circle City. It was dark and cold, though not as cold as it had been on the Fortymile. By 6 a.m. they had reached Trout Creek. The front-runners were still camped there, but when Mac and Rebecca pulled in, they were quick to ready their teams and depart.

''Did you see that?'' Rebecca said to Mac while they prepared their dogs' breakfast. ''Their teams were looking tired. I don't think they'd been here more than two hours. I think we should stay for three.''

''Three? I thought you planned on two.''

"We cut our rest short in Eagle. If we shave things too close, our teams will be exhausted."

"Wilton and Beech only stayed four hours in Eagle. We stayed six," Mac pointed out.

"We'll rest here for three and see how they do on the run to Biederman's. If they slow down too much, we'll rest four hours there."

Mac nodded slowly. "You're the boss."

"I think if we push too hard now, we'll burn them out," Rebecca said. "We still have a long way to go, and I want to keep my dogs happy. I want them smiling when they cross that finish line."

A three-hour rest was barely enough time to tend the dogs, eat their own meal and ready their gear for the next haul. They sat together on Rebecca's sled, side to shoulder, leaning against each other. Mac handed Rebecca a piece of smoked salmon and Rebecca handed Mac his portion of chili. They communicated with a series of grunts and gestures. No need for words. Words wasted too much energy.

Rebecca's eyes burned with fatigue, and the cold was a constant torment. She had shipped hundreds of chemical warmers in her food drops to the checkpoints, and she doubted there would be a single packet left by the end of the race. Being warm was a fantasy she indulged in when she drifted toward sleep. She chewed wearily on the piece of salmon and, eyes closed, leaned against Mac's shoulder. Mac. She couldn't imagine life without him. For the past several days she had shared an incredible odyssey with him, and it seemed as though he had been a part of her life forever, as much a part of it as the dogs and the race and the checkpoints and the miles and miles of trail. Whenever she dozed off, she'd awake with a jerk, wondering if she'd overslept, wondering which checkpoint she was heading for—or was already in. Wondering where Mac was, and if he was okay.

What would happen when the race was over? Would they go their separate ways, politely shaking hands and maybe giving each other a chaste farewell kiss? Would Mac leave the Territory as Brian had predicted? And if he did, would he miss her? Would he ever think about what they'd been through in this wild arctic land, running behind a team of Alaskan huskies while a blue norther drove winter deep into both of their souls?

Rebecca drew a deep breath of polar air into her lungs. Probably not. He would most likely do just as Brian had said he would. Be drawn by forces more powerful than the land, more seductive than a woman. Technology and big bucks. Maybe Sadie would drift with him on her way to becoming a doctor. Maybe Sadie and Mac would marry.

"Fruitcake?" Mac said, interrupting her thoughts.

She poured the tea while he divided the last of the precious fruitcake. They ate and drank. The dogs curled on their snowy beds and slept. By the time Kinney and Gurney drove their teams to the Trout Creek cabin and stopped for a break, Mac and Rebecca were ready to depart. They exchanged a few words with their fellow mushers but were soon back on the trail. There was no time for socializing. No time to share a cheery campfire and the camaraderie of the long trail. This was a race, after all, and the finish line was a mere 365 miles away.

The pressure was on.

CHAPTER TEN

THE RUN TO BIEDERMAN'S cabin was nasty, with strong, gusting winds pushing their sleds around on an icy river trail. A light snow made visibility poor, in spite of the strengthening daylight. Rebecca was glad they weren't making the run at night. Beech and Wilton must have had a rough time of it. She and Mac kept to their schedule of hourly stops to snack and check their dogs, and when Biederman's cabin came into view five hours after leaving Trout Creek, both were startled to see two dog teams staked outside it. Rebecca, whose team was leading, turned on her runners. "Do you see what I see?" she asked, a surge of excitement purging the fatigue and frustration from her.

"Let's burn right on by without stopping," Mac said. "That'll shake 'em up good, maybe force them to cut their rest break short."

Rebecca knew Mac was right, but she longed to stop. She wanted to sit beside a warm stove and toast her cold bones. She could see smoke whipping out of the cabin's chimney and she closed her eyes. "All right, Raven," she commanded through frozen lips. "On by, Thor. Good dogs!"

There was a ripple of noise from the staked teams as they passed, and the cabin door opened. A man stepped out and waved to them. Rebecca waved back. There was a ham-radio operator stationed at Biederman's for the duration of the race, and he would relay information about which mushers had passed by. "Reed and MacKenzie!" she shouted to the man, who waved again in acknowledgment. He stepped back inside and shut the door against the cold. Rebecca closed her eyes again. Warm cabin gone. Her teeth chattered and she clenched them together with a vengeance. "Wimp," she muttered to herself.

Mac was right about the race strategy. She turned to look back at the cabin. Mac was watching, too. Just before the bend in the river obscured the cabin, they saw the door open again and two mushers emerge, moving quickly to their teams. Mac's teeth flashed in a triumphant grin. "Told you so," he said, and she laughed and turned her back to the strong wind.

In less than an hour Beech and Wilton had caught up and passed them. They had strong teams, there was no denying it. But how long could they run on so little rest? It took them some time to pull ahead of Mac and Rebecca's teams. Only when Mac and Rebecca stopped for their hourly snacking did they disappear completely.

"We'll definitely see them again at Slaven's," Mac said as they shared a cup of tea. "We can't be far from there now. And we'll be right on their heels coming into Circle. I was hoping we'd pass them before then, but now I'm not so sure. It all depends on how their teams hold up."

"It looked as if some of their dogs are not liking the pace."

Mac nodded. His scruffy beard and the fringe of hair that escaped his hat were coated with ice. The steam from the tea turned to ice on his eyelashes and he rubbed it off impatiently. "When this race is over, I'm going to sleep for at least a month,'' he said. ''Maybe two, depending.''

Rebecca bit her tongue to keep from asking him where he'd be sleeping. Would it be California or Great Britain? A wave of emotion swept over her so unexpectedly that tears were freezing on her cheeks before she could stop them from forming. Mac was in the act of lifting his cup for another drink and he stilled. ''Rebecca? What is it? What's wrong?''

She shook her head and swiped the back of her mittened hand across her cheeks. ''Just tired, I guess.'' She turned away and walked to the head of her team to finish her tea in privacy, leaving Mac to watch and wonder.

On the trail again, she struggled with her wildly fluctuating emotions. One moment she'd think everything was fine, that her dogs were doing great, that maybe Mac was right and they might win. The next moment her throat would close and she'd struggle against tears, thinking about how cold and tired she was, how much she hated racing and would never, ever race again, and most of all, how much she dreaded losing Mac.

Losing Mac? How could she possibly lose what she'd never had to begin with?

Wake up, Rebecca! she'd chastise herself. *Quit feeling sorry for yourself!* And then she'd concentrate on her dogs, on the trail, on the next bend in the river and the bend after that, the miles passing slowly in a blur of wind-driven snow as daylight faded into dusk.

THERE WAS A PLANE parked on the river below Slaven's Roadhouse. It was a big yellow deHavilland Beaver on the obligatory skis, and Mac admired it as they drove their teams up the riverbank and tied them off beside the roadhouse. The plane hadn't been here long. Snow hadn't yet dusted its leeward side, and the landing tracks were still clearly defined. Mac's eyebrows raised. It must have been a bumpy landing. The river was a mile wide here but jumbled with chunks of ice. The plane had come to a stop right along the shoreline, almost on top of the race trail. The river ice was smoother there, but a far cry from flat.

Two snowmobiles were parked near the entry door. Beech's and Wilton's teams were staked on the far side of the roadhouse and the smell of wood smoke was a welcome invitation to the warmth that waited within. Rebecca desperately needed that warmth. Mac walked to where she was already firing up her dog-food cooker. "I can do that for you. Go thaw yourself out," he offered. "I'll call you when it's ready to serve up."

She shook her head, unsheathing her ax to begin the painstaking process of chopping the block of frozen meat into the smallest pieces possible and throwing them into the cooler. As she worked she scooped snow into the water pot to melt. "I'm all set," she said. "See to your own dogs." She glanced at Beech's and Wilton's teams. "How long do you figure they've been here?"

Mac glanced over at the other teams and shrugged. "At least long enough to have fed their teams, but not all their dogs are sleeping yet. An hour, maybe?"

The roadhouse door opened. Wilton stepped out. "Hey!" he shouted. "Either of you two got any medical experience?"

Rebecca stood up, still holding her ax. "What's wrong?"

Wilton shut the door behind him and walked toward them. "We've got the pilot of that plane in here. He landed about twenty minutes ago. I don't know much about this stuff, but he looks pretty sick to me, you

know? He was on his way to Circle and put down here
when he saw smoke coming from the chimney. There's
no radio at this cabin, just a couple of folks keeping the
place warm for us. We could send one of them by snowmobile back to Biederman's to radio for help from there.
I guess that's the best bet."

"There must be a radio in the plane," Mac said.

Wilton shook his head. "We asked. The guy said it
didn't work. It's an old plane." He shrugged helplessly.
"I think it's his heart. His face is gray."

Mac glanced at Rebecca. "I'll go check on him," he
said. "You finish up here."

Rebecca watched him walk back to the roadhouse and
felt a knot forming in the pit of her stomach. She looked
at the plane parked down on the river ice, its yellow
wings rocking in the wind. She stood there watching it
until one of her dogs whined impatiently, and she
dropped back down to her knees to finish making supper
for the dogs.

WILTON WAS RIGHT about the pilot of the plane. He was
conscious and he was talking, but he was obviously in
a great deal of pain, all of it in his chest and left arm.
There were two race volunteers who had arrived the day
before to get the roadhouse warmed up and provide a
huge pot of stew for the mushers who would stop there.
The pilot, Guy Johnson, was sitting at the table. Mac
dropped into a chair across from him and cut to the
chase.

"How much fuel is in your plane?"

"Filled her up in Circle," Johnson muttered. He lifted
anxious eyes to Mac's face. Sweat beaded his pale brow.
"I was on my way to Eagle when—" he drew a few
shallow breaths and swallowed "—I had to land."

"Do you have charts in the plane?"

Johnson nodded.

"But no radio?"

Johnson shook his head. "Meant to get it fixed. Don't need one much around here."

"Okay, here's the deal," Mac said, leaning over the table. "I'm no doctor but I can fly a plane, and if yours is gassed up and ready, I can get you to Fairbanks. They have a good hospital there. What do you say?"

Johnson lifted his head. Hope flickered in his eyes. "You can fly?"

"I have over three thousand hours in navy jets. If you can show me how to start that old girl, I can sure as hell fly her."

Johnson nodded. "Let's go," he said.

Mac got to his feet. "Wrap him up in blankets or a sleeping bag and carry him down," he said to Wilton and Beech, tough mushers and more than capable of the task. Mac pulled his parka back on and headed out to where Rebecca crouched over her cooker. She stood as he approached. "Listen up," he said. "I'm going to fly this guy to Fairbanks. He needs to get to a hospital right away. I hate to ask it, but I need you to feed my dogs for me." He fumbled with the parka's zipper and pulled it up. "With any luck I should be back before noon tomorrow, but I don't want you to wait for me. I want you to haul yourself out of here in eight hours, just like we planned. Snack my team before you go and tell the folks up at the cabin to keep an eye on them till I get back." He paused and eyed her keenly. "Are you listening to me? If I get back here and you're still hanging around, I swear I'll kick your ass down the trail." Her blue eyes were so blank that he grabbed her shoulders and gave her a gentle shake. "Rebecca?"

"You can't do this!" she blurted. "You can't fly that plane! You haven't flown a plane in a long time and you've never flown *that* plane! The radio doesn't work. How will you let Fairbanks know you're coming in? What's going to keep you from crashing into jetliners when you get near the airport? If the radio doesn't work, what else might be broken? Its almost dark, and—"

"Rebecca, eight hours and you're out of here!" The roadhouse door opened and Beech and Wilton emerged, carrying Johnson in a sitting position in the cradle of their joined arms. "I have to go. Take care of yourself, Rebecca, and beat those two guys, okay? That's an order."

He let go of her and trotted down the riverbank toward the Beaver. The engine was still warm so she'd probably start just fine. He bled the fuel line and did his preflight walk around the old aircraft with fatalistic calm. There was no way of knowing how well the plane had been maintained. Rebecca was right. If the radio didn't work, what else might be wrong with her?

Beech and Wilton hoisted Johnson into the passenger seat and helped him get strapped in. "Hey," Mac said, buckling his own harness, "send one of those volunteers back to Biederman's. Have the ham-radio operator call ahead to Fairbanks airport and let them know we're flying in. It's 1600 hours now, our ETA should be 1730 or somewhere thereabouts. It'll be darker than hell. Tell 'em to leave the lights on for us and have an ambulance standing by."

He started the Beaver's engine—no problem there— then let it idle while he pored over the air charts and plotted his course. "It's going to be a bumpy takeoff," he warned Johnson, who nodded weakly and muttered that it had been a bumpy landing.

Magnetos, oil pressure, fuel gauges, everything checked out. No time to waste. He put aside the charts and checked rudder, ailerons, flaps. "Here we go, old girl," he said, advancing the throttle and settling himself into the seat. "Let's rock and roll."

The stiff wind made for a short takeoff roll on the rough terrain, which was probably the only reason Mac didn't lose all his fillings, but the old engine roared smooth, deep and sweet, all nine cylinders firing well, and when he pulled back on the yoke, the Beaver lifted obediently off the ice and climbed steeply into the darkening sky. Mac caught a glimpse of Slaven's Roadhouse as he banked around and took a compass heading of 240 degrees south of west. He saw Rebecca standing on the riverbank, looking very small and defenseless. Saw her lift her arm in a wave and he dipped the plane's wings in response. And then the roadhouse was behind him. Rebecca was behind him. Something deep inside him churned with a particularly intense anguish all the way to Fairbanks.

REBECCA STOOD rooted in place long after the plane had disappeared. She couldn't believe he was gone. Just like that! One moment they were starting to feed their dogs, and the next he was climbing into an old yellow plane and flying off into the gathering darkness. She felt completely abandoned and alone, standing on the bank of the frozen Yukon River and staring westward across the vast, snow-covered wilderness. It was the cold that galvanized her into action. The cold and the sound of a snow machine starting up, revving its engine repeatedly and then speeding down to the river and back toward Biederman's.

Feed the dogs, Rebecca, feed the dogs, insisted the

nagging voice inside her head. Was it Mac's voice or hers? No matter. She set to the task of feeding her own team and then Mac's. She put coats on all the dogs, and when they were curled up and sleeping, she took her sleeping bag and her supper sack and walked to the roadhouse on leaden feet. Beech and Wilton were still up. She sat down at the table and thanked the volunteer who promptly set a bowl of stew in front of her. She spooned it automatically into her mouth, not tasting, not hearing the bantering words around the table, not seeing the faces. Thinking only of Mac. What if the engine failed? What if the plane crashed? What if he was killed?

"Hey, Beck," Wilton's voice prodded. "Becky. That guy. What's his name again? MacKenzie? How long's he been driving dogs?"

"Less than a year," she replied dully.

Wilton whistled. "No kidding!" he said. "He's pretty good. He was starting to make me nervous. We figured he'd burn his team out a long time ago. I don't mind tellin' you that I'm glad he can fly a plane. Too bad for him, though. He's blown any chance he had, and he had a damned good chance."

"Yes." Rebecca nodded. "He did."

"What about you, Becky? You gonna give us a run for our money?"

"You can count on it," she said without conviction.

"Oh, I do," Wilton said, pushing out of his chair. "You've had us on the run for the past two hundred miles. I didn't think you were planning to give us any rest." He kicked Beech's chair. "C'mon. Let's get some quality snore time in before Rebecca rousts us out of here." The two mushers climbed upstairs with their sleeping bags in hand.

Rebecca finished her stew. It was nearly 7 p.m. She

was due to depart the roadhouse at midnight. Without Mac. She would sleep until 10 p.m., then begin the preparations for leaving. She'd feed her own team and Mac's one more time before heading for Circle. Mac should be in Fairbanks by now. If only she knew whether or not he'd arrived safely! She poured herself a cup of tea and drank it slowly, then poured a second one and drank it, too. She should be sleeping, like Beech and Wilton, but how could she sleep when Mac might be in trouble?

She poured herself a third cup of tea and slumped over the table. She was dizzy with exhaustion and there was a constant buzzing in her ears—or was it the sound of an approaching snowmobile? She lifted her head and listened. Yes! It approached rapidly, climbed the steep riverbank, and the engine cut out. Moments later the second volunteer tramped into the roadhouse, shrugging out of his heavy clothing.

"Well," he said before anyone could speak, "the ham-radio guy at Biederman's got the message sent okay. I hung around to see if they made it into Fairbanks and they did. Guess it was a pretty tricky landing, too. Snowing like crazy there and blowing hard. That storm must be heading this way fast."

"He's okay?" Rebecca asked, relief flooding her.

"I don't know. They trucked him off in the ambulance. But he was alive when he got there," the volunteer replied, thinking she was talking about the sick pilot. Then he grinned. "There was a message for you," he said. "The guy who flew Johnson into Fairbanks. MacKenzie, is that his name? He said for you to check out of Slaven's at midnight and not a second later."

Rebecca couldn't help but smile. He was safe. Mac was safe! She swallowed the last of her tea and stood, holding her sleeping bag in one hand. Her feet seemed to weight fifty pounds apiece and she climbed the stairs slowly, the muscles in her thighs burning with the effort. She picked an empty bunk and unrolled her sleeping bag. Beech and Wilton were both snoring, but not loud enough to keep her awake. She pulled off her boots and bibs and crawled into her sleeping bag. Her head spun as she lay down, and she felt as exhausted as she ever had, but her own discomfort didn't matter. The race didn't matter. All that mattered was that Mac was safe.

"CAN'T YOU MAKE this thing go any faster?" Mac asked the oil-truck driver, who glanced at him and grunted.

"Impatient sum bitch, ain't you?" he said, his upper lip bulging with Copenhagen snuff.

Mac slumped back on the truck's cracked vinyl seat. The headlights beamed into the darkness but did little to penetrate the wall of wind-driven snow. The Steese Highway, connecting Fairbanks to Circle City, was 162 miles of narrow, twisting, treacherous unpaved road that in the middle of summer had some flatlanders clutching their steering wheels with white-knuckled grips. He'd been lucky to find a ride at eight o'clock at night. A race official in Fairbanks had offered to take him to Circle the following morning, but Mac hadn't wanted to wait that long. Instead, he'd parked himself inside an all-night gas-station-and-convenience store on the edge of town and asked every trucker who passed through where he was headed. Most of them weren't going anywhere until morning, but the oil-truck driver had an emergency delivery in Circle.

With any luck they'd make Circle by midnight, Mac thought as he stared out the windshield at the strip of road ahead. He'd shanghai a snowmobile to get him the fifty miles to Slaven's Roadhouse, and by morning he'd be on the trail again with a very well-rested team of dogs. Of course, by that time the front-running teams would be miles and miles ahead of him, and there was no way he could make up that lost time.

"Nope," the truck driver, Wardlow, said suddenly. The truck was slowing. Slewing a bit as it did, but not out of control. Just sliding gently on the snow-covered surface. Wardlow downshifted, downshifted again. "Nope," he repeated with conviction, rolled down his window and spat, rolled it back up again. "It'll just have to wait till morning." His big fists were turning the steering wheel, and then Mac was looking at a big log building with a sign out front that read Chatanika Lodge.

"No!" Mac sat up straight. "We can't stop! The road's not that bad. There can't be more than six inches on the ground!"

"You ever been over this road before, son?" Wardlow said, parking the big rig in front of the long line of guest-room doors. "You ever been over the Summit in a bad snowstorm?"

Mac stared back. "What about the family that's out of oil?"

"They won't freeze to death. Most of 'em have woodstoves. Indians, you know. Most of 'em that live in Circle are. Survivors. Anyway, I'll call 'em. Tell 'em I'll be there in the mornin'." Wardlow climbed down out of the cab and looked at across the seat at him. "C'mon, son, I'll buy you a drink or two. You can drown your sorrows, and a hot shower sure wouldn't do you no harm, come to think of it."

Mac followed him reluctantly into the lodge where they settled side by side on bar stools in the saloon. Mac had exactly twenty dollars, Canadian, in his pocket. When he told Wardlow that, the older man just chuckled.

"Save it," he said. "I'm buying. Consider me one of your race sponsors. I've always admired you crazy sum bitches, driving those crazy dogs across all those miles through all that country in all that bad weather. Never understood it and never wanted to do it myself, but I always admired your sand. Now belly up to the bar, son, and enjoy yourself."

Mac hadn't eaten anything in over twelve hours nor slept much at all since Dawson, and by the time he finished the third generous drink that was set before him he was almost too far gone to lift his head off the bar. Wardlow propped him up on the way to their room, leaned him against the log wall while he fished the room key out of his pocket. When he'd gotten the door open, he dragged Mac inside. There were two twin beds and Wardlow steered him toward the closest one. The bedspread was cream-colored, and as it floated up toward him, Mac thought that he'd better get his parka off. It was dirty, would make the bedspread dirty… Too late! The bedspread hit him in the chest and there was a soft mattress beneath it. Mac closed his eyes and never did get his parka off.

BY MIDNIGHT, the wind had died. The silence was vast and palpable. Rebecca stood by her team and breathed ice into her lungs. It was time to go. Her dogs were ready, everything was packed up, her sled bag was cinched down tight. No snow, no wind. Maybe they'd been wrong about the storm. Maybe it had changed directions and was heading out to sea. She punched her headlamp's bumper switch, and bright light flooded forth. She panned her team, all of them on their feet and awaiting her command. She panned behind to where

Mac's team remained picketed. Merlin was standing, gazing solemnly at her.

She drew a deep breath and faced front again. Maybe she should wait here until Mac returned. What if the volunteers in the cabin forgot to feed Mac's team and they all starved to death?

Come on, Rebecca, the little voice chided. *Get your team in gear.* Wilton and Beech had left a good two hours ago. Kinney and Gurney had arrived an hour ago and would probably rest four hours at least. The night was calm and still, perfect for traveling. *Come on, Rebecca...*

One last look at Mac's dogs. Merlin was still watching her. She felt a twinge of guilt as she pulled her snub line and freed her sled. "All right, Raven," she said, and her team moved forward, trotting over the steep riverbank and onto the river trail.

An hour later a gust of wind came out of nowhere and nearly flipped her sled over. After that, the night became a desperate struggle against the wind and the snow, which fell lightly at first, then with increasing strength. Her team's pace slowed with the worsening trail. She stopped hourly to snack them, to switch dogs around, to give Raven a break and try another dog up front. None of them was happy. It was a wild night and getting wilder. The hours dragged, and what should have been a four- or five-hour run into Circle took her almost seven. It was 7:30 a.m. when she arrived in the tiny settlement on the banks of the Yukon. The checkpoint was at the Yukon Trading Post, and she was gratified to learn from Kanemoto, who anxiously awaited her, that Cookie was doing just fine and that Wilton and Beech were still there. In fact, though they had left Slaven's

two hours ahead of her, they had arrived in Circle
scarcely an hour before she did.

"It's going to be a heck of a storm," the checker told
her. "Supposed to last a couple of days. We're expecting
at least a foot of new snow, maybe two."

The vet checked her team, and as soon as they were
strawed and fed, Rebecca took advantage of the hospi-
tality and hot meal offered at the Trading Post. Mac had
not arrived yet, but road reports were that the drifts were
very bad over the Summit and the plows were working
hard to clear them. She wouldn't leave Circle until noon.
Mac was sure to be here by then.

Noon came, and still no Mac. Rebecca's team was all
dressed and ready to go, and still she watched the road,
waiting and hoping. The checker walked over and
handed her the sign-out sheet. She took the pen and
clumsily scrawled her signature, noting that Wilton and
Beech had left two hours ahead of her. Her dogs were
getting a lot more rest than theirs, and she hoped her
strategy would keep her in striking distance. She released her snub line. "All right, Raven. Good girl,
Thor."

Her team trotted out of Circle. They looked good, and
while a long rest might have been an extravagance at
this checkpoint, she thought it would pay off on the long
slog to Central. It was still snowing hard, and that would
slow the teams down considerably. She would stick to
her schedule and try not to think about Mac.

Of course, trying not to think about Mac was like
trying not to think at all.

Maybe that wasn't such a bad idea.

"NOW SEE HERE, son," Wardlow said the following
morning when Mac returned to the oil truck, shovel in

hand and weaving a little—both from the onslaught of the fierce wind and the unsteadiness of his legs. "You can't shovel your way through sixty miles of snowdrifts. Get into the cab and relax. You heard me radio the plow truck. They're almost here."

Mac climbed slowly into the cab. He stashed the shovel behind the seat and closed the door. He let his head tip back and his eyes close. He felt awful. It was more than just a hangover, much more. It was the idea of Rebecca out in this storm by herself, and also his team being looked after by people he didn't know. It was the certain knowledge that he was out of the money, that he wouldn't win a damn cent when his team crossed the finish line. He wouldn't be able to pay Rebecca with his race winnings because there wouldn't be any. He'd have to sell his Rolex again—maybe he'd get a better price in Fairbanks—and then he'd have to hope for some kind of financial miracle.

And of course there were the dogs. *His* dogs, not Brian's. They belonged to him, and yet Brian was going to sell them. Mac would probably never see them again after this race, never feel the power of Merlin's loyal gaze on him or the incredible rush of driving fourteen top dogs in the toughest sled dog race on earth.

How could he have fallen so far so fast? Just yesterday morning he'd been counting his chickens, and now he was finding out that none of them were destined to hatch. Rebecca had warned him against doing that and she'd been right. As usual.

"Well, now," Wardlow said. "She'll be comin' around the mountain, didn't I tell you, son? Sure enough, here she comes! Sum bitch!"

Mac opened his eyes. Wardlow pointed. A spume of snow was arcing high into the air, being caught by the cold, stiff wind and whipped to the side. The huge plow truck itself was invisible until it was nearly upon them, and then it veered slightly to clear the oil truck. They caught a glimpse of a driver, the flash of a brief wave, and then the plow truck swept on.

Wardlow started the oil truck. He waited for the oil pressure to come up and then put it into low gear. "Don't you worry, son," he said as the big truck eased forward through what moments before had been a six-foot-high drift. "We'll get you to Circle in time to catch your taxi."

BY THE TIME they got to Circle it was 2 p.m. Kanemoto was still there, and when he spotted Mac, he rushed toward him. "She's gone!" he said, pointing out of town. "Gone to Central. Waited for you, hoped you'd come. Left two hours ago!"

Mac looked around. "There's supposed to be someone here to take me back to Slaven's," he said. "The race official in Fairbanks said he'd arranged it."

Kanemoto nodded. "He is at the Trading Post. He waits there for you."

"How is she? How was she? I mean, was she okay?" Mac felt foolish asking, but Kanemoto would know.

Kanemoto looked at him and nodded somberly. "She's okay. Her dogs are okay. But I think, Mac-Kenzie, she misses you."

IT TOOK THREE HOURS for Mac and his snowmobile driver to reach Slaven's Roadhouse. It was a slow, fumbling slog through whiteout conditions, the trail markers obscured by the heavy snowfall. By 5 p.m. darkness had fallen, and Mac was beginning to despair. They'd passed five oncoming teams, each of the drivers anxious to ask about the trail ahead of them. Mac felt his spirits sink lower. There were now seven mushers between him and Rebecca. He had fallen hopelessly behind. His spirits picked up a bit when they rounded the curve in the trail and the glow of oil lamps framed by windows beckoned through the stormy darkness. He'd made it to Slaven's.

His dogs were extremely energetic, having had a full twenty-four hours of rest since he'd left them. They whirled around on their short picket lines and howled their joy at seeing him again. Merlin jumped up and put his paws on Mac's chest and stared into his eyes. "Hey, Merlin. Give me a few minutes to get things together and we'll be out of here."

The volunteers at Slaven's Roadhouse had taken excellent care of his dogs. They had been fed every six hours, religiously, in the exact way that Rebecca had specified before she left. They looked good. Hell, they looked great. Mac bootied them in record time, and less than one hour after arriving at the roadhouse he was back on the river with his team, heading for Circle and hoping he wouldn't finish this race dead last.

REBECCA REACHED Central ten minutes behind Wilton but fourteen minutes ahead of Beech. The run from Circle had been tough. Birch Creek was without a doubt the most twisted, contorted river she'd ever run. No wonder it was an eighty-mile run, when by road the distance was a mere thirty-three miles. She had stopped her team twice to feed, and four other times to snack, and still she had caught up with the front-runners. Kanemoto met her at Crabb's Corner, the Central checkpoint, and before she could ask, he said, "Mac's okay. He's back with his team by now, and he says for you to kick ass." Kanemoto grinned.

Rebecca felt more like lying down and sleeping. The storm was intensifying, and the final few miles into Central had seemed endless. It was midnight, and she felt as though she hadn't slept in years. Worse, throughout the entire run she'd been anticipating the next leg of the trail, the most dreaded stretch of all, Eagle Summit. In this weather it would be unbelievably nasty. Her only hope of getting over it was to tuck in behind Beech and Wilton when they checked out.

"Kanemoto," she said when both the checker and the veterinarian had given her team a thumbs-up, "I'm going to try and grab a little nap. Watch Wilton and Beech. When they start getting ready to leave, wake me."

Kanemoto nodded vigorously. Kanemoto wanted her to win. He would watch Wilton and Beech like a hawk, and when one of them so much as stirred, he'd wake her. Rebecca felt confident enough in this that she was able to lie down on a warm mattress in the checkpoint's back room and fall asleep instantly.

To be woken instantly by a shake on the shoulder. "Rebecca!" Kanemoto said. "They are getting ready!"

She felt miserable. Her muscles ached, her eyes burned, and she was nauseatingly dizzy. "How long...?"

"They have only been here three hours," Kanemoto said. "But you told me to wake you."

Three hours! Rebecca had hoped that given the severity of the weather conditions, they would have waited longer. She sat up. Kanemoto handed her a cup of something hot. She took a sip. Coffee, black and strong, and Lord, it tasted good. In spite of her resolve not to drink any caffeinated beverages, she downed that cup of coffee in jig time.

By 4 a.m., Wilton, Beech and Rebecca were signing

out of the Central checkpoint. Rebecca's dogs were disgruntled. She had broken some unspoken pact between them, cheating them out of much-needed rest, but without Cookie she couldn't see how this team would ever get over the summit. The weather was just too fierce. If they could follow Wilton and Beech, they might just make it.

AT MIDNIGHT Mac was checking into Circle. He was a good eighty miles behind Rebecca. In this dirty weather that meant at least twelve or fourteen hours, not counting the time he'd have to spend at Circle feeding and resting his team. It was little consolation that three of the teams he'd passed on his snowmobile trip back to Slaven's were still at Circle. He wanted to be in Central, where Rebecca was.

By 4 a.m. he was on the move again, his team trotting into the stormy darkness. The trail was soft, visibility was nil, and the wind strong enough to sap the heat from his body and suck the breath from his lungs. Merlin kept on, never once questioning Mac's judgment. The husky's courage was humbling. Five thousand dollars? Hell, Merlin was worth ten times that. How did one put a price on the best sled dog that ever lived?

Only by winning the race could Mac have afforded to buy the team, and he had lost all hope of that the moment he'd offered to fly Johnson to Fairbanks. He didn't regret his actions; he'd had no choice in the matter. But the thought of losing the team, losing Merlin, was the same as his fear of losing Rebecca. He'd never really possessed either, but in the past four months his entire life had become the sum of both.

THERE WAS NO UP or down to the world, just the endless white and the polar cold and the sound of the wind howling across a treeless landscape. There were no dogs to be seen, just the dark blotch of her sled bag. There was no trail to follow, just the punchy, blown-in trough left by the teams ahead, and the teams ahead were running blind.

Running? Hah! Walking. One step at a time.

Up and up. Higher and higher. Each upward step brought a stronger wind, a more blinding snow. Rebecca stopped her team and labored to the front. She pulled off one mitt and held her hand across Raven's eyes to melt the ice that had frozen them shut. She did the same for Thor. Moments ago she had caught a glimpse of what she had assumed was either Wilton or Beech, but now she was as alone as she had ever been, and in the most awful weather she had ever seen.

The conditions would get even worse, for the Summit was still four miles away. Four miles of uphill struggle in a blistering wind that topped seventy miles an hour. She couldn't believe that her dogs were still moving forward. She wouldn't have blamed them at all for quitting on her. "You're a good girl, Raven," she said, her voice wavering in the wind's onslaught, her words whipped from her mouth and shredded into unintelligible fragments. She turned her back to it and sank to her knees to catch her breath, leaning backward to keep her balance on the steep grade. If it got much worse, they'd have to stop, though stopping on this barren dome was not something she wanted to do. The longer she waited here, the farther ahead of her Wilton and Beech would get. She opened the bag of snacks and worked her way slowly down the team, tossing each of the dogs a chunk of meat mix. When she reached the sled, she caught hold of it to steady herself and stuffed the snack bag back inside. She peered ahead through her goggles. The front end of her team was completely obscured in the blowing snow. "Ready?" she shouted, and she saw her wheel dogs stand up, leaning into the wind. "All right!"

The gang line tightened and the huskies began to move forward, using all their strength, endurance and agility to battle their way toward the summit. Rebecca walked behind the sled, her hands gripping the driver's bow so tightly that they began to cramp. She stared down at her feet as they plodded slowly forward. Her leg muscles burned. She gasped for breath. She counted out her steps in a muttered monotone, "...eight, nine, ten...," and knew that these next four miles would be the longest four miles of her life.

Ten minutes passed. Twenty. Forty. The minutes seemed like hours. The wind increased and Rebecca's hands tightened. If she let go, she'd be blown clear to the moon. Her dogs were belly deep in the snow, pulling hard, giving everything they had to give, and somewhere up in the front of the team, invisible to her, a small black female named Raven was leading them on. She was about to stop the team for another snack break when of their own accord they halted. This was it, then. They were quitting on her.

Rebecca fished the snack bag out of the sled. She crawled on her hands and knees up the length of the gang line, handing out liver snacks this time, giving each dog a brief rubdown, a word of encouragement over the howl of the wind. At the front of her team she snacked Raven and Thor. "It's okay, Raven," she said into the leader's ear. "I don't blame you for stopping."

And then she heard something. A muffled shout. She looked ahead and saw the figure of a man emerge from the whirl of snow. He, too, was crouching on his hands and knees to avoid being knocked over by the wind. It was Wilton, and if she looked half as bad as he did, they were all in sorry shape.

"Our leaders have quit on us!" he shouted when he had drawn near enough for her to hear. "Do you think yours will go ahead?"

Rebecca was astounded. She looked back at her team. "I don't know," she shouted back. "They've been doing all right, but we've been following your tracks. I'm going to give them a breather, and then we'll see."

"Okay," Wilton shouted. He turned around and crawled back up to where his sled was stopped. She could barely see it through the snow even though it was no more than a few feet ahead of her.

She gave her dogs a ten-minute break and then made her way back to the sled. "Ready?" she shouted to the team. She watched her wheelers stand, brace themselves sturdily and shake. "All right!"

The gang line tightened and once again the team moved forward. Step by slow step they pulled ahead, veering out around Wilton's sled and passing his dogs one pair at a time. "Good luck!" Wilton shouted as she passed his sled. Beech's team was right in front of Wilton's, and Raven passed them, too. Here was the true test. Would her young leader be able to feel out the trail beneath a foot of new snow? Would Raven have the motivation to keep the team moving without Wilton's and Beech's teams up ahead? Could she possibly keep forging ahead into the teeth of this awful blizzard? Rebecca didn't think that any dog could, yet Raven was trying. "Good girl, Raven!" Rebecca shouted, hoping she would hear. "Good girl!"

Ten feet, twenty feet. Ten minutes, twenty. Climbing steadily until it seemed as though they must be near the top and yet it was still just out of reach. Rebecca knew she couldn't lift her foot for one more step, but she did. She knew that Raven and Thor were going to quit on her, but they didn't.

Then something happened that changed everything. A freak accident that occurred for no other reason than that they happened to be in that particular place.

The trail to Eagle Summit curved as it climbed, until instead of climbing straight into the wind, they were at an angle to it. Rebecca's sled, its bag stuffed with gear and drawn taut on the sled frame, acted like a sail, catching the full force of the wind. By walking on the uphill side of the sled, she was able to lean her weight against the driver's bow and keep the sled from flipping away from her and back down the hill, but the struggle was a mighty one, and it was a struggle she ultimately lost in one awful moment, one slip of a foot, one ferocious gust of wind. She felt the sled jerk over and there wasn't enough of her to counterbalance the wind's force. She clung on desperately and went over with the sled, her feet flipping into the air.

The rest was a blur of dizzying motion and the sickening sensation of falling, tumbling, rolling forever and ever until all at once everything stopped, and there was nothing, nothing at all.

CHAPTER ELEVEN

MAC'S TEAM POSTED the fastest run from Circle to Central. He checked in at Crabb's Corner at 3 p.m. with a trail time of just under twelve hours, in spite of the slow conditions. He'd passed two teams in the past three hours, and Kanemoto was still in Central when he pulled in. This surprised him, because Kanemoto should have been driving Rebecca's dog truck up to Mile 101 on the Steese Highway. Mile 101 wasn't an official checkpoint, but it was a place where spectators and handlers could watch the teams as they came over the summit, and it was also a place where mushers could drop dogs if they had to.

"The road is still closed," Kanemoto explained. "Rebecca checked out of here at 4 a.m. but no mushers have passed Mile 101."

Mac paused in the act of firing up his dog-food cooker. "What?" he asked stupidly.

"No mushers have passed Mile 101," Kanemoto repeated. "Officials think the storm is so bad that they're all stuck up there. It has happened before. One year they say the teams were backed up for more than twenty-four hours."

"Mile 101 is only forty miles from here. They've been on the trail for nearly twelve hours and they haven't reached...?" Mac's voice faded into silence. He lit his cooker and the flames burned hot. There was water to be had at Crabb's Corner, so at least he didn't have to melt snow. "It must be hellish up there," he muttered, putting the water on to boil. He began chopping his frozen block of meat while Kanemoto watched. Lord, he was tired. His movements were sluggish, his thoughts equally so. When he'd arrived at the checkpoint, he'd stood on the runners of his sled for several idiotic moments, wondering what he should do next.

Rebecca had kept a cheat sheet, small and laminated, clipped to the driver's bow. On it was a concise list of what to do upon reaching each checkpoint or stopping to feed the team. Mac had laughed when he'd first seen it, way back at the beginning of the race when clear and conscious thought came easily, and she'd gotten all fired up. "Just you wait," she'd said. "A week from now you'll wish you had one of those."

Once again, she was right. Kanemoto had to coach him through the act of feeding his dogs, taking off their booties, staking them out on beds of straw. Without Kanemoto's polite and carefully worded suggestions, Mac might never have gotten his team fed. He ate something inside the checkpoint, muttered unintelligible responses to questions asked by reporters, checkpoint staff and race followers, and told Kanemoto to wake him in two hours. Kanemoto nodded gravely. Two hours. Not much time to sleep.

No, Mac thought, closing his eyes. Not much at all. But Rebecca was only forty miles away. So close...so close...

REBECCA OPENED HER EYES on a strange world. She felt odd, as though something was lying on top of her, pressing down on her, smothering her. She moved cautiously and a bolt of pain shot through her right arm. The pain was bad enough to make her ears ring and her stomach turn over. The object that was smothering her was the sled. Somehow she'd gotten underneath her sled, but why would she have done that?

A jolt of adrenaline rushed through her as she remembered what had happened. Her sled and her team had been blown off the summit! She moved abruptly, shoving with her left arm and twisting out from beneath the heavily loaded sled. Daylight! Relief helped her deal with the incredible pain of moving. At least she could see, although darkness was approaching.

She was on her knees and moving through the deep snow, holding her bad arm against her side. "Raven! Thor!" At her shouts there was movement all around her, and where before there had been only snow, she now saw heads poking up. She counted them. They were all over the place, no semblance of a team, but all the heads were there. All her dogs were alive and looking back at her. Relief weakened her muscles, and she slumped against the overturned sled. Tears flooded her eyes and froze on her cheeks. Her dogs were okay. Nothing else mattered.

She'd been underneath her sled long enough for her team to curl up and be covered by the snowfall. They'd be hungry. She'd better get them sorted out and snack them. She looked around—it was still snowing hard. Had Wilton and Beech seen her sled go over the side? Did anyone even know she was down here?

She tried to shift the sled but couldn't with just one arm, and so she reached underneath to grab the snack bag. It took her a long time to get to each dog, untangle the lines and harness, unsnap the tug line and deliver a snack. They all seemed fine, but she couldn't be sure because they were standing chest-deep in snow. She didn't know exactly where she was, but at least the wind in this gully wasn't nearly as bad as it had been on top; they were protected from the brunt of the storm. Rebecca unhooked Raven, and her little black leader followed her to the sled. She made a place to sit in the lee of the wind. She leaned her back against her sled, and Raven curled close beside her. Rebecca closed her eyes. Her head ached terribly and her arm throbbed with pain. She tried to move her fingers but couldn't. The entire appendage hung uselessly at her side like the arm of a stranger, but the pain definitely belonged to her. If she'd had the energy and the ambition, she might have felt sorry for herself. Instead, she sat with her good arm around Raven, her bad arm hanging by her side, and watched the stormy sky grow darker.

"HERE'S THE SCOOP, Merlin. Rebecca's out in that mess somewhere and we're going to find her. Not only are we going to find her, but we're going to beat Beech and Wilton across the finish line. Got that? Okay, let's do it." Mac stood up from a private consultation with his lead dog and shook Kanemoto's hand. "Quit worrying," he said. "She'll be fine. Get the truck to Mile 101 as soon as you can and wait for her there if she hasn't already passed through. If she has, head down to Angel Creek."

Kanemoto nodded. Anxiety and sleeplessness made the prosperous Japanese businessman look much older than his forty-five years. He watched while Mac walked back to the sled, giving each dog a brisk rub and a cheerful word. He stepped onto the runners as Merlin's blue eyes watched from the head of the team. "All right," he said, untying the snub line. The team surged forward into the darkness.

Anxiety had a firm hold on Mac, as well, but he didn't want to make Kanemoto any more concerned than he already was. The storm was predicted to blow itself out by morning, but that still left another twelve hours of pure misery to deal with. "All right, good dogs," he crooned, coaxing them along at a solid trot. They plowed ahead as the trail began to ascend Eagle Summit. Forty miles wasn't far, but Mac had already learned that a mile can be traveled so many ways, not all of them swift. Not by a long shot.

His headlamp beam focused on a narrow vortex of swirling snow. Watching it made him dizzy, so he switched the lamp off, only using it periodically to check for trail markers. He didn't have to worry about Merlin losing the trail. The grand old leader could probably run it blindfolded.

In an hour he had passed two more teams, both of them bogged down in the wicked wind. One of them tried to get his team to follow but soon gave up, and Mac was alone again on the steepening trail. He didn't stop the team to snack. He broke all his own rules in that run up Eagle Summit. He worked harder than he ever had before, running beside the sled in the deep, soft snow, pushing the sled to help the dogs up the steeper sections, righting the sled when the wind blew it over.

Had there ever been such a wind as this? He'd already seen one of his dogs swept right off its feet. The others were creeping on their bellies, each making itself as small a target as possible for the fierce gusts. The darkness was both a curse and a blessing, a curse because he couldn't see a damned thing, and a blessing because if he could, he might have become discouraged at his slow progress. "Good dogs!" he praised frequently. "Good boy, Merlin!"

A strange feeling began to build inside him, pressing upward against his diaphragm. As he slogged ahead into the stormy darkness, the pressure continued to build until it became difficult to breathe. He pushed his team harder, and his voice carried an edge that he'd never used before, a curt, demanding sharpness that left no doubt as to what he wanted. Merlin gave his all, head down, eyes closed against the sting of the wind and the ice and the snow, feeling out the trail with his paws and pulling for all he was worth. His teammates followed suit.

Rebecca was in trouble. Mac was as sure of this as he'd ever been sure of anything. She was in terrible trouble somewhere up ahead. The minutes stretched like hours and each step only brought him twelve inches closer to her. Sled-dog racing! he fumed. Whoever thought up such a ridiculous sport! Who in their right mind would ever willingly indulge in such torture? *He* had, true, but only because he hadn't known any better. Never again would he race a team of dogs. He was finished with it. When this race was over, he was going to turn his back on all of this craziness. "All right!" he bellowed angrily. "Get up!" The team struggled valiantly on his behalf.

Where the hell was the summit? They must be getting close! They were nearly seven hours out of Central. The summit must be just up ahead, had to be! "Merlin! Get up!"

When Merlin stopped, unbidden, a mindless rage filled Mac. He struggled up to the head of the team, cursing the loyal dogs who had pulled so hard for him. He reached Merlin and raised his mittened hand to swat the dog's rump in angry retribution, and all of a sudden his arm froze. He looked ahead into the swirling darkness. Was that a sled right in front of them? Mac took one step forward and reached out his hand. It connected with the solid wood of a driver's bow. "Hey!" he shouted. "Rebecca!"

The top line of the sled bag ripped open in the wind, and a man sat up. It was Wilton. His face had the blank expression of a man who had reached the limits of his endurance.

"Where's Rebecca!" Mac roared.

Wilton shook his head and pointed. "Down below! She and her team got blown off the summit. It was quite a while ago, just past noon."

Mac turned to look where Wilton pointed. The slope dropped steeply away into the darkness. He pushed past Wilton's sled, and sure enough at the head of Wilton's team was another sled. "Hey, hey! Get up!" He was so full of rage and fear that he nearly jerked Beech up and out of the sanctuary of his sled bag. "Where's Rebecca!"

"Down below! We couldn't see her, the snow was too thick. We saw her sled get blown over, and her team got dragged down with it. We couldn't see how far down they fell."

"Where was her sled when it went over?"

"Just ahead of me, in front of my leaders," Beech shouted.

Mac stared down into the bottomless void. How in God's name would he ever find her in this whiteout? She could be anywhere along this slope. Or she might have tumbled clear to the bottom, wherever that was.

He turned and plunged back through the deep snow, falling several times as the wind knocked him over. His team was lying down, trying their best to get out of the wind. Mac rummaged in his sled bag for the first-aid kit Rebecca had given him for Christmas. He shoved four spare batteries and a flare into his parka pocket, threw each of his dogs a chunk of meat, tipped his sled over to reduce the wind's effect, and walked back to the front of the team, where he unhooked Merlin from the gang line.

"Merlin, come!" he shouted to the dog over the howl of the wind. Merlin rose to his feet, his blue eyes somber in the light of the headlamp. "Come, Merlin," Mac repeated, then turned his back on the husky and began a careful, step-by-step descent of the slope, panning the beam of his headlamp back and forth as he went.

Looking for Rebecca.

REBECCA OPENED HER EYES on the darkness. She didn't know how long she'd been sleeping, but something had woken her. What? The wind was howling at the same demonic pitch and the snowfall was just as heavy. What had changed? Raven stirred beside her, lifted her head from Rebecca's lap. Rebecca turned on her headlamp and panned the area around the sled. Nothing. Her dogs were invisible again, buried in their snowy beds. She switched her headlamp back off and leaned back against the sled. Raven sat up, and in the dark Rebecca could feel the rigidity of the animal's small muscular body as she strained to see or hear something in the night. "What is it?" Rebecca murmured. "What do you hear?"

Something came at them out of the darkness. Raven let out a rumbling growl, and Rebecca flashed her headlamp back on. Two eyes glowed bright red in the glare of it. Her first thought was wolves, but then the eyes moved and she saw the black-and-white of the furry coat and the familiar handsome mask. "Merlin?" She stared, incredulous. "Merlin, come here! Good boy! Come here!"

Mac's lead dog closed the distance between them. His cold nose brushed against Rebecca's cheek and then he whirled and disappeared back into the darkness. "Merlin!" she called after him.

A moment later she heard a faint shout and she answered it. She left her headlamp on, and before too long she spotted the dim glow of another headlamp working its way toward her. She knew it was the man who belonged to the dog. His calm, low voice was a balm to her, his presence an intoxicating elixir. Mac! He was here! He was beside her now, kneeling down, talking to her, saying something she couldn't quite make out. "Mac?" she said, reaching to touch him, her mittened fingers grasping. "Mac, is that really you?"

"Rebecca!" His voice was right in her ear. "Are you all right?"

"I'm fine," she said. "But I think my right arm is broken."

She heard him swear. "You're not fine if your arm is broken!"

"I can't believe you're really here!" she said. She felt as though she were floating, as if she were looking at Mac from some distance above him, watching as he bent over her and very carefully manipulated her right arm. The intense pain cleared her head and brought her back down to earth with a jarring crash. "Hurts!" she gasped. "Don't touch!"

"Can you move your fingers at all?" he asked.

"No."

"I have a splint and a sling in my first-aid kit," he said clearly into her ear. "I'm going to put it on your arm, right over your parka. Can you tell me where it hurts the most?"

"My forearm. Glad you came. Wind blew us off the trail."

"I know. Wilton and Beech told me. They're still up there."

"You can still win this race, Mac. Get going. You could still win!"

Mac rummaged in the first-aid kit. "I don't give a damn about the race. I don't care if I ever race again! This is going to hurt, Rebecca, but I have to move your arm. Lean forward just a little. Good girl." He wrapped the splint around her forearm. She bit her lip hard to keep from crying out. In spite of the cold, her forehead was slick with sweat, which iced almost instantly. She closed her eyes against the pain when Mac adjusted the sling around her neck and moved her arm into it. There was a loud ringing in her ears, and Mac's voice seemed to come from very far away. "Dammit, don't you pass out on me! I need you to stay awake. You hear me?"

"You owe me a lot of money. If you don't leave right now, you'll never be able to pay me back."

He ignored her words, holding her until her head cleared and she was able to sit up on her own. "I'm going to get you back up to the trail," he said. "We can't be that far from Mile 101. I'll load you in my sled and take you there. Your dogs'll be fine right where they are until I can get back and get them out. Can you stand up?"

He helped her to her feet. Her head spun and she was afraid she was going to be sick. "I don't think I can walk that far. Maybe in a minute or two..."

"I don't intend for you to walk," he said, scooping her gently into his arms. "Merlin, you come," he said unnecessarily to the dog who hadn't left his side.

"Put me down," she protested weakly. "You can't carry me. The slope's too steep and I'm too heavy."

"Heavy? When I first met you, Rebecca Reed, I thought to myself, 'I bet a strong gust of wind could blow that little lady clean away.' And I'll be damned if it didn't," Mac said as he began the painstakingly slow process of climbing back up the steep incline with Rebecca in his arms. He dug one booted toe into the slope to make a step, then the other. "If that little bit of wind was strong enough to blow you down this hill, I guess I'm strong enough to carry you back up it. Hell, you don't weigh much more than one of your scrawny sled dogs."

The pain of being moved one jolting step at a time was so intense that Rebecca could not always stifle her gasping moans. The climb lasted forever. She kept her left arm curled tightly around Mac's neck, her head tucked beneath his chin, and tried to make herself as light as possible for him. The slope was very nearly steep enough to require ropes and belays, and with the wind screaming across the face of it, she couldn't imagine where he found the strength or the balance to stay on his feet.

For the most part he did. He stumbled twice, but Rebecca only remembered the first time. The second time he went to his knees, the impact sent such an explosion of pain through her arm and shoulder that she could no longer keep herself from falling into the black abyss. She no longer wanted to try.

"REBECCA?" A STRANGE VOICE summoned her from a faraway place. "Can you hear me? I'm Dr. Stamm, your admitting physician. Can you squeeze my thumb, Rebecca? Squeeze my thumb if you can hear me."

Rebecca opened her eyes, blinked them into focus and saw a young doctor gazing down at her, a nurse standing to one side with a look of pleased surprise on her kindly face.

"Well, now, that's a pretty sight," Dr. Stamm said. "Her eyes are blue and they're lookin' right at me. Pupils equal and very reactive. And best of all, she's just about breaking my thumb. Let go, Rebecca. I know you're a strong lady. You don't have to prove it to me."

"Mac," Rebecca said. "Where's Mac? Where am I?"

"You're in the emergency room at Fairbanks Memorial. You had an accident on Eagle Summit. You have a fractured radius, a mild concussion and numerous bruises that shouldn't have any lasting ill effects. You arrived here approximately two hours ago, pretty incoherent, in and out of consciousness. We've done all the X rays and put a cast on your arm, so the hard part's over with. All you have to do now is behave yourself. I'm keeping you overnight as a precautionary measure. We're going to give you another unit of fluids, because you were pretty dehydrated when we admitted you."

"How did I get here? Where's Mac?"

"How much do you remember?" Dr. Stamm asked.

Rebecca's forehead furrowed as she thought. "I remember the sled blowing over and starting to fall, and Mac finding me. He carried me back up that slope. I don't know how he did it. It was so steep." She moved her head on the pillow. "I don't remember much of anything else."

"Well, from what I understand, you were brought into Mile 101 riding inside someone's sled bag at approximately 4 a.m. Someone with a ham radio called for emergency ambulance service. By then the storm had pretty much blown itself out, so they sent a chopper after you. You've been here since five-thirty. It's almost nine o'clock now."

"Where's Mac?"

"I take it Mac is the guy who rescued you?" Dr. Stamm shook his head. "I don't know, but there's another guy out in the waiting room. Japanese. I believe his name is Kimono."

"Kanemoto," Rebecca corrected. "Can I see him?"

Relief flooded through her when Kanemoto walked into the room. His face was drawn and somber, but he tried to smile when he saw her. Rebecca propped herself up on her good arm. "I'm sorry, Kanemoto. I can't finish the race. My arm is broken and the doctor says I have to stay here overnight. Where are my dogs? Are they okay?"

Kanemoto stood beside the gurney and touched her cast very gently with his fingertips. "The dogs are fine. You are fine. Don't think I am disappointed. I think next year you will win and I am very proud! Mac brought you to Mile 101. He left his team there and went back to get your dogs. I'm going to drive back out with the truck and meet him at Mile 101. It will take him a long time to get your dogs. The trail is still very bad. A race volunteer went to help him. He sent me here to check on you and told me to come back as soon as I knew, so I will go back now and wait for Mac at Mile 101."

"Take good care of my dogs," Rebecca said. "And, Kanemoto, stay with Mac. Stay with Mac the same way you would have stayed with me. Okay?"

Kanemoto nodded. "Okay."

IT WAS STRANGE, really, how things worked out. Mac had spent the last eighty miles thinking about all the choices he'd made, all the roads he'd traveled, all the things he'd regretted doing and the things he wished he'd done but hadn't. He tried to think of what he'd do differently if he had it all to do over again, but when it came right down it, there weren't many things he'd change. There weren't many he *could* change. Sometimes a man's path is laid down by forces greater than himself, and Mac was bound by his sense of honor and duty to walk his no matter how difficult it was.

He felt that way, sometimes, when he thought about his naval career and his father. He'd had no choice but to do what he had done, and he had no regrets. Well, almost none. He wished he hadn't had to kill the two Iranian pilots. But he wouldn't have traded those years of flying for anything. As for his father, the old man might come to realize that he'd been wrong about his son. It was possible. All things were possible. It was even possible that Rebecca might fall madly in love with him, though by the time she did, he would probably be a very old man.

"We're in the home stretch, Merlin. Not far now." Mac pulled up the sleeve of his parka to glance at his watch. It was exactly 1400 hours, and the afternoon was clear and sunny, a balmy zero degrees. He had seen his first houses a few miles back along the Chena River, and he had returned waves to a few spectators lining the Chena Hot Springs Road. He had no idea what day it was. He did know that he was at least two days behind the winners and about twenty miles from the finish line, and the way he was feeling, if he could just hang on to the sled and keep his eyes open for the next two hours of river trail, he'd be doing fine.

He hoped these last miles would be easy miles. He hoped that soon he'd be seeing Rebecca with his own eyes, be able to touch her, feel the warmth and the life

of her and know that she was really and truly all right.
Kanemoto had assured him she was fine, and in fact,
Mac had spoken to her by phone on his Angel Creek
layover. She had left her number with race officials
there, and he had dialed it with his heart in his throat.
A motel operator answered and connected him to her
room. "Mac!" she had said when she heard his voice.
"Mac! Are you okay?"

She'd been worried about him? What was wrong with
that girl? Didn't she realize that she was the one who'd
been hurt? She had told him she was fine, but knowing
Rebecca, he knew she'd say the same thing if she'd been
told she only had one day to live. He needed to see her.
He needed to be sure she was really all right. That awful
night he'd carried her up the hill, that terrible, mind-
numbing moment when he'd stumbled to his knees, and
she'd gone limp in his arms...

He'd never driven his team harder than he'd driven
them to reach Mile 101. It had taken more than two
hours for them to travel a mere six miles, each step an
immense struggle. His dogs had collapsed in their harnesses, completely played out, when they'd finally
reached the checkpoint. If it hadn't been for Kanemoto,
Mac never would have survived the horror of that night.
Stress took on a whole new dimension when a loved
one's life hung in the balance.

It was daybreak before he persuaded a snowmobiler
to take him back to where Rebecca's team had been
blown off the trail, and the steepness of the slope
astounded him. He was glad it had been dark when he'd
carried Rebecca up it. Had it been daylight he might
have deemed the task impossible. It was a good 150 feet
to where her sled had come to rest against an outcrop-
ping of rock. He and the race volunteer spent an hour

getting the dogs up, and then the sled had to be unloaded and its contents carried up to the trail before they could haul it, step by agonizing step, back up that hellish stretch of mountain. They'd reloaded the sled, hooked in the dogs, and then Mac had driven Rebecca's team six miles to where Kanemoto waited with the dog truck and news of Rebecca. By the time Mac was finally on the trail to the Angel Creek checkpoint with his own team of dogs, it was nearly 6 p.m. and he was once again way behind the front-runners.

"All right, Merlin. Steady as she goes. Good dogs." For having just completed a one-thousand-mile run, his team looked good. They were still moving along well, and in spite of the stress of the past few days, they still seemed happy to be trotting down the trail.

Rebecca had told him about Guy Johnson, the sick pilot, when Mac called her from the Angel Creek checkpoint. She'd given him a blow-by-blow description of the diagnosis, the emergency open-heart surgery and the prognosis. "He's doing nicely, but it was touch-and-go for a while. You saved his life! The doctor said if you hadn't gotten him there when you did, he'd have been a goner. Johnson and his family know it, too. They want to thank you in person.

"And, Mac, did you know that Guy Johnson was the pilot who took over Sam's mail route when Sam retired? Don't you think that's quite a coincidence? Oh, and by the way, Sam and Ellin won't be at the finish—Ellin caught Sam's cold—but I promised I'd let them know just as soon as you arrived. How's your team doing? How's Merlin?"

Mac had never heard Rebecca talk so much all at once, her words tumbling out in a bright, breathless rush.

"The dogs are fine but they're tired. I'm going to stay right here until they tell me it's time to go. I know it's only eighty miles to the finish, but I pushed them too hard coming over Eagle Summit. I really burned them out. Don't expect me for at least another day or so."

At the end of their conversation he replaced the phone in the receiver and sat for a few moments, his head spinning. "I don't care about Guy Johnson and his mail route!" he'd wanted tell her. "I only care about you!"

Not that he had anything against Guy Johnson. Well, he did resent the fact that if Guy hadn't had that damn heart attack, Mac and Rebecca would probably be counting their race winnings right now. None of that was Johnson's fault, of course.

Mac raised his arm in response to a riverside wave. More and more people were turning out along the riverbank as he drove his team nearer to town. A stray dog ran out onto the ice, yapping at the team, but his dogs ignored it, trotting steadily on. He wondered if they would travel like that forever, this incredible team of dogs who had been his loyal companions for the past fourteen days.

He had stayed a long time at the Angel Creek checkpoint, fussing over his team, feeding them special treats, apologizing to them for the way he'd driven them over Eagle Summit. He didn't pull out of there until all of them were ready to roll, and he'd babied them on this last stretch of trail, stopping every hour to snack, to rub tired muscles, to tell them what grand and glorious dogs they truly were.

Mac heard a noise coming from up around the next bend in the river. He thought at first it was the sound of water rushing over a dam or a strong gusting wind that never diminished. His dogs heard it, too, and checked their pace so much that he had to step on the section of snowmobile track dragging between the runners to keep the brush bow of the sled from bumping into his wheel dogs. "All right," he said reassuringly. "All right." They pulled forward again, but their ears were pricked and their tails were raised. The noise grew louder as they approached the curve. More people were lining the riverbank waving to him, and he wondered what all the commotion was about. He turned to look behind him, but the river trail was empty. He knew there were no mushers between his team and the finish line. He'd left Angel Creek nearly a day behind the last group of middle-of-the-pack mushers, and the back-of-the-pack mushers were another day or so behind him. He'd had the trail to himself for the past seventy-five miles.

Merlin rounded the corner and trotted in his bold, brisk way, leading the team. Mac's first impression was that he was driving his team into the midst of some kind of parade or winter carnival. There were people everywhere, thousands of people, more than there'd been at the start of the race. People were waving little Canadian and American flags and jumping up and down and raising their voices in one continuous roar as his team trotted toward them. The massive crowd parted to form a long, ragged chute and as they did he suddenly saw, at the end of it, a big banner strung on high with huge black lettering against a white background. The letters spelled out just one word, but it was undoubtedly the sweetest word he'd ever read from one hundred yards away.

FINISH!

"My God," he said, amazed. He found it difficult to comprehend that this crowd of people was standing here waiting for him to finish the race. Why would they be so interested in a musher who was running so far back? He was in sixteenth place, or so he thought. Maybe even seventeenth. This had to be some awful and embarrassing mistake, or maybe the first group of mushers had gotten lost and were somewhere out on the edge of nowhere, running their teams in circles for days while desperately trying to find the trail to Fairbanks.

Well, a man could always dream.

Merlin's nose crossed the finish line to a deafening roar and an intimidating stampede of the crowd. The dogs spooked and bolted, ducked and cowered, and Mac had no idea what to do. He stepped on the sled brake and stared around at the wall of unfamiliar faces, felt the slap of unfamiliar hands on his back and shoulders, saw several microphones and large video cameras zooming toward him, and wondered where Rebecca was. He took the clipboard from the checker and signed his name while a race official checked his sled bag for the mandatory gear.

And then he heard a high, excited voice. A foreign voice. Japanese. He caught sight of a small, slender man, forcing his way through the crowd. Kanemoto emerged, out of breath. "Mac!" he said, and bowed, reaching at the same time to pump Mac's mittened hand, a unique Japanese-American greeting. "Congratulations!"

"Excuse me," a sonorous voice interrupted, and a microphone was pushed closer. "Could you tell the crowd how you feel at this moment? What emotions are running through you as you stand at the finish line, after having just completed such a long and challenging journey? How did you feel when you carried that young woman to safety and when you flew Guy Johnson to

Fairbanks, knowing that you'd given up any chance of winning this race?''

Mac felt acutely embarrassed. "It feels good to be here," he said. He looked at Kanemoto, ignoring the reporters and their microphones, cameras and questions. "Where's Rebecca?"

Kanemoto pointed vaguely and then walked to the front of the team, grabbed Merlin's harness and trotted through the crowd, leading the team while Mac handled the sled as he threaded his way to the dog truck. The truck was Rebecca's. Where Brian was, Mac hadn't a clue. Maybe he was at class. Maybe it wasn't a Saturday or a Sunday.

And then it didn't matter where his brother was, because suddenly he saw her. She edged her way through the crowd, walked up to Merlin, knelt and gave the dog a warm, one-armed hug. She grinned at Mac as she rose to her feet. He knew he should be tending his dogs, seeing to them first, but for the moment he only had eyes for the woman standing at the head of his team. He walked toward her and didn't stop until he had pulled her very gently into his embrace. He felt her good arm squeeze him fiercely and he heard her say in a choked voice, "Oh, Mac!"

The crowd had followed them to the truck. People thronged around, their voices an unintelligible babble, asking questions and patting the dogs while Mac and Rebecca clung wordlessly to each other. Finally, he set her back at arm's length and looked her up and down. She looked alive and well, he thought. Hell, she looked beautiful. "I'm so damn glad to see you!" he said. "I missed you like crazy!" He knew by the bright, shining joy in her face that the feeling was mutual, even if she didn't voice it. He wanted to tell her a hundred things, a thousand things, but first he had to tend to his team, those loyal, courageous dogs who had brought him safely across a thousand miles of rugged wilderness, from Whitehorse, Yukon Territory, to Fairbanks, Alaska.

"My dogs," he said, knowing that she would understand.

"They're in good hands," she said, nodding behind him. He turned. Beech was helping Kanemoto unhook the team and tether them around the truck. The dogs' food bowls were out and Wilton was already dishing up their snack. He stared for a moment, then turned back to Rebecca, perplexed. "Why are all these people here?"

"They're all here," she explained patiently as if he were a very young child, "because everyone wanted to see you finish. What you did out there on the trail made them want to be a part of your race. You're a hero, Mac, and heroes are a rare commodity these days."

He pulled her back into his arms and bent his head over hers, intoxicated by her nearness. "Rebecca, are you all right? I mean, really all right?"

"One hundred percent," she said.

"You can't be one hundred percent if your arm is broken," he said with mock exasperation. They drew apart and looked at each other, grinning like idiots.

"Well, ninety percent, if you want to get technical. You, on the other hand, look like you could use a hot meal, a cold beer and about two or three months of sleep. But, Mac, be forewarned. You have less than two hours until the awards banquet, and you absolutely have to attend. It's mandatory. You can't skip out, and you can't fall asleep. I have a hunch you're going to be the star of the show."

Mac reached out for her again. "Rebecca, listen," he began.

She shook her head again. "Not now, Mac. We'll have plenty of time to talk later. At the banquet."

Talk! He didn't want to talk! He wanted to wrap her in his arms. He wanted to kiss her so badly that he was giddy with desire. He was about to grab her and do something in front of all these people that might just shock the hell out of them when someone behind him apparently caught her attention. She looked over his shoulder and raised her arm in a beckoning wave.

"It's Sadie," she said. "She's been here since early this morning, waiting for you to finish."

Mac whirled around. Sure enough, there she was. Sadie Hedda, making a determined beeline through the crowd toward them. She caught Mac's gaze and waved her hand wildly, grinning from ear to ear as she approached. Drat and damnation! "Look, Rebecca—" he said.

"Later!" she repeated. "Right now I think you'd better pay some attention to Sadie. Here," she said, pressing a key into his hand. "Brian got you a room. He was around here just an hour or so ago but some friends of his showed up and they drove off to get something to eat. They should be back soon. You can walk to the room from here, and the banquet's in the same building. Don't worry about your dogs. We'll take good care of them. And I'll see you at the banquet."

"Rebecca!" he said as she nimbly eluded his grasp, ducked beneath an approaching video camera and disappeared behind a wall of humanity.

"Mac!" Sadie was calling his name, but Mac was staring after Rebecca and thinking about later—later being that long-awaited time when they could finally be alone together, when he could finally tell her all the things he'd been thinking about and wanting to say for the past thousand miles.

Later! Could he possibly wait that long?

CHAPTER TWELVE

REBECCA SAT ON HER BED in the motel room she'd been holed up in for the past two days and nights and stared at the wall. It was time to leave for the banquet. Any moment now Kanemoto would tap on her door and drive her to the place where all the mushers and race fans would be gathered. Mac would be there. Sadie would be there. Sadie would be at Mac's side. Sadie and Mac. Rebecca had always known it would work out between the two of them. They were a good match for each other. She should be happy for them, but instead, she was immersed in self-pity. She didn't want to go to the banquet, sit with them, watch them, listen to them. She didn't think she could bear seeing how Sadie looked at Mac, how she reached out her hand and laid it on his arm whenever she spoke to him. Oh, God, in spite of all her precautions, Rebecca had fallen in love with Bill MacKenzie, and she had no one to blame but herself for the way she was feeling now.

She had sworn she would never love anyone the way she had loved Bruce, but she had forsaken the memory of her husband. Worse, she no longer felt the guilty sting of her transgression. Bruce was dead. Mac was alive. Loving Mac felt so good, so right. But it was too late! She'd driven him into another woman's arms, and with Sadie he would find all the loving he needed. He'd soon forget about her and the dogs and the wild and lonely land known as the Yukon.

The tap at the door startled her even though she was expecting it. She stood up, reached for her parka and wondered if she could beg off the banquet. Nobody would care if she didn't go. After all, she hadn't even finished the race. She'd tell Kanemoto she was ill. He would understand. She dropped her parka on the sofa, drew a measured breath to compose herself and opened the door.

"Mac!" she said to the man who stood before her, freshly showered, shaved and dressed in decent clothes. His face was drawn with fatigue, and there were two small patches of frostbite, one on the bridge of his nose and the other over his left cheekbone. Rebecca thought he'd never looked sexier. She raised a hand to the side of her face and stared. "What on earth are you doing here?"

"Good to see you, too," Mac said. "Mind if I come in?" She opened the door wide and he stepped past her into the room. "For the past hour I've been sharing the same hotel room with my brother, but all he wants to talk about is how broke he is and how desperately he needs to sell the team, so I told him that you were my date and I was taking you to the banquet. He gave me the keys to the dog truck and here I am. Hope you don't mind too much."

Rebecca's heart rate accelerated. "But—" she glanced outside the door before closing it, spying his dog truck parked next to hers with no one sitting in the passenger seat "—where's Sadie?"

"Sadie?" Mac said with a puzzled look. "She stayed long enough to congratulate me and then headed back to Dawson, but before she left she gave us this to

share!'' He held up a bottle of champagne with a triumphant grin, which slowly faded in response to Rebecca's frown and long silence. ''It's good champagne,''
he said.

''I don't understand,'' Rebecca said. ''I mean, why
would Sadie give us champagne? Why did she leave?
She's crazy about you and—''

Mac set the champagne bottle on the desk and reached
out to her. His strong hands closed on her shoulders.
''Listen to me very carefully, Rebecca. I told you before
and I'll tell you again—there's nothing between Sadie
and me. She wishes us all the best. She really does! Why
in God's name are you looking at me that way? When
are you going to realize that you're desperately in love
with me? And when, for the love of Pete, are you going
to ask me to kiss you? Dammit, woman, these last few
days without you have been the loneliest of my life!''

Rebecca could scarcely draw breath. His words addled
her tormented mind and wreaked havoc with her heart.
Her eyes stung with tears. He cared about her! In spite
of all the cold shoulders she'd given him, in spite of a
total lack of encouragement, in spite of all the awful
things she'd said, he still cared about her! She'd treated
him badly from the very beginning and repeatedly
pushed him in Sadie's direction, and yet he'd come back
to her. He was here, standing before her, pledging a loyalty she didn't begin to deserve but a loyalty she craved
more than anything else on earth.

''Mac,'' she said, a quaver in her voice. She raised
her hand, her fingers closing lightly around his powerful
wrist. ''Mac, I—''

Another tap at the door. This time it was Kanemoto.
He stuck his head around it, beaming at the sight of them
together. ''Okay, okay! Time to go! Quick!'' he said,

pointing at his watch. "We'll be late! I want to get pictures! Lots of pictures!"

MAC COULDN'T REMEMBER a thing he ate or drank during the long, drawn-out process of feeding hundreds of people crammed into a hot, stuffy banquet hall, followed by the even longer and more drawn-out process of awarding prize monies and trophies to the top-placing fifteen mushers. It seemed that every musher had to make a long speech that encompassed the race's high and low points, and there were a lot of high and low points over a thousand miles of wilderness trail. And then, of course, they had to thank all of their sponsors, and the luckier ones had a list of sponsors as long as the race itself.

The awards started with the fifteenth musher. It was a good sixty minutes before they awarded the first-place prize to Jim Wilton, who then proceeded to talk on and on about the race trail, the checkpoints, the veterinarians, his sponsors, his dogs, himself, until finally, finally! he ran out of steam. But instead of leaving the podium, he leaned toward the race officials and they murmured together for a few moments. Mac leaned his shoulder into Rebecca's and said, "Can't we cut out of here? It must be about over."

Rebecca shook her head. "Special awards are next," she told him. Mac closed his eyes and groaned. He'd never last. He was sinking fast. "Get me some toothpicks for my eyes," he said, and Rebecca laughed.

Wilton was talking again. He talked glibly and well, making humorous comments that provoked bursts of laughter from the crowded banquet hall. "I've always thought that there were 5,280 feet in a mile," he said, "but up on Eagle Summit they've added about five thousand additional feet to each mile, and every one of them is vertical. You know, there's a musher here tonight I've always envied because she don't weigh no more'n one of my legs. I always thought Rebecca Reed had quite an advantage on all us fat old men, but after watching her sail off Eagle Summit in that stiff breeze I've changed my mind. Rebecca, next time you run the Summit, I suggest carrying some ballast in your boots, like about fifty pounds of lead sinkers in each.''

Wilton rustled some papers in front of him on the podium and took a drink of water. Mac groaned again. This guy was settling in to talk all night.

"I've asked the race officials if I could say a little something about this next award. The Sportsmanship Award, as most of you know, is presented to the musher who demonstrates the best sportsmanship along the trail. The vote is made by fellow mushers, and there's been years when some of us scratched our heads trying to figure out who in hell the nice guy was, but this year's choice was a shoe-in. The vote was unanimous. For those of you who might have been born a few minutes ago, I'll fill you in on a few minor things this particular musher did.

"Me and Beech were camped at Slaven's Roadhouse when Guy Johnson landed his plane right out on the river. It wasn't a good place to land a plane, and the landing was pretty damn rough. Johnson stopped there because he was having some real severe chest pains and he couldn't catch his breath. We carted him up to the roadhouse and were wondering what to do when all of a sudden this rookie musher drives his team up, walks inside, looks old Guy Johnson over in the most steely-eyed way I've ever seen, and the next thing you know he's flying Guy Johnson to Fairbanks. He might be a rookie musher, but he ain't no rookie pilot. From what I understand, he did a long stint in the navy flying planes onto boats. Guy Johnson's doing okay—he's at Fairbanks Memorial—but he'd be dead right now if he hadn't gotten there as fast as he did.

"So this rookie saves Guy Johnson's life. By hook and crook he manages to get back to where he left his team at Slaven's Roadhouse and he's back on the race trail. Now, when he took Guy to Fairbanks, this musher was running in third or fourth place, right behind me and Beech. But now he's way behind. No chance of winning. That doesn't stop him, though. He gets to Central and finds out we're all pinned down on Eagle Summit, so he fires up his team and charges up the hill. He catches up to us and we tell him about Rebecca Reed being blown off the summit. So what does he do? You guessed it! He rescues her. I mean, this guy would put Superman out of business in about a week! He carries the little lady up a slope you and I couldn't walk up with crampons and an ice pick, loads her into his sled and drives her to a rendezvous with a rescue helicopter at Mile 101. And another thing. This rookie's lead dog is undoubtedly the most phenomenal dog in the race. No one's team was moving on that summit, but this rookie musher says one word to his leader and they're outta there. Me and Beech followed right behind him, and his team broke trail for us clear to Mile 101.

"Did he keep going after he dropped the injured musher at Mile 101? Nope. Me and Beech did, but this guy stayed until the chopper came, and then the next morning he and a race volunteer went back and got Rebecca Reed's dog team and brought it to safety. Only then did he continue on and finish the race.

"This rookie musher's face is plastered over all the

major newspapers in Canada and the United States, and all that publicity paid off for you, Bill MacKenzie, because not only do we have a beautiful fur musher's hat and five hundred dollars donated by MAPCO Alaska Petroleum, but we also have an anonymous donation of ten thousand dollars for this year's Sportsmanship Award winner. Come on up here, Mac, and get your loot!''

Mac sat rooted to his chair. Wilton's speech had paralyzed him. He felt Rebecca squeeze his arm. ''Go on, Mac!'' She spoke gently into his ear. ''Get up there! You deserve it.''

He stood to thunderous applause and earsplitting wolf whistles. The entire room stood with him. He walked up on wooden legs and awkwardly accepted the hat and the check, shook hands with Wilton and the race officials, and was trying to escape when Wilton dragged him in front of the podium for a mandatory speech.

''Thank you,'' he said. ''Thank you all very much!'' He started to turn away, and Wilton grabbed him again.

''You might as well stand right here, MacKenzie,'' he said. ''You got another one coming.''

The race marshal stepped up and took over the mike. ''This next award is given to the musher who best exemplifies the spirit of the Yukon Quest. I guess I don't have to explain how the race officials came up with the nominee this year, proof positive that this is a race where you don't have to finish first to be a winner. Bill MacKenzie, it is my honor to present you with the Challenge of the North Award and a check for two thousand dollars. I sure hope we see you on the trail again next year!''

Mac accepted the trophy and the check, mumbled his embarrassed thanks once again, but was prevented yet a second time from making his escape as the race's head veterinarian approached the podium and took her place behind the microphone. She gave Mac a warm smile before beginning her speech.

"Each year the race veterinarians vote on the musher who demonstrates the most humane treatment and over-all excellence in caring for his or her dogs throughout the race. This award is a legacy for aspiring mushers to emulate in the treatment and care of their team. I think it's the first time in the history of the Yukon Quest that a rookie musher has won this prestigious award, and I'd like to say that personally, I wouldn't mind being one of Bill MacKenzie's sled dogs. He kept all of his four-teen dogs happy and healthy throughout the entire race, and not only that, he recovered Rebecca Reed's team from a perilous place and brought them to safety at the cost of his own race. Mac, I'm proud to present to you this year's Vet's Choice Award of three thousand dol-lars, along with this beautiful plaque. I hope you hang it on your wall in some prominent place, because it's something for you to be very proud of."

Once again he was dragged in front of the podium. He stared out at the blur of faces, dry-mouthed. When the applause eased, he leaned forward. "Thank you again. I have to admit that I'm a little overwhelmed. I wish my dogs were here right now, because they deserve all this praise, not me. They may not have won the race, but they're the winningest team I'll ever have the priv-ilege to drive. As far as my lead dog, Merlin, goes, there's no better dog on the face of this earth. Amen. Thanks also to Sam and Ellin Dodge for sponsoring me right down to the ground, to Donny for all his smoked salmon and to Rebecca Reed for sponsoring my ex-tremely, incredibly excellent dog food, as well as the tastiest homemade thousand-mile chili I've ever eaten and eaten and eaten!''

He returned to his seat amidst the thunder of applause and another standing ovation, and studiously avoided looking at Rebecca.

Brian leaned toward him. ''*Your* dogs, Mac? The least you could have done while you were up there is announce that the team's for sale!''

''Shut up, Brian!'' Rebecca snapped, startling the hell out of both Mac and Brian. Her cheeks were flushed and her eyes bright with indignation. ''Now is hardly the time for that kind of talk!''

Mac turned his gaze to her, astounded and enormously pleased by her response to Brian's comment. ''No, it sure isn't,'' he agreed. ''It's time for bed. Hell, it's past time for bed. Way past. You coming?''

Rebecca's eyes widened. She glanced to see if anyone had overheard. Kanemoto was talking animatedly to someone on his right, and Brian had jumped out of his chair in a sulk to find himself another drink. She looked back at Mac. ''Let's go,'' he said. He stood up and reached for her hand. When Kanemoto turned to look up questioningly, Mac said, ''Here's the key to my truck, Kanemoto. It's parked out back. I'll drive Rebecca back to the motel in her truck and take care of her dogs, if you'll take care of mine.''

Kanemoto nodded. ''Okay,'' he said. ''I'll see you in the morning, then.'' And he smiled a big smile as he watched them leave.

Mac kept his hand on the small of her back as he guided her out of the crowded banquet hall where the special awards were still being given out. The cold night air embraced them when he opened the door for her and they stepped into it, drawing it gratefully into lungs that hadn't known that much hot stuffy indoor air in a long, long time. They began walking along the side of the building toward the back parking lot, and when they passed into a dark alley, Mac pulled her to a stop. He didn't say a word, he just backed her up gently until her shoulders bumped against the building behind her. He braced his hands on either side of her and lowered his head, stopping just shy of kissing her.

"I promised you a long time ago that I'd never kiss you again unless you asked me to," he said, "but God help me, I've been wanting to do this for the past thousand miles. I'm afraid I'm about to break my promise."

Rebecca felt the strong masculine warmth of his nearness, and a delicious, sensual shiver rippled through her. "Oh, no you're not. For the past thousand miles I've been hoping you'd kiss me," she said.

He drew his head back to look at her in the near darkness. "Really?"

"For the past two thousand," she amended. "So please, please, William MacKenzie, kiss me."

"At last," he breathed, lowering his head again.

Finally! Rebecca thought as his lips touched hers. The kiss was so electric she was surprised sparks didn't fly. She reached up with her good arm to curl her fingers around the nape of his neck and stood on tiptoe to bring him closer. Their lips parted simultaneously, and Mac's tentative, questing mouth insinuated itself upon hers with growing passion. Rebecca lost herself in the icy, hot tingling sensation of Mac's long-awaited kiss. At the same time she felt the empty, aching feeling in the pit of her stomach—that had been with her since Bruce died—dissipate. She lost all track of time as Mac's mouth awakened feelings inside her she had thought long dead. Her knees buckled abruptly and he dropped his arms to grab her against himself. They broke apart, gasping for breath. Mac groaned as if in agony. "Where in hell's your room?"

"It's clear across town, remember? What about the dogs?"

"What dogs?"

"We have to drop my dogs, remember?"

"Oh, yeah." Mac slumped against her, bracing one hand against the wall and running the fingers of his other through the hair over her left temple. "Damn! I forgot about the dogs…"

He kissed her again in the shadow of the building and once more at the dog truck, once at each stoplight on the drive across town and five times while he let twelve dogs out of their dog boxes to stretch their legs one last time before being boxed for the night. Rebecca's room was a typical motel one, but there was plenty of hot water and they could park the truck right outside the door, which is where they left it when Mac finished reloading the team and took the room key from Rebecca.

Once inside the room, he locked and chained the door, flipped on the bedside light, closed the curtains and began undressing as fast as he could. Rebecca stood for a moment watching him and then began to laugh. He stopped in the act of pulling off his boots, standing first on one leg and then the other as he hopped around the room. "What's so funny?" he said, boot in hand.

"You're in an awful hurry," she said. "You're beginning to make me a little bit nervous."

He dropped the boot on the floor with a heavy thump. "Why's that?"

She crossed to where he stood and reached up her hand to trace the side of his face. "Because I was kind of hoping that this was going to last all night."

LATER SHE AWOKE in the dimly lit room and stifled another rueful laugh. All night? He'd barely lasted ten minutes before collapsing beside her, sound asleep before his head hit the pillow. No one could blame him. He hadn't really slept in more than five days, and the physical exertion he'd expended on the race would have wiped out a handful of lesser men. Rebecca curled on her side and contemplated him from a delicious twelve inches away. He was lying on his stomach with his arms flung out, taking up most of the bed. He was naked, the bedsheet bunched at his waist. His back and shoulders were exquisite. The muscles in his upper arms and shoulders were rounded and powerful, and in his back they were perfectly knit over his ribs. She longed to touch him but didn't dare. He needed sleep so desperately.

The bedside clock read 4 a.m. She rolled onto her back with a silent sigh and then made an awkward one-armed clutch at the mattress as she felt herself start to slide off the side of the bed. She hit the floor with a muffled thump and a startled cry, dragging most of the bedding with her. Above her on the bed Mac groaned. He reached his arm out, encountered nothing and came awake with a lunge that propelled his upper body over the edge of the bed. "Rebecca? What the hell are you doing down there?" He helped her back up onto the bed. "Are you all right? Did I push you off? Is your arm okay?"

"My arm's fine. I slid off, that's all."

He knelt over her, one leg on either side of her thighs, and examined her closely. "You sure?" She nodded. "Well, you look okay to me," he said in a voice barely above a whisper. "In fact, you look pretty damn wonderful." He lowered his head and kissed her very gently, drawing back for a moment. "You taste pretty damn wonderful, too." He grinned slowly. "If you don't mind, I'd like to try something."

"What's that?"

"I'd like to try making love to you again without falling asleep before we even get started."

"Think you can do it?"

He turned his head to look at the bedside clock and then looked back at her. "The way I've got it figured, I should be able to keep you entertained for at least four hours. I've been sleeping since midnight or thereabouts. Equal run, equal rest, isn't that right?" He lowered himself carefully on top of her, keeping his upper body braced to avoid the cast on her arm.

"That formula was devised for sled dogs," Rebecca said, catching her breath as he slid his body sensuously against hers. "I don't know how it translates to mushers."

"Well, let's try it and see," Mac said, with a grin. "You could write a column on the results for the *Whitehorse Star*," he suggested.

"I'm not sure they'd print it," Rebecca said, smiling and then laughing aloud as he kissed a ticklish spot on her neck, just below her ear.

"I'm not sure I'd want them to." Mac moved his head until his mouth covered hers. She reached up to pull him closer, savoring the exquisite sensations, the very nearness of him. Ten minutes later, she was muffling her moans into a pillow...and the column was the last thing on her mind.

THE SHRILL RING of the bedside phone was a very rude interruption of a very beautiful moment. Rebecca was awake, relishing the sensation of Mac's warm, hard body spooned against hers. His legs and arms embraced her, his warm breath and the rise and fall of his chest made her feel incredibly safe. Yet, at the same time, he made her feel like a deliciously wanton wench. He made her feel that she wanted very much to love again, something she swore she'd never do. Mac hadn't said he loved her, and a small voice inside her begged caution, but a much louder voice demanded audience, for she was desperately, deeply, hopelessly in love with Bill MacKenzie and there was absolutely no denying it.

The abrupt ring of the phone destroyed the quiet and woke Mac. She felt him stir as she reached for the receiver. "Yes?" she said.

"Becky? Brian. Mac there?"

She glanced at the bedside clock, surprised to see that it was nearly 9 a.m. "Yes," she said. "Hold on." She twisted in Mac's arms. "It's your brother," she said.

"Hang up," Mac moaned, his arms closing around her.

"I can't!" she whispered, muffling the receiver. "He knows you're here!"

"So? He probably just wants to tell me about some wonderful person who wants to buy the team. Hang up."

"Talk to him." Rebecca thrust the phone into his hand and he reluctantly took it, rolling onto his back.

"What!" he said in a decidedly gruff voice. Rebecca let herself melt against him, breathing the wonderful scent of him, relishing his warmth and his sheer masculine strength. "*What?*" Mac said again, and she felt his body tense. He sat up and swung his legs over the edge of the bed. "Why would he call here? What could he possibly have to say to me?" Another pause while Brian spoke, and then Mac said, "Well, I have nothing to say to him!" Mac's voice had a hard edge to it Rebecca had never heard. She could hear Brian's voice on the other end, but not what he was saying. Only that whatever it was sounded urgent. "Are you sure about this?" Mac said, his voice a curious blend of skepticism and hope. There was a long pause and then, "Okay. I'll talk to him." Mac hung up the phone and looked at Rebecca. She watched him, eyebrows raised questioningly. "My father," he said. "He's going to call here. He wants to talk to me. It's…important."

"Oh," Rebecca said, recalling what Brian had told her about the relationship between Mac and his father. "That's good, isn't it?"

"I don't know," Mac said. He smoothed his fingertips along the side of her face. "It's been more than a year since we spoke," he said. "I did something while I was in the navy that pissed him off and got me court-martialed, and he hasn't acknowledged me since." Mac uttered a bitter laugh. "The last thing he ever said to me was, 'I'm glad your mother wasn't alive to see this day.'" Mac brushed a stray wisp of hair to the side of her face. "Frankly I don't care if I ever talk to him again." The phone rang and he turned to look at it. It rang again.

"Answer it, Mac," Rebecca said. "He's your father. A year is long enough."

He raised the receiver reluctantly, and for the next five minutes Rebecca was privy to one-half of a very formal and stilted conversation between a father and son. She had never heard a grown man address his father as "sir" before.

"I understand, sir," Mac said toward the end of the conversation. "Thank you. It's more than I could have hoped for." One last pause while his father spoke, and then Mac said, "I will, sir. As soon as possible." He replaced the receiver very gently, sat for a few moments in absolute stillness, then dropped his head into his hands and heaved a great sigh that bordered on a moan.

"Mac?" Rebecca touched his shoulder gently. "Is everything all right?"

He lifted his head to look at her. "Yeah, I guess. He congratulated me on finishing the race." He drew another deep breath and stared across the room. He was within arm's reach of her and yet he was a million miles away. She felt something start to build inside her, an icy premonition bordering on panic.

"Mac?" Rebecca said, her mouth dry. "What is it? Tell me!"

He hesitated, then turned to look at her. "I have to go back East."

The awful premonition had become reality. Rebecca's hand tightened its grip on the bedsheet. "Oh," she said, her voice faint.

"My father told me that new testimony has come up that sheds a different light on my case." Mac shook his head as if he didn't believe his own words. His keen eyes locked on hers. "I shot down two Iranian planes, Rebecca. I was flying cover for a search-and-rescue mission over the no-fly zone and all of a sudden these two fighters appeared... It all happened so fast. So fast! You see, there was this radar in my plane..." Mac gave up trying to explain. "Jesus. I didn't do anything wrong." He dropped his head into his hands again and sat for a few moments gathering his thoughts.

"It's okay," Rebecca said, touching his shoulder. "Brian told me about it."

He raised his head and glanced sidelong at her. "Apparently a motion has been made for a retrial and it's gone to the court of appeals. My father tells me that I'm going to be acquitted. He must know—he has an inside ear. My God, Rebecca, do you realize what that means? He's asked me to come back while they make my pardon official, and I guess I owe it to him. I have to go.''

Rebecca gazed at him. ''Of course you do,'' she said. But her something inside her was dying all over again, and the anguish was almost more than she could bear.

CHAPTER THIRTEEN

> Let the lone wolf-cry all express...
>   thy hearts abysmal loneliness...
>   Robert Service, from "The Land God Forgot"

IT TOOK THEM two days to drive back home. They arrived on a Tuesday evening and Mac stayed just long enough at Rebecca's to make sure that everything was unloaded from the truck, her dogs were fed and Donny was agreeable to helping out while she was recuperating. Mac was solicitous and tender toward her, as he had been for the entire journey home, but Rebecca kept him at arm's length with excuses about feeling poorly. Relations between them had become increasingly strained, and while Mac seemed totally baffled by her behavior and had made repeated attempts to break through her reserve, Rebecca was desperate to be free of his company. She couldn't bear the nearness of him, the warm touch of his hand on her shoulder as he passed behind her in the cabin on his way to fill the wood box, the sound of his deep, resonant voice within the cabin's walls. She hated herself for falling in love with him and blamed only herself for the pain she was feeling. Brian had tried to warn her, but she had ignored him. "Don't count on him sticking around," he'd said. And now Mac was leaving the boonies, just as Brian had predicted.

"Right," he said, preparing to leave. "Everything's

all set here. I put Cookie in the special pen. She's look-ing very maternal and she's eating like a horse again. I'm going to go take care of my own dogs and get them settled, then I'll come back and make sure you're all right. Rebecca?'' His hand on her shoulder again, turn-ing her toward him. His eyes were piercing, questioning. ''What in hell is bothering you? You're as pale as a ghost and you've been acting like I'm some kind of cold-blooded pathological killer for the past two days.''

''I'm fine,'' she said, dropping her gaze. ''I just don't feel well, that's all. My arm hurts. Please don't bother to come back tonight. I think I'm just going to go to bed. I need...sleep.''

His hand fell away from her shoulder, and he nodded, turning toward the door. He paused there and looked back. ''I'll tell Donny and Kanemoto not to bother you,'' he said. ''Ellin left you a casserole and some fresh-baked rolls on the counter. You saw them? Good. Heat them up and eat a good supper before you go to bed.'' He paused again in the act of opening the door. His eyes were hurt, puzzled. ''Rebecca, if I've done anything wrong, anything to offend you...''

Rebecca shook her head. ''You haven't. Please just leave, Mac. I really need to be alone.''

MAC REELED OUT into the cold, his mind a turmoil of anguished thoughts. Rebecca didn't love him. She didn't want him around. His brother had tried to warn him. ''I can't imagine her as being anything but a lone wolf grieving for her dead mate,'' he'd said. As Mac climbed into his rusting dog truck and turned on the ignition, his heart was on the ground. Two nights ago they had shared the most intimate and tender of moments. Two nights ago he had drowned himself in the intoxicating sweetness of her after months of dreaming of those precious moments. He loved her more than life itself, yet now she was acting as cold and aloof toward him as the day they'd first met, in spite of all they'd been through together.

"Don't get your hopes up," Brian had warned, and yet two nights ago his hopes had been somewhere up in the stratosphere, just about as high as they'd ever been or would ever be again. He had been so sure she felt the same way!

Who could figure the heart of a woman?

REBECCA LISTENED to the truck engine start, listened as Mac drove out of her life. She felt numb, as if the cold had finally had its way and permanently frozen her heart and soul. She moved listlessly to the counter, gazed down at the offerings Ellin had left, along with a brief note. "Welcome home, my dear girl! I'll be over first thing in the morning to hear all about your adventures!"

Tuffy's cold nose nudged her hand sympathetically, and the old dog pressed her body against Rebecca's leg, offering what comfort she could.

Rebecca ate no supper and wondered dully if she would ever feel hungry again. She climbed the steep ladder to the sleeping loft where she collapsed on her bed, wrapped her arms around Tuffy and wept inconsolably until the cold gray light of dawn brightened the frost-shrouded windows.

IT WASN'T ELLIN who visited Rebecca first thing in the morning. It was Mac. His knock on the cabin door took her completely by surprise, and for a moment she forgot her manners and just stared. When she reluctantly motioned him inside, he stood in silent disbelief, staring at her. Finally he spoke. "Your hair," he said. "Your beautiful hair!"

Rebecca raised her fingertips self-consciously to the ragged ends of her shorn locks. She nodded. "I couldn't comb or braid it with one hand, so I cut it off. I had to, you see."

"My God, Rebecca!" Mac said. She was clearly distraught, and he couldn't imagine that cutting her hair was the sole reason. Impatiently she motioned him into the cabin and he stepped inside. He stood near the woodstove and looked around the room, trying to gather his wits. Rebecca was behaving like a stranger, and there was something different about the cabin, too. Her husband's things were gone. His coats on the hooks behind the door, his boots lined up in back of the stove, the clothes hanging on wall pegs, the pictures on top of the bureau. And all those trophies, those big, gleaming testimonials to his mushing prowess, had vanished. All of it gone! Mac glanced at her left hand. The wedding band, too, had vanished.

Rebecca Reed had finally buried her husband.

He turned to look at her. There were dark hollows beneath her eyes, and her face was pale. She looked awful. "Has Kanemoto gone?" he asked.

"Yes," she replied stiffly. "He left early this morning. Donny drove him to the airport."

Mac stood flat-footed, uneasiness building within him. "Are you really all right?" he asked.

"I'm fine."

He wanted to tell her that she didn't look fine, but he didn't dare. "I came to say goodbye," he said. "I'm flying out of Dawson in a few hours."

She nodded, stone-faced. "Well, say it then, and be on your way. I have lots to do."

He stared at her. She was as frigid as the February morning. He nodded slowly. "All right, then. Goodbye, Rebecca."

"Goodbye," she replied, walking to the door and opening it for him. He stared at her a few moments more and then walked out. Behind him the door closed with a sharp, hostile bang. He stood in the arctic entry and felt his bewilderment transform rapidly into desperate anger. Without thinking of what he meant to do or say, he turned and burst back into the room. She was standing right beside the door and he nearly ran right over her. She took two steps back and looked up at him.

"I can't believe you're treating me this way! Two nights ago you were treating me a little differently!"

A spark kindled in her eyes. "Two nights ago you weren't going back East! Brian tried to warn me that you'd never stick around a place like this. He said that after the race you'd probably take a high-paying job flying for British Airways, that you'd never stay out here in the boonies, as he called it. He warned me that something like this would happen. And it's all right, Mac. I understand. I really do. You don't have to explain anything to me. I don't blame you. Just please go. Don't make this any harder than it has to be!"

Mac drew a deep breath, counting silently to ten. When he spoke, his voice was calm and controlled. "Did it ever occur to you that Brian might not know what the hell he's talking about? Did that thought ever occur to you, Rebecca?" He was angry. Angry enough to stalk the perimeter of the little cabin as he spoke. He stopped before her and his voice lost a little of its self-restraint. "I came out here of my own accord, didn't I? I stayed, didn't I? I finished a race you told me I shouldn't even have started, *didn't I?*" The last sentence ended on a raised and angry note. He wheeled around and stalked to the door, ripping it open and then changing his mind and slamming it shut again hard enough to make her jump. He spun around, whipping an envelope out of his pocket.

"Oh, I almost forgot," he said, extending it toward her. "The rest of the money I owe you, including what you had to shell out to get the watch back. I paid a little visit to that crook during our Dawson layover, so I know just how much he gouged you for it. I promised I'd repay you and I'm finally doing it, with interest. Bet you never thought I'd do that, either!"

When she didn't take the envelope from him, he flipped it onto the tabletop and turned toward the door again. He opened it and stepped through into the arctic entry, where he turned around one final time. "You're wrong about me, Rebecca. This may be the first time in your life you were wrong about anything, but you're wrong about me. You're way off base! And I'll be back," he said. "As soon as this mess gets straightened out, I'll be back. We can finish this argument then!" He was halfway to his truck when he heard the cabin door open behind him.

"Mac?" Rebecca said in a small voice.

He stopped reluctantly, his blood hot with anger and frustration. He didn't know how to talk to her, didn't know what to say to her to make her understand, didn't know how to love her the way she obviously needed to be loved. He had never felt as completely inadequate as Rebecca made him feel. At length he turned and looked back at her because he didn't want to leave her this way, with all the harsh words spoken aloud and all the tender thoughts unvoiced.

"You didn't tell me you were planning to come back," she said in a voice that trembled with emotion.

He stared at her for a few moments in disbelief. "How could you possibly think I wouldn't come back?" he said with an exasperated wave of both arms. "I'm in love with you, dammit! How could you possibly not know that?" His voice softened as he pleaded with her to understand. "I love you, Rebecca. I've never felt this way about anyone before, so maybe I'm not good at showing it, but I spent the second half of that hellish race thinking up names for our first child. I thought we might call her Sarah Elizabeth MacKenzie. Sally. A girl named Sally would have spark and spunk enough to be as strong as her beautiful mother."

He looked up at her, standing there on the porch with her arm in a sling and her shorn hair curling around her face. The wind tugged a sad sigh from the spruce trees around the cabin and blew loose curls of dark hair about her eyes. She smoothed them away with her hand and stood like that, looking down at him with her hand pressed to the side of her face and an expression he couldn't begin to fathom. She shook her head slowly.

"You don't like the name Sally?" Mac said.

"I didn't know," she said in a voice barely above a whisper. "I didn't know you felt that way. I didn't know!"

"Rebecca, the reason I'm going back is because it means a lot to me to have my name cleared." He stared out across the distance, as if searching for the right words to explain it to her. "I thought I didn't give a damn about that anymore, but the truth is, I do." He gestured futilely again. "Oh, hell! It's not about getting away from this place, and it sure as hell isn't about getting away from you! Why can't you believe that?"

She looked down at him from the cabin porch and suddenly, right before his disbelieving eyes, Rebecca collapsed. She raised one hand to her face to shield it from him and half turned as if to flee back into the cabin, but her devastation was so complete that she sank slowly to her knees on the cabin porch and crumpled over herself. She knelt in rigid silence for several painful moments while Mac stood dumbfounded, transfixed by the sight of one of the strongest people he had ever known in a state of total collapse.

He took the steps two at a time and knelt beside her. "Rebecca, it's all right. Please don't cry. There's no reason for you to cry." He drew her into his arms and she turned and clung to him, sobbing like a heartbroken child while he comforted her. He knelt with her for a long time before he raised her gently to her feet.

"I thought you were leaving," she said, her slender body trembling in his embrace. "I thought you'd walk away from here and I'd never see you again."

His strong arms tightened around her. "I'll never leave you, Rebecca. I'll die first."

His ill-chosen words did little to comfort her. "Don't you ever die on me, Mac," she said, lifting her face to him. It was streaming with tears and the sight brought the sting of tears to his own eyes. "Promise you'll never die on me!"

"That's a mighty tall order," he said, "but I will if you will."

She hiccuped, blinked the tears out of her eyes and gazed up at him for a silent moment, realizing how impossible a promise that was to keep. "Okay," she said, smiling through her tears. "I promise I'll do my best not to." She snuggled close to him, pressed the side of her head against his chest, listened to the strong, steady beat of his heart, felt the rise and fall of his breathing. She drew a shaky breath of her own. "I'm sorry I doubted you, Mac. I guess I just don't understand what happened to you in the navy."

Mac shook his head. "That's a long and sordid story. When I get back, maybe you could invite me over for dinner. I'll bring a bottle of wine, we'll tuck up close to your woodstove, and I'll tell it to you. I didn't do anything wrong, Rebecca. I swear to you, I did nothing that would ever shame you."

"I know that, Mac," she said, speaking softly and with absolute conviction. "You're the most honorable man I've ever known."

Her words moved him deeply, and again his eyes stung with tears. He tightened his grip on her and bent his head over hers, breathing the sweetness of her. "I'll be back as soon as I can, as soon as it's over. I'll call Sam and Ellin and give them the number where I'll be staying. You can call me there. Collect. Call me every day. Promise me!"

"What about your dogs?" she said. "What if Brian sells them while you're away?"

Mac shook his head. "Too late. He already has."

Rebecca looked up at him and her face mirrored her dismay. "Oh, Mac, no! I didn't think he'd do it! You'll never drive another team of dogs any better than that one. And Merlin...you'll never have a better leader!"

"I know. That's why I bought the whole team, lock, stock and barrel," he said, grinning at her reaction. "Now listen up, because I'll miss my flight if I don't leave soon, and I don't want to leave until you know the rest of the story.

"When I get back I'll be staying at Sam and Ellin's because they've asked me to, and because I finally got them to agree to accept rent payments from me on that little cabin. Guy Johnson's getting out of the hospital next week, but he'll never fly again, so the powers that be called me up just last night and asked if I'd be interested in flying his mail route." Mac grinned again at her expression. "So there you have it, Rebecca Reed. There's the high-paying job Brian told you I'd get. It's not quite the cash I'd rake in flying for British Airways, but I can sleep in my own bed nearly every night, see you as often as you'll let me and still find time to train a team of dogs for next year's race."

"You told me you never wanted to race again," she said, her voice sounding faint and faraway.

"Now that I've had a few days of sleep, I've changed my mind," he said. "And there's something else you should know."

"What's that?"

"You're going to be training and racing right along with me."

"I am?" Rebecca said.

"You are."

And it seemed to Mac as he bent his head to kiss this marvelous woman that all the paths he had followed all his life had been leading him to this very place at this very moment. Standing here with her in the cold, crystalline light of a Yukon morning and kissing her against the background of her forty huskies raising their voices together and singing the wild, primordial song of the pack, was the one of finest things he had ever done.

He tasted the salt of her tears, kissed her closed eyes, kissed her cheeks, kissed her trembling lips. "I have to go," he said.

"I know."

"When I get back, I'd like to ask you something."

Her lashes were still sparkling with teardrops, but the beginnings of a smile trembled at the corners of her mouth. "What might that be?"

"I'd like to ask you if you'd let me dry my boots behind your woodstove."

Her lips curved. "I'll have to think about that."

"And while I'm at it, I'd like to ask you a few other things, too. I'd like to ask if maybe I could fill your wood box and carry your water on a regular basis. If I could help you with your finances until you get back on your feet and get that book of yours written. If we could train our teams together this fall, run the Quest together next February and get married in Dawson on our thirty-six-hour layover."

"In our mushing gear?"

He nodded. "Standing on the runners of our dog-sleds."

Rebecca laughed shakily. She tipped her head back and gazed into his eyes. "I'll think about all of the above," she said.

Mac kissed her tenderly. "Promise?"

"I promise. You'd better get going. You'll miss your plane."

"That's it?" he said, eyeing her. "Aren't you going to give me a hint as to how you might answer any of those questions?"

"I told you I promised to think about them while you're gone," she said. "The sooner you go, the sooner I can start thinking, and the longer you're gone, the longer I can weigh the pros and cons."

Mac tucked a stray curl behind her left ear. "I don't know as I like the sound of that," he said. "How much time do you think you're going to need?"

"Oh—" her brow furrowed as she gazed past his shoulder, calculating "—at least sixty seconds."

Mac nodded gravely. "I see." He bent to give her tear-streaked cheek a chaste, parting kiss. "Goodbye, then, Rebecca," he said.

"Goodbye, Mac. Safe journey."

He turned and started down the steps, walked out to his truck and wrenched open the sagging door. He pulled himself up and in, slammed the door shut behind him and turned the key in the ignition. The old engine groaned and sputtered and finally caught. Mac adjusted the idle and sat in the cab for a few moments, his breath frosting the windshield. He pushed back the sleeve of his parka, glanced at the face of his watch and rolled down his window.

"That's sixty seconds on the dot," he said to the woman who stood on the cabin porch, watching him with a bemused expression.

"You don't give a woman much leeway, do you?" she said. "Supposing this takes a little longer than I thought?"

"That's seventy seconds."

"I mean, those were some pretty serious questions, Bill MacKenzie. A woman ought to be allowed a few extra moments to think about them, wouldn't you agree?"

"Eighty," he said.

"If you sit there any longer, you're apt to miss your plane. You keep the navy waiting and they just might revoke your pardon."

"Coming up on ninety seconds."

She laughed then, reaching her hand to smooth her hair back from her face while the wind did its best to defeat her. "All right, then, yes," she said. "Yes, yes,

yes, yes and yes! But as for standing on the dogsleds for the nuptials, I haven't made up my mind about that one yet.''

Mac let out a whoop that started the dogs barking. He leaped from the truck, covering the distance between them at a gallop and sweeping her into his arms. He kissed her again and again and again until she was dizzy and laughing and crying and so full of love and joy that all she could do was gasp his name.

"I love you, Rebecca," he said, folding her into the protective embrace of his strong arms. "Dammit, I love you so much it hurts!"

"I love you, too," she said. "So much it scares me."

"I thought the only thing that scared you was falling through the ice," Mac said, setting her gently at arm's length.

"Falling through the ice and falling in love. Equally terrifying."

"But vastly different," he countered. "One makes you very, very cold, whereas the other…" He drew her close. "We'll have plenty of time to perfect the other," he said as he bent his head to kiss her.

"Mac, you'll miss your flight!"

"Woman, the only thing I'm going to miss is you." He kissed her again and she pushed him away, laughing and breathless.

"Go, please, I can't stand goodbyes! Hurry up and leave so I can start thinking about you coming back again."

"Okay. You might start planning our wedding while I'm gone. I'd really like Merlin to be the ring bearer, and you really do look kind of cute in Bunny boots."

She laughed again and gently guided him down the steps. "I told you, I'll have to think about that."

"I'll give you as much time as you need," he said as he climbed into the truck for the second time. "You can let me know when I get back."

"I will," she said softly as he put the old truck in gear and started down the long, snow-covered drive that led out to the Klondike Highway. "I promise."

The
Shannon Sisters

A Trilogy by C.J. Carmichael
The stories of three sisters from Alberta whose lives and loves are as rocky—and grand—as the mountains they grew up in.

A *Second-Chance* Proposal
A murder, a bride-to-be left at the altar, a reunion. Is Cathleen Shannon willing to take a second chance on the man involved in these?

A *Convenient* Proposal
Kelly Shannon feels guilty about what she's done, and Mick Mizzoni feels that he's his brother's keeper—a volatile situation, but maybe one with a convenient way out!

A *Lasting* Proposal
Maureen Shannon doesn't want risks in her life anymore. Not after everything she's lived through. But Jake Hartman might be proposing a sure thing....

On sale starting February 2002

Available wherever Harlequin books are sold.

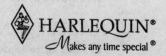

HARLEQUIN®
Makes any time special ®

This Mother's Day Give Your Mom A Royal Treat

Win a fabulous one-week vacation in Puerto Rico for you and your mother at the luxurious Inter-Continental San Juan Resort & Casino. The prize includes round trip airfare for two, breakfast daily and a mother and daughter day of beauty at the beachfront hotel's spa.

INTER·CONTINENTAL
San Juan
RESORT & CASINO

Here's all you have to do:

Tell us in 100 words or less how your mother helped with the romance in your life. It may be a story about your engagement, wedding or those boyfriends when you were a teenager or any other romantic advice from your mother. The entry will be judged based on its originality, emotionally compelling nature and sincerity.
See official rules on following page.

Send your entry to:
Mother's Day Contest

In Canada
P.O. Box 637
Fort Erie, Ontario
L2A 5X3

In U.S.A.
P.O. Box 9076
3010 Walden Ave.
Buffalo, NY
14269-9076

Or enter online at www.eHarlequin.com

PRROY

HARLEQUIN MOTHER'S DAY CONTEST 2216
OFFICIAL RULES
NO PURCHASE NECESSARY TO ENTER

Two ways to enter:

• **Via The Internet:** Log on to the Harlequin romance website (www.eHarlequin.com) anytime beginning 12:01 a.m. E.S.T., January 1, 2002 through 11:59 p.m. E.S.T., April 1, 2002 and follow the directions displayed on-line to enter your name, address (including zip code), e-mail address and in 100 words or fewer, describe how your mother helped with the romance in your life.

• **Via Mail:** Handprint (or type) on an 8 1/2" x 11" plain piece of paper, your name, address (including zip code) and e-mail address (if you have one), and in 100 words or fewer, describe how your mother helped with the romance in your life. Mail your entry via first-class mail to: Harlequin Mother's Day Contest 2216, (in the U.S.) P.O. Box 9076, Buffalo, NY 14269-9076; (in Canada) P.O. Box 637, Fort Erie, Ontario, Canada L2A 5X3.

For eligibility, entries must be submitted either through a completed Internet transmission or postmarked no later than 11:59 p.m. E.S.T., April 1, 2002 (mail-in entries must be received by April 9, 2002). Limit one entry per person, household address and e-mail address. On-line and/or mailed entries received from persons residing in geographic areas in which entry is not permissible will be disqualified.

Entries will be judged by a panel of judges, consisting of members of the Harlequin editorial, marketing and public relations staff using the following criteria:
- Originality - 50%
- Emotional Appeal - 25%
- Sincerity - 25%

In the event of a tie, duplicate prizes will be awarded. Decisions of the judges are final.

Prize: A 6-night/7-day stay for two at the Inter-Continental San Juan Resort & Casino, including round-trip coach air transportation from gateway airport nearest winner's home (approximate retail value: $4,000). Prize includes breakfast daily and a mother and daughter day of beauty at the beachfront hotel's spa. Prize consists of only those items listed as part of the prize. Prize is valued in U.S. currency.

All entries become the property of Torstar Corp. and will not be returned. No responsibility is assumed for lost, late, illegible, incomplete, inaccurate, non-delivered or misdirected mail or misdirected e-mail, for technical, hardware or software failures of any kind, lost or unavailable network connections, or failed, incomplete, garbled or delayed computer transmission or any human error which may occur in the receipt or processing of the entries in this Contest.

Contest open only to residents of the U.S. (except Colorado) and Canada, who are 18 years of age or older and is void wherever prohibited by law; all applicable laws and regulations apply. Any litigation within the Province of Quebec respecting the conduct or organization of a publicity contest may be submitted to the Régie des alcools, des courses et des jeux for a ruling. Any litigation respecting the awarding of a prize may be submitted to the Régie des alcools, des courses et des jeux only for the purpose of helping the parties reach a settlement. Employees and immediate family members of Torstar Corp. and D.L. Blair, Inc., their affiliates, subsidiaries and all other agencies, entities and persons connected with the use, marketing or conduct of this Contest are not eligible to enter. Taxes on prize are the sole responsibility of winner. Acceptance of any prize offered constitutes permission to use winner's name, photograph or other likeness for the purposes of advertising, trade and promotion on behalf of Torstar Corp., its affiliates and subsidiaries without further compensation to the winner, unless prohibited by law.

Winner will be determined no later than April 15, 2002 and be notified by mail. Winner will be required to sign and return an Affidavit of Eligibility form within 15 days after winner notification. Non-compliance within that time period may result in disqualification and an alternate winner may be selected. Winner of trip must execute a Release of Liability prior to ticketing and must possess required travel documents (e.g. Passport, photo ID) where applicable. Travel must be completed within 12 months of selection and is subject to traveling companion completing and returning a Release of Liability prior to travel; and hotel and flight accommodations availability. Certain restrictions and blackout dates may apply. No substitution of prize permitted by winner. Torstar Corp. and D.L. Blair, Inc., their parents, affiliates, and subsidiaries are not responsible for errors in printing or electronic presentation of Contest, or entries. In the event of printing or other errors which may result in unintended prize values or duplication of prizes, all affected entries shall be null and void. If for any reason the Internet portion of the Contest is not capable of running as planned, including infection by computer virus, bugs, tampering, unauthorized intervention, fraud, technical failures, or any other causes beyond the control of Torstar Corp. which corrupt or affect the administration, secrecy, fairness, integrity or proper conduct of the Contest, Torstar Corp. reserves the right, at its sole discretion, to disqualify any individual who tampers with the entry process and to cancel, terminate, modify or suspend the Contest or the Internet portion thereof. In the event the Internet portion must be terminated a notice will be posted on the website and all entries received prior to termination will be judged in accordance with these rules. In the event of a dispute regarding an on-line entry, the entry will be deemed submitted by the authorized holder of the e-mail account submitted at the time of entry. Authorized account holder is defined as the natural person who is assigned to an e-mail address by an Internet access provider, on-line service provider or other organization that is responsible for arranging e-mail address for the domain associated with the submitted e-mail address. Torstar Corp. and/or D.L. Blair Inc. assumes no responsibility for any computer injury or damage related to or resulting from accessing and/or downloading any sweepstakes material. Rules are subject to any requirements/limitations imposed by the FCC. Purchase or acceptance of a product offer does not improve your chances of winning.

For winner's name (available after May 1, 2002), send a self-addressed, stamped envelope to: Harlequin Mother's Day Contest Winners 2216, P.O. Box 4200 Blair, NE 68009-4200 or you may access the www.eHarlequin.com Web site through June 3, 2002.

Contest sponsored by Torstar Corp., P.O. Box 9042, Buffalo, NY 14269-9042.

PRRULES

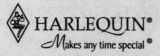

Meet the Randall brothers…four sexy bachelor brothers who are about to find four beautiful brides!

WYOMING WINTER

by bestselling author

Judy Christenberry

In preparation for the long, cold Wyoming winter, the eldest Randall brother seeks to find wives for his four single rancher brothers…and the resulting matchmaking is full of surprises! Containing the first two full-length novels in Judy's famous *4 Brides for 4 Brothers* miniseries, this collection will bring you into the lives, and loves, of the delightfully engaging Randall family.

Look for WYOMING WINTER in March 2002.

And in May 2002 look for SUMMER SKIES, containing the last two Randall stories.

HARLEQUIN®

Makes any time special ®

COMING NEXT MONTH

SSECNM0302